BEWARE
OF
GREEK
BEARING
GIFTS

LUKE
CHRISTODOULOU

BOOKS

Vinci Books

vinci-books.com

Published by Vinci Books Ltd in 2026

1

The publisher and the author have made every effort to obtain permissions
for any third party material used in this book and to comply with copyright
law. Any queries in this respect should be brought to the attention of the
publisher and any omissions will be corrected in future editions.
A CIP catalogue record for this book is available from the British Library.
Paperback ISBN: 9781036712617
The EU GPSR authorised representative is Logos Europe, 9 rue Nicolas
Poussion, 17000 La Rochelle, France contact@logoseurope.eu

By Luke Christodoulou

Murderous Greece

Pandora's Box
Achilles' Heel
Beware of Greeks Bearing Gifts

Greek Island Mysteries

The Olympus Killer
The Church Murders
Death of a Bride
Murder on Display
Hotel Murder
Twelve Months of Murder

Dedicated to the refugees of the world.
May your heart find a place to call home...

Chapter One

PARGA, GREECE

Spring, 1913

Iphigenia stood by the open window, allowing the fresh sea air to rush into her small cottage. It carried the sweet smell of blossoming Greek flowers mingled up with the sharp salty scent of the Ionian Sea. The stone-paved streets below welcomed hundreds of joyful Greeks as they celebrated their union with the free state of Greece. Greece had emerged victorious from the Balkan War, and Ottoman rule came to an end after centuries of harsh occupation.

Iphigenia could not care less.

She slammed the blue wooden shutters, fastened the rusty lock, and slid down the old, decaying wall. Curled up on the cold floor, she gazed around the dark room. The two empty beds before her pierced her soul. Her handsome twin boys, both dead in the war. She carried them inside her for nine months and proudly raised them for eighteen years, and one letter from the front changed all that.

She was no longer a mother.

Iphigenia did not believe in crying. She cursed God and pushed herself up from the wooden ground. She dragged her feet out of their room and stood in the hallway. From the ajar door creaking in the spring breeze, she witnessed her husband sobbing in his armchair, an empty vessel of the man she once knew. Two months had passed since their boys' passing to the other world, and her husband had not left the house.

'You need to go tend to the land,' she had urged him.

'Why? Who will inherit us, Effie? Who?'

'We need to eat, and frankly, we need to move on. Life is for the living...'

'I'm already dead. I have no reason to be alive.'

Iphigenia closed her eyes and sighed deeply. She quivered her head to shake away the memories of his words. She turned around, picked up her knitted jacket, and rushed out of the house. She wrapped her hazelnut hair inside her purple scarf as she walked by her neglected garden, and with her eyes lowered, she made her way through the ecstatic crowds dancing the evening away. Shorter than most, she moved through them, avoiding eye contact. Iphigenia headed away from the village's center; her eyes were set on the restless sea opposite. A row of rocky islands stood proudly in the cool waters of Parga. Saint Mary's chapel stood alone on the largest of the isles that nested in the small bay.

The planks of the dock squeaked as Iphigenia made her way toward her uncle's fishing boat. Born upon a ship to a family of fishermen, Iphigenia had no trouble untying nautical knots and releasing the boat from its chains. Both were soon free upon the short-lived waves of Parga Bay. With her hands firmly gripped around the paddles, she steered the small boat to the shore of the church-owned island.

Father Gregory stood behind the church's colored window, admiring the will of the woman with whom he grew up with. His teeth travelled along his thin lips as he scratched his left eyebrow. '*Well, well. What has the Lord have in store for me on this glorious day?*'

He opened the wooden door and rushed down the dirt path leading to the rocks that served as the islet's dock. He nodded to Iphigenia as he stepped in the shallow waters to help bring her boat nearer to shore. He offered his hand, and Iphigenia's icy hand grabbed hold of him, and as many times before, she jumped to land.

'Good evening, Father.'

'Went looking for me at St. Nicholas?' he replied and coughed.

Iphigenia wiped her hands on her black dress; the dirt on her hands left behind lines of mud as it blended with the droplets offered by the splashing of the Ionian. 'I know you well. You're not one for much commotion. Also, you're not one to miss a spring sunset from Saint Mary's island. One look at the clear sky above, and I did not even bother to go look for you at your church.'

Father Gregory's thick beard was lifted by a sincere wide smile.

'Come in,' he said and sauntered back up the path. 'What is on your mind?' he asked as he stood by the door, waiting for her to enter the high-ceilinged church. Iphigenia fought back tears as she did the sign of the cross upon her body and made her way to the first row of wooden stools. 'Must be hard to find joy in our liberation, but you must rest assured that your boys are by our creator's side. Jesus once said …'

'It's not my boys that I worry about, Father. It's Giorgo,' she interrupted him.

Father Gregory sat down by her side. He placed his hand on her trembling fingers. Iphigenia took a deep breath and sighed. 'I think he is going to do something crazy. I think he is going to take his own life. He will not listen to me. I feel his demons lingering in our house, in his head. You must talk to him!'

The following day, the bright Mediterranean sun found Greece nearly double in size. White smiles glowed on people's olive-skinned faces. Freedom, that once-elusive dream, was theirs to relish and savor. Tears fell from Father Gregory's green eyes as he praised Jesus for the euphoria of the people in his town. He ambled uphill through stone cottages and wished a good morning to all that greeted him. Children's laughter filled the air as they ran by him waving Greek flags. Soon, Father Gregory was leaning on the rusty gate of Iphigenia's home. He heard her shout out to her husband. 'Giorgo, I'm off to my aunt's.'

Iphigenia forced a smile as she nodded to him. 'Don't worry,' he managed to say as she sprinted off down the street. Father Gregory closed the gate behind him and paused to enjoy two merry swallows building their nest in the corner above the front door. He never married. He never truly understood why. Every time his parents mentioned a good Christian girl to him, he would come up with an array of excuses. Now, at thirty-seven, with his parents deceased and Greece a free country, he felt lonelier than ever.

'Good morning, Giorgo,' he said in a cheery voice as he popped his head through the open front door.

'What's so good about it?'

Father Gregory swallowed the lump forming inside his throat and entered the gloomy living room. The stuffy air housed the smoke from Giorgo's cigarettes, and the closed shutters blocked out the singing from the spring birds outside. He took out his Bible and sat by the sad man's side. He opened the Good Book. Nehemiah 8:10.

Chapter Two

Iphigenia felt the first sun rays of the day dance upon her pale face. She pushed back locks of tangled hair from her forehead and stretched her arms. Startled, she opened her eyes and sat up. She was alone in bed. Giorgo never awoke before her.

'Giorgo?'

Silence.

'Giorgo?' She raised her voice as her feet landed on the wooden floor. Living room, kitchen, boys' room. She was home alone. On her bare tiptoes, she leaned outside of the bedroom window and called out her husband's name once more.

'Lost your man, Effie?' her neighbor asked, poking her head through the sheets she had just hung up to dry in her narrow back yard.

'Seems so, Helena.' A faint smile spread along her tired face. 'Could it be?'

She rushed back into her bedroom to dress. Maintaining

the same speed, Iphigenia exited her cottage and hastily set off for their land. Above, the sun painted the flock of inno-cent-looking clouds gathering in the blue sky. The long dirt road seemed longer to her as she paused by a stubborn olive tree growing out of a rocky surface, trying to catch her breath.

'Good morning, Iphigenia,' Jacob, the cheery farmer, called out. 'Off to your vineyard?' he asked; hints of sorrow came tangled in his words. He dared not mention the neglected fruit trees and the dying —most likely already corpses- vegetables. It had been months since he saw anyone on their land.

'Good day to you too, sir. Yes. I'm off to meet Giorgo.'

A wide smile lifted the farmer's thick mustache. 'Giorgo is back? That's great. Early as always, huh? I did not see him pass by.'

Iphigenia replied with a short-lived smile and a quick nod and continued down the road as the morning breeze circled her, raising clouds of dust around her running feet. Iphigenia stopped by the open gate and made her way through overgrown weeds, wild orchids, and sweet-smelling daffodils. The wind grew stronger as she entered the shadows of the rows of fruit trees. A gust swept the cold sweat forming on the back of her neck. Iphigenia froze. Like an ancient statue of a Greek Goddess she stood still, not moving a single muscle. Her eyes were fixed on the life-less man hanging from a tall carob tree in the distance. His feet swung two feet from the ground, and his head lay on his right shoulder. She took a few steps forward, exhaling deeply. Her eyes followed the rope from the snapped neck up to the thick branch. More steps forward. An old wooden stool lay on the dry ground. She moved sideways, her eyes watering up. The face of the man she married at the tender age of seventeen. The blue eyes she once found herself getting lost in, now scared her. Two hollow, blood-red eyes, wide open, decorated a face of shock. Crimson saliva snake-lined from the corners of his purple-blue mouth. Iphigenia sat down in the dirt opposite his swinging corpse. She closed her eyes and let her senses travel around her land. The flowery aroma of spring would soon be ruined by the odor-iferous, putrid smell of a dead body. The songs of the choirs of April's birds would soon be covered by her mother-in-law's loud cries.

Minutes passed before she placed her pale hands on the ground and lifted her body and spirit up. Emotionless, she stumbled out back onto the road and walked up to Jacob.

'Hey again! How's Giorgo doing?'

'He's dead,' she said and bit her bottom lip. 'I... I can't...' she stuttered as she sat down. 'Please go tell his brother,' she managed to say in one breath of a sentence before fainting in front of the shocked farmer.

Two days later, she would faint again. This time in Father Gregory's arms as he held her a foot away from her husband's final resting ground. The sky, even though spring, dressed for the occasion. Dark grey clouds roamed above the crowd crying as four men lowered the wooden coffin into the ground. Iphigenia knelt in the soft soil. Her fingers ran through the dirt. She raised her fist above the hole and watched as the casket settled six feet below. Her right arm trembled violently; her fingers were clenched into a fist, holding prisoner the earth inside. She shook her head. 'I can't...'

Father Gregory took a step forward and knelt by her side. 'Effie, you have to say goodbye. It's time for ...'

Thunder covered his last words. Iphigenia opened her fist, watched as crumbs of dirt dived down to Giorgo, and just as the first drops plummeted from the sky, she fainted into Father Gregory's arms.

Chapter Three

Spring, 2010

Susan stared at her phone's screen as she sat alone on her old brown sofa in the attic of her three-bedroom home. Her teary eyes gazed at the four-year-old's lifeless little body, lying face down in the golden sand as the Aegean Sea washed him out on the Turkish coast. The news hit too close to home for her to handle.

Five months had passed since she last saw a child's body.

Her little Eugene would have been two if alive. Tears formed rivulets on her cold pale cheeks as she closed her eyes. She relived the moment often. She stood above her boy's cot and looked into his still eyes. She screamed frantically animal-like cries as she picked him up and shook his little body. He was cold and a sickly shade of white. Blood no longer ran through his veins. His tiny heart no longer gave a beat.

'Mum? Mum?'

Her teenaged daughter's calling pulled her out of the

nightmare. Her trembling arm reached out and flicked on the lights, scaring the darkness and the nightmare world away. She wiped her eyes and swallowed the lump in her throat. 'Yes, dear?'

'Where's my black jacket? I left it in the hallway and …'

'In its place, Sophia.'

Silence.

'Your wardrobe!' Susan continued.

'Thanks, Mum. You're the best. See you later!'

Loud steps echoed toward Susan as she pictured Sophia running down the stairs, leaping them two-by-two. 'Why do I bother with the news? It's just all doom and gloom, doom and gloom,' Susan mumbled as she dropped her phone on the sofa and stood up, rubbing her aching lower back. 'Yeah, the bloody forties are the new twenties. Woo-fucking-hoo!'

Her bare feet slipped into her warm moccasins as she kneaded her neck and carelessly fixed her hair. 'It's seven o'clock already,' she said in one breath and made her way down to her modern rustic kitchen. Susan always had an eye and a heart for home design. Before having her four children, nothing could please her more than shop-hopping to find the perfect wooden counter or the cushion she had envisioned for a client's living room. She quit her job two days before Eugene's funeral. Andrew had held her in his strong arms and looked straight into her blue eyes while stroking her golden locks. 'You can't quit. You love your job. Psychologists say we must keep our minds busy at such times…' He began to recite some *bullshit* -as Susan referred to it- he had read online. 'The world is grey and cold and awful and hostile. My eyes are incapable of seeing color. How will I set up a home? I am an empty vessel,' she drunkenly replied.

The crackling of the sausages brought her focus back to the meal she was preparing. Susan poked them with the fork in her hand and rolled them over. Her eyes watched the boiling oil furiously roaming the black pan. She brought her palm above it; the heat attacked her skin. 'I need to feel,' she whispered, and she gradually lowered her hand toward the deep-frying pan.

The loud buzzing of her doorbell made her jump. She took a clumsy step back and breathed heavily. '*Get a grip, Susan!*'

The front door banged against its door stopper as its hinges retaliated to the force used by her son, Christopher. The fair-haired boy kicked off his shoes and threw his jacket in the direction of the metal coat rack. He missed. His sister, Maya, wobbled in behind him, a happy grin permanently occupying her round face. Andrew followed, shaking his head at the sight of the pair of shoes and the sports jacket that ruined the catalogue-picture-perfect tidiness of his home. It did not take much to awaken his OCD.

'Why do you always ring the doorbell when you have keys?'

'Hey, Ma! What's for dinner?' Christopher asked, ignoring her complaint.

Susan forced a large smile across her tired face. She stroked her son's hair and kissed his forehead. 'You're in high spirits.'

'I broke my personal record today. Fifty-six seconds!'

Susan hugged her ecstatic youth. 'That's amazing. Well done, Christopher!'

Christopher pulled out a wooden chair with aluminum tips and dramatically fell back on it. 'You didn't answer my question though.'

'Sausages, cabbage and chips. Your favorite!'

Susan felt two little arms wrapped around her right leg. 'Chips!' her three-year-old daughter repeated.

'Well hello, my baby. How was your day?'

Maya replied with a dance. She tip-toed the length of the kitchen, twirling her body around while her hair swirled, covering her face.

'I'll take that as a good sign,' Susan commented, her eyes on her husband walking in with Christopher's jacket and shoes. He threw them all on his son's lap. 'This' -he waved his arms three-hundred and sixty degrees- 'is not a pigsty. Go put them in your room.'

Christopher rolled his eyes but did not speak. He arched his back and dragged his feet past his parents.

'And wash your hands,' his mother added, while accepting a gentle kiss on her cheek. 'Where's Sophia?' Andrew asked as he remained close to her, rubbing her back. Susan remained still. 'At Katie's, down the road. She will eat there and be home later.'

'Great. I have news for you. *Just you.*'

Twenty-five minutes later, they both stood by the open dish-washer. Susan had tried to read her husband's enigmatic expression during dinner, and after various thoughts came alive in her head, she gave up on her personal guessing game and waited to hear his news. The hot water fell on her hands as she wiped the plates, keeping her warm from the cold air invading through the slightly opened window. The thin white curtains swayed to the rhythm of the wind, revealing the breeze growing in strength. As she handed the first plate to Andrew, droplets of icy water splashed against the glass.

'My mum has Alzheimer's.'

Susan continued pushing away a blob of ketchup. 'Thought you said you had news. As in something *new* to tell me.' She turned to his direction. 'Oh, no. *You* are starting to forget, *too!*' she joked, opening her eyes widely.

Andrew hid his annoyance and laughed. It was not often that he saw his once joyous and bubbly wife in high spirits. 'I spoke to the nursing home today. They called about some change in their payment methods, and I got an update on her health. She's getting worse. It seems to be all downhill from now on.'

'Poor Penelope. She used to be so... so vibrant, you know?'

Andrew nodded as he shut the window, taking in a deep breath of fresh air. 'It got me thinking...'

'You want to go to Greece to see her?'

Andrew bit his bottom lip and stared straight at her. Susan watched his thumbs play around with his fingers. 'Go on, spit it out.'

'I wanna us all to go. For the entire summer...'

Susan dropped the knife she was wiping into the soapy pool of the sink. Andrew never understood why she washed the dishes so well if she was going to place them in the dish-washer anyway.

'The *entire* summer?'

'Think about it,' Andrew said, raising his voice. Susan saw the spark in his round eyes come to life.

'Oh, God. Another one of his project ideas.'

'My mum inherited her grandma's old mansion. It stands on a great piece of land. We go for the summer, stay in the place, visit my mother and draw up plans to renovate the place. We are an amazing team. Projects are what we do best. Architect and designer superpower!'

'That doesn't even make sense.'

Andrew lowered his raised arms and placed his hands on her shoulders. 'I can only think of benefits. Others would give an arm and a leg for a summer in paradise, in Greece. The sun, the sea, the air... it will do us all good. My half-Greek kids should know more than a simple kalimera and efcharisto. We need this as a family. And you need to work, to design. And, I'll get to spend my mother's dying days by her side...'

'Nice play, Mr. Fotopoulos.'

Andrew chuckled and scratched the back of his neck. 'And, think about it. Greece's economy is finally on the rise again. Prices are going up. That mansion will one day be ours. Ours to sell. This could be two new cars for us. And all college expenses for all three of them. And all our future holidays.'

'What a wonderful future you paint. For all *five of us*. While *one of us* was placed in a small wooden box and thrown into the cold winter ground...'

Andrew pulled her into his arms and squeezed her upon his heavily breathing chest. 'I miss him, too. Every single day. I close my eyes, and there he is. His cheeky smile, and his shiny eyes. His uncontrollable laughter echoes in my ears. But we owe to our living kids, to our marriage, and to our mental health to do something. Anything! This is our home. Not a mausoleum.'

'And yet, you want to escape it.'

Chapter Four

GREECE

June, 2010

'I see land!'

Sophia removed her brand-new possession: her headphones. 'Shhh, Christopher! The whole plane doesn't want to hear your high-pitched shriek of a voice,' she said. Her body seemed to not react, yet her keen wide eyes journeyed west in search of a view out of the excuse for a window. The scintillating sun transformed the airplane's window into the Eye of Sauron. She narrowed her eyes and raised herself inches off her seat. Islands were spread out below, like still leaves floating in a clear lake. Sophia's heartbeat accelerated, accompanied by Drake's latest beat, yet her teenage expression drowned out all newborn excitement.

'Wow! Look at all those islands,' Christopher continued as if not a single word his sister uttered managed to reach his ears. He leaned closer, dropping his mythology book right off his lap.

In the row of seats behind them, their sister, Maya,

hopped on her father's legs, pushing his glued-to-the-glass Greek nose out of the way.

'All I see is clouds!'

'Look down, jellybaby,' Andrew said as he stretched out his arm and laid his sausage fingers upon his wife's slender hand. He forced his puffy eyes to wink. His inner spark got jumpstarted by Susan's first *real* smile in ages.

'I knew Greece would do us good. Cold, colorless England... in its grounds I buried a son and my wife's joy and will to live... Greece can't bring back my boy, but damn it, it will bring back my Susan... God, I miss being in your heaven... I hope Mama remembers us...'

Scattered thoughts meandered in his mind. He closed his red sleepless eyes and felt comfort at war of the sting from his deprived eyelids. His village came to life in his brain's private cinema. Blocks of countryside joined as the puzzle of his childhood background formed.

'Ladies and gentlemen, this is your captain speaking; we have just been cleared to land at Corfu International Airport. Please make sure one last time that your seat belt is securely fastened. The flight attendants...' The pilot's guttural voice interrupted his childhood memories. It also spread smiles to the Fotopoulos gang. Even to Sophia who tried to hide her excitement behind a *'finally'*. She eagerly awaited to be able to reopen her phone and post on her MySpace. Her friends would be so jealous of her summer in sunny Greece. She hoped Gary and his dreamy eyes would see her photos. A whole year being in love with him and all she could master was a plain *hi*. All she did was like his Facebook posts. Not all, of course; she did not wish to appear desperate or a loser. Or worse, both. Teenage problems in a teenage world.

'What time are we taking the ferry?' Susan asked as she played around with a rebellious strike of hair in front of her eyes. She was growing fond of her new color. Fiery red suited her.

'In two hours. Plenty of time.'

'And the bus?'

'In the evening. So we will have time for lunch and a stroll in Parga. Remember how much you loved my dad's village when you first came?' Andrew replied, crunching his knuckles. She hated that noise.

'Hope tourism hasn't murdered its beauty,' she commented in a low voice as she forced all freedom-fighting hair back into her black band.

Sophia poked her slim face between the seats and squinted her vivid eyes. 'Seriously, where the heck are you taking us? A plane, a ferry, and then a bus? What's next? A car to the donkey park and from there on we ride into the sunset in unchartered lands?'

Susan released a soft laugh. 'She's definitely your daughter!'

Just then, the plane shook them and the black wheel made contact with the cracked cement ground.

'Mesopotamos. Your grandma's village. Small, but not unchartered, I assure you!' Andrew answered his daughter's sarcastic question.

'Mesopotamos? Middle river?' Christopher translated.

'Yes, wise one.'

'Are we heading to Middle Earth?'

'Why, yes, my young hobbit!'

Chapter Five

PARGA

The night after the funeral
1913

The moonless night suited her fine. The empty streets and the serenity floating in the subtle breeze brought a faint smile to her pale face. Iphigenia could not remember when she last left the house at such an hour. *Midnight.* Maybe this was the first time. Fear caused her spine to shiver. She was a woman walking the dark, silent streets alone. The ebbing tide was gently caressing the sand as the crash of the surf on the rocky islets of the bay broke the silence. Saltwater aroma filled her nostrils to the point she could taste the Ionian on her dry tongue.

Suddenly, horny cats rushed by her feet. Iphigenia quickly brought her hands to cover her mouth and drown a breathy scream. Voices traveled to her cold ears as she paused to exhale. Men were returning from the only well-lit building at such an ungodly hour -the fisherman's pub. Iphigenia sprinted and hid behind a fig tree to her right. She brought her arms to her side and remained still as the clearly drunk men trudged by her hideout. Their ode to freedom came uproariously out of the intoxicated lungs and echoed down dark alleyways. Such a path, Iphigenia chose. The church was near. Father Gregory's room was nearer.

The rusty gate stood taller than the one-meter wall that ran around the Holy grounds. No one hardly used it. No need to use the back entrance. No need to sneak into church. Iphigenia had no interest in the centuries-old building. Her eyes were fixed on the wooden door to her left. A simple hut where Father Gregory slept. Iphigenia scanned her surroundings. Apart from a majestic owl and an eerie song of the wind, she was alone. She took steady, determined steps toward the door. A deep breath helped calm her nerves. Her right hand formed a punch and came close to the door. She was not ready to knock. She placed her forehead on the door and contemplated the madness. *'Madness is all the heart can produce.'*

Father Gregory loved the owl that took up home in his garden. He considered himself a sort of night bird, too. Even though his days began early, he found it impossible to switch off his mind and surrender into Morpheus' sweet embrace. He sat on the edge of his single bed and looked down at his books. Books had conquered his small room. Always three or four of them would lay on his wooden bedside table -built by his late father, bathing under the light of tall church candles. The rest of his books formed towers around the humble habitat.

His round glasses with the thin frame sat upon his nose as his eyes ran along the words of Homer's Iliad. He had not read the epic poem since he was a teen. He was amazed at how many details he had missed the first time around. His youthful eyes then rushed to the battle scenes, the descriptions of heroes, and even if he felt guilty to the Lord to admit, to the raucous sex scenes. Now, a mature man, his mind foraged for words, for meaning. Fate, free will, friendship, honor and love raised above bloody battle scenes.

Knock. Knock.

He was not sure if he heard well. It surely could not be someone at his door. He stood up. Another faint knock and a slight wobble of his old door. Fear was his first emotion. After living ninety-nine percent of his life under Ottoman rule, his first thought was of war. '*The Turks are back.*'

'Hello?'

A long pause. A silence that fed his trepidation.

The timid female voice shocked him. 'It's me. Iphigenia.'

He looked down at his body. Only a white shirt and his underpants covered him.

'Wait. Let me dress.'

'Please let me in before anyone sees me.'

Father Gregory took a reluctant step toward the door. He opened it and hid his body behind it. With a deep, loud exhale he closed it; his mind running wild thoughts. A lady in his chambers. That was a first.

'Iphigenia, this is highly inappropriate,' he began to say, still facing the door.

Iphigenia stroked her face, her palms collecting cold globules of sweat and moved behind him. 'I can't stand that mausoleum of a house. I'm alone. More alone than ever before.'

'Go to your aunt's in Corfu for a few days ...'

'I need to feel wanted.'

His eyes widened. 'Effie, please. Do not taunt me.'

He shivered as her hands touched his broad back. His entire spine shook as she placed her head upon him.

'Effie, stop. Your husband is still fresh in the ground.'

'Dead. To be eaten by worms. I'm alive. Giorgo was a good man and a great father, but I never loved him…'

Father Gregory swung around. 'Don't say that.'

'It's the truth. He was my father's choice. Not mine. My heart had long chosen you. *You*. The sweet boy with the careless curly hair and a smile that brought shame to the brightest night sky. The boy who gave me my first kiss. The boy that took my virginity…'

'Iphigenia!'

'I have always been yours,' she continued, and the gap between their trembling bodies diminished and vanished. She could feel his erection growing, pushing up against her. 'Body and soul.'

'Jesus Christ, show mercy,' he said, his eyes closed. He felt her fingers under his shirt running upon his pores, journeying downward. His underpants soon fell to the stone ground and his breathing turned heavy. The tip of his penis touched bare skin and he realized Iphigenia's dress also fell victim of gravity. It was going to be the second time in his life to be with a woman. The first being twenty years ago with the same girl. The girl that his heart would skip a beat or two every time he laid eyes upon her autumn hair and sun-kissed skin.

Iphigenia pulled him toward her, and together they fell back on his narrow bed. Between the white tangled sheets, she exhaled with delight as she felt him in her. She was once again that careless teenage girl that loved nothing more than to run through the meadows, collecting flowers and absorbing energizing rays from the generous Greek sun. Her nails dug slightly into his buttocks, and she pushed him down, forcing him deeper inside her. She inhaled his manly scent. Father Gregory's instincts took over him, and he thrust faster and harder. Iphigenia fought to control her need to yell. The Father was well-endowed, nearly double Giorgo, the only other man she had had between her curvy legs.

The few minutes seemed like hours to her. She was right where she wished to be. Now, to only find the right time to say the right words. The speech she had rehearsed many times before at her home. Suddenly, in the midst of her musing, Father Gregory abruptly pulled out of her and with a muted grunt he awkwardly came on her thigh and sprinkled the clean sheets. Iphigenia sat up and hugged him, her cool body against his burning skin. He quivered in her embrace and clasped her close to his beating heart. His eyes looked up at the almost bare wall opposite him. Christ remained still on his wooden cross, yet Gregory could sense His eyes staring at him, piercing through his soul. He almost whispered 'I'm sorry', though surprisingly guilt never took hold of him. He felt like he was where he was supposed to be. He felt closer to Heaven than ever before. '*Blasphemy, Gregory!*'

Neither of them spoke for a while. Slowly, they fell back onto the thin mattress, their heads sharing the single pillow. Their breathing settled and returned to normal, aiding the rule of silence in the low-ceiling room. Iphigenia waited for him to speak first. Minutes passed before his lips parted and words departed from them.

'This was wrong.'

'No, it was not. A God of love…'

Father Gregory moved away from her and sat up, his back against the old wall. Candlelight danced upon his face, distorting his friendly image. His eyes looked dark. 'Please, do not bring God into this. I am an embarrassment to our religion, to my church.'

She placed her hands upon his. 'Then quit.'

His eyes, wide and still, came forward to the light. His jaw hung low. No word came out of his open mouth.

'You're a good priest. And you served the Lord during hard barbarous years. You kept our faith and taught the next generation. You gave Him all of you. Maybe it's time someone else took over. Peace has arrived, and you deserve to enjoy it. To live the rest of your life with me.'

'A priest marrying a widow? The people here would …'

'Who cares? We will not stay here.'

Father Gregory scratched his eyebrow. 'And where would we go?'

Iphigenia smiled at his question. He was considering her proposal. 'Mesopotamos. I have a large piece of land there which I inherited from my late grandmother. Away from everyone. We will build ourselves a castle with walls capable of protecting us from all the cruelty of the world. I've had enough of hardship. I want you. Only you. Us! King and Queen in our own fairytale.'

'And live on what?'

She ran her fingertip along his cheek. 'Always the practical man.' She giggled. 'I'm not sure your heart and mind can cope with another shock.'

'Test me,' he replied, rejoicing in his new-found confidence. He felt alive. He felt a man.

'With the gold you have below the church. The money hidden by people trusting their fortunes here rather than risk the Turks getting their filthy hands on them. Folk that have been dead for centuries.'

'That belongs to the church.'

Iphigenia shook her head. 'No, it belongs to its owners. Most of which don't even have living relatives anymore. We won't take it all. Just enough to build a house and a sufficient amount to live out the rest of our days carefree. No more working the rough land. I want to be a woman at home. Your woman,' she said and leaned forward to kiss his lips. She continued kissing him. Down his neck she went, her tongue traveling down his chest, heading between his legs.

The sensation fogged his mind. He was not sure about her plan, but he was positive that he longed to be inside her again.

Chapter Six

MESOPOTAMOS

2010

A storm in the stomach plagued the ladies of the Fotopoulos gang.

The twenty-year-old bus with the faded colors and the peeled paint sped along the uneven country road with the dried-up bushes. Nothing able to withstand the ferocious summer sun. The magical images of *touristy* picturesque Corfu and Parga faded in their minds as endless fields connected as a puzzle to fill their view. Dirt and olive trees were in abundance all the way to the thin line touching the clear turquoise sky.

Andrew gently ran his fingers through Maya's soft blonde hair as she leaned on him, trying hard to keep her calamari and chips lunch within her tiny body. Sophia also struggled to keep her vegan lunch in and sat up straight with her eyelids sealed.

'Not even your stomach wants the crap you eat in it,'

Christopher said, shaking his sister. 'Feed me meat! Feed me meat!' he joked.

'Chris, stop it,' she said with a soft voice. He knew that tone well. And she did say Chris, not Christopher. 'Okay, okay. But seriously, we are in Greece, and we are going to a remote village. Meat is on the menu daily out here. What you gonna do? Graze the grasslands with the only other vegan animals out here?'

Behind them, their mother sat silently next to an elderly lady dressed in all black. Her vague stare did not focus on anything particular. The background was just lines of shades of green and brown. The tempest in her stomach did not come from delicious seafood but from her agitated mind. Thoughts and thoughts. Thoughts and thoughts. *'Please, shut off.'*

'I used to worry,' the old lady said in Greek. Susan sighed and turned to her direction. Crow's feet set off from her kind, beady eyes and connected with rivulets of deep wrinkles and scars. 'Not anymore. Life is too short to stress about things not in our control. Enjoy the ride now that you are young, my dear. You have a beautiful family. The future is not always kind. Live the now, my red-haired beauty.'

Susan nodded and forced a slight smile at the enigmatic woman.

'Do you understand Greek?' the woman continued, probably expecting more of a reply than body language.

'A little,' Susan replied, glad her children could not hear her and laugh at her bizarre -according to them- Greek accent. 'My husband is Greek.'

'Lucky you. Mine died in the war.'

Susan rolled her tongue across her teeth before opening her mouth. *'When was Greece in a war last? Did he fight in*

27

Cyprus? Member of NATO's peace force somewhere in a troubled land? Susan, shut it off, she is waiting for a reply!'

'And he brought you out here to see the corner of heaven in which he was raised? the old lady beat her to it.

'Sorry to hear about your husband. My condolences,' Susan said and continued with answering her question. 'Yes, yes. We saw Parga. What a marvelous place. Now, we are off to Mesopotamos.'

'That small village? Don't expect much. Nothing like Parga. Though if you ever get bored, take the kids to Ammoudia. Wonderful beach, good restaurants, too.'

Susan smiled widely. 'Thank you. That's very kind of you to mention.'

The woman closed her eyes and leaned back as if ready to take a nap. 'Anything to keep them away from the dangers at the manteio.'

Susan had no idea what the old lady's last word meant. The woman seemed to have fallen asleep.

'There's Daddy's village,' Andrew said and watched as Maya opened her eyes to take a peek out of the window. Light bounced from the glass and made her violet eyes shine, awakening their peculiar purple color. Christopher had read that less than one percent of the population had violet eyes, while Sophia always said that with golden hair and violet eyes, Maya could be a successful influencer on social media one day. Envy normally dressed her comment. She and Christopher had inherited most of their father's characteristics. Brown eyes and large noses were not ideal for Instagram fame. Christopher, at least, had their mother's fair hair. Hers were as black as her first cat, Chimney. Another Greek present from her father's side.

Maya giggled. 'Town small.'

'Yes, jellybaby. The town is small. It's called a village,' he replied, glad to be released from her hold. He crunched his knuckles and then opened his arms wide. His upper back clicked and clacked. 'I think I am turning into a Transformer.'

Christopher laughed out loud. For a young boy with such a high-pitched voice, his laughter carried a lot of bass. It was also contagious. Even Susan could not resist a chuckle.

'Finally! Our trip to the middle of nowhere is coming to an end.'

'Actually, Greece was considered by many in the ancient world to be the center of the Earth so that would ...'

'Aaaagh,' Sophia grunted and rolled her eyes. 'Zip it, Living-Encyclopedia.'

Christopher laughed again. 'You say that as if it is a bad thing.'

Susan took in a deep breath at the sight of the small village with the few scattered houses surrounded by vast grasslands running up to the line of dark, dull mountains. They paled in comparison to the highlands where her Scottish grandfather used to live. '*From what attitude are they considered mountains? What criteria make you a hill? Mental note for later: Ask the Google you gave birth to,*' she thought as she focused on Christopher giggling as his sister tickled him. She felt the closest to possible joy as she saw her three kids all smiling: energetic and carefree under the strong vibrant rays. Eugene's death took a toll on them as well. A sense of guilt lingered above them the first few months after his passing. Guilt to play, to laugh, to live. Yet, gradually, they returned to themselves, restored to their default state of childhood. At first, this angered Susan. They were forgetting him, while she found it impossible to move on. Maya asked for her brother often. He was her playmate. It broke Susan's frail heart to hear her search for Eugene, but at least she had someone to hug and feel pain with. Andrew avoided showing emotions. Andrew avoided her in the beginning. Now, to see them all happy made her realize that they needed to move on. She rolled her eyes. '*Aaaagh, Andrew was right. Again!*'

The German-made bus came to a halt outside of a small cafeteria. The silent driver with the big, thick mustache that covered a large percentage of his lower face waited for the cloud of dust and black smoke of the exhaust to be carried away from the weak wind before pushing the button that opened the door. He switched off the engine and rushed out. Susan spied on him as he made his way to the lavatory door. At that moment, her eye caught a sunburned, lanky man with ripped jeans and a checkered shirt apparently missing half its buttons. A thin chain housing a golden cross hid between thick grey chest hair that escaped from within the top of the red and blue shirt. A toothpick bobbled as his yellowy teeth played with its end. None of these though were the details that surprised her. It was the sign in his hands. A white piece of paper with *FOTOPOULOS* written upon it with a black marker. A blue smiley face had been drawn it the corner. Andrew was already outside, lifting their luggage out of the quiet beast's belly. He rolled up his shirt's sleeves, his muscles stretching as he lifted Sophia's heavy bag, glowing from the sweat welcoming the bright sun. The countryside was cooler than Corfu and Parga, but it was still a high enough temperature to be considered a heat wave by any permanent resident of cloudy London. Their three kids stood behind him, all looking around at the small houses with the large gardens that run along the side of the road. Around them, green dominated. They had not seen so much green since their holiday in Scotland.

'Dear, look,' Susan said, stepping off the vehicle.

Andrew wiped his forehead and focused in the direction of his wife's hand.

'You must be the Fotopoulos family, eh?' the man with the sign said in a rather good English accent. 'I am Harry. Harry, the taxi man,' he introduced himself and pointed to the green cab parked under the shade provided by a towering carob tree. 'Your mother, Penelope, sent me to pick you up. Your house is not exactly near to the village.'

'How far is it?' Sophia asked, each word louder than the last.

'Oh, not too far, my sweet one. A short drive, yet with all your luggage, Penelope, bless her heart, did not wish for you to walk through the fields with this sun above you,' he replied as he shook Andrew's sweaty hand and listened to him introduce each family member. 'Leave your luggage to me. Go enjoy my strong aircon.'

Susan squeezed into the back seats with her three children while Andrew sat shotgun. The air was indeed cool, too cool. Cold. Icy. Maya even blew out air to see if it would form a cloud. Strange music came from the audio system - rough, strong, sharp sounds from a seemingly out-of-tune orchestra. A skeleton key-ring hung from the rearview mirror, sandwiched between two furry red dice and a donkey doll with *I LOVE GREECE* printed on its side.

Bang.

The slamming of the car's trunk made Susan jump, offering a much-needed giggle to her worried children. Their sense of adventure had diminished with each scale of their journey, from the large coastal town of Corfu to the marvel of Parga to the nothing-to-do-or-see village of their grandmother's.

Nothing could prepare them though for the sight of the dirt road through endless twisted olive trees that lead to the one-hundred-year-old mansion. Not a single house could be seen in the distance. Trees all the way to fields, and fields all the way to mountains. They parked upon the marble tiles that covered a large chunk of the house's front garden. Weeds and wildflowers grew out of each crack. You saw more flora than man-made floor.

Christopher opened his door first and a gust of thick hot air rushed into the confined space of the taxi. The young boy leaped out of the car and gazed upon the two-story home. 'It sure has seen better days, huh, Dad?'

Happy crickets and broken wooden shutters provided the soundtrack to their shock. 'Maybe it's nicer on the inside,' Andrew replied walking up to his son and placing his arm upon Christopher's skinny shoulders. 'And, don't forget,' he continued, turning toward his wife, 'we are here to fix it up. Think! All this land is ours.'

Susan gazed around her. *Their* land stretched for a least a mile in all directions until it reached the stone-built wall that ran around *their* property. *Theirs*. She repeated the word a few times. Out of amazement or to help the notion settle in her mind better, she did not know. Each rock in the wall housed a considerable amount of mold -a sign of wet winters- and Greek Ivy crept through the crevices of the old wall. Susan shivered at the idea of how the uninhabited-for-years home would look on the inside.

Sophia dared to go up the seventeen marble steps that led to the long veranda. Skeletal shrubs in old pots were placed by each column. Corpses of a beloved garden long lost. Her sweaty palm landed on the cool door handle. 'It's locked!' she yelled out. 'Of course it is, Sophie. Wait. I've got the key here somewhere,' her father replied and started to pat the pockets of his faded-blue jeans.

'Of course, it is,' she mimicked his voice softly. 'What the hell for? There's no one for miles, and who in their right minds would break into the place? I doubt Mesopotamos has many squatters or crack addicts,' she mumbled as she walked around the place, stopping by a dirty window. She created an oval shape upon the glass and tried to gaze inside. Darkness owned the place. She guessed she was starring at the back of thick curtains.

'How much do we owe you?' Andrew asked the driver, key and wallet in his right hand.

A small grin appeared on the driver's face. 'Oh, everything has been paid for beforehand,' he said and looked up at the mansion. 'Enjoy your stay,' he continued as he unloaded their luggage.

'Paid for?' Andrew asked with young Maya pulling on his trousers, eager to explore.

'You'll see,' the driver replied and winked.

Andrew was beginning to feel annoyed. He opened his mouth, yet he had no time to put his thoughts into words as the driver spoke loudly. 'First surprise, my friend,' he said and raised his eyebrows, bowing gently forward, pointing to the house. A window on the top floor opened, creaking on its rusty hinges. 'Welcome, welcome!'

Andrew took a step back and blinked twice. An awkward smile came to life. 'Mum?'

The elderly woman waved enthusiastically from the window. 'I'll be right down. Oh my, how they have grown!'

Susan walked up to shaken Andrew. 'What is she doing here?'

He shook his head and raised his hands. 'Beats me. I

thought she was in her nursing home in Preveza. I was planning on all of us taking the bus down there tomorrow to visit and then to surprise you all with a day at the beach.' With the word surprise, his mind went to the taxi driver. He looked back and realized the car was gone. Funny, he heard no noise. He must have been focused on his mother.

The mansion's majestic, thick, sun-bleached, green wooden door opened before their eyes, and a short, dark-complexioned lady limped out into the light. Her purple cane banged against the ground, and she wobbled her extra weight towards them.

Andrew swallowed his sorrow at the sight of the silver-haired woman with deep wrinkles. Once his robust mother. He rushed up the steps, laid his strong arms around her, and kissed her three times. 'What are you doing here, Mama? Are you alone?' he asked, wiping a few tears forming in the corners of his eyes.

'Always worrying. I am perfectly capable of taking care of myself if that's what you are asking, young man. This is my home. I feel just right here. I told them; I have family coming...'

'And they let you go?'

'My, my, they have grown. My Sophia. My Christopher!'

Andrew's eyes opened wide. He looked back at Susan. 'She remembers them,' he whispered as his children fell victims to their grandma's attack of kisses, hugs, and cheek pinching. Susan walked up the steps with Maya in her embrace.

'Hello, my dear,' Penelope said quickly and turned her attention to the child looking down. 'We have never met, my little one. I am your grandmother, Penelope, and you must be...'

'Maya,' Susan said, killing the long pause.

'Oohh, magical name, my little bird. Fitting...'

'Mama...'

Penelope walked straight by him, placed one foot inside, and proudly declared, 'My family, welcome to Fotopoulos Manor!'

One by one, they took the plunge and walked into the darkness.

'Silly me. Let me open the curtains,' Penelope said. The five stood together, trying to make out what the dark shapes were around them. A divine flowery smell invaded their nostrils, reminding Susan of one of her favorite fragrances - Jo Malone No.42. *Bang, bang, bang.* The purple cane yelled. The banging got faster as Penelope quickly beelined to the first curtain. She drew the drapes. 'Viola! Let there be light!'

A gasp of shock came from the Fotopoulos gang as strong light spread around the vast hall. The decrepit outside had prepared them for the worse, yet in front of them stood the inside of a palace. They exchanged confused looks as their eyes ran from the perfect spiral staircase with the oak steps to the antique pedestal table with the expensive silver candlesticks and the Persian vase filled with red roses.

More light invaded the room as, one by one, Penelope opened the thick, Syrian curtains, allowing the Mediterranean summer sun to push the darkness into the corners. The floor sparkled below them, and fresh air plundered towards them as Penelope opened the last window.

'Mama, where did all this furniture come from? Please, tell me you haven't been cleaning all day. At your age...'

'Pa pa pa pa,' she said, covering her ears and running - as much as her weak knees allowed- toward the three children. 'Don't believe a word he says. I'm not a day older than sixty. Now, let me show you the kitchen. Guess who bought ice-cream!'

Penelope walked backward, enjoying the smiling youths following her, and with a Spanish dance move, she banged her bottom against the kitchen door. The cherry-wood door receded from view, revealing a long mahogany table. A straw bowl overflowed with seasonal fruit, and little porcelain plates sat around it. 'See? I have healthier choices, too.' Penelope laughed as her son and daughter-in-law came into the grand kitchen. 'But for now, ice-cream as promised. My first of many gifts, my loved ones,' she said, caressing Christopher's jaw. 'I plan on spoiling you silly. The Gods know when I will be seeing you again. Oh, I wish I had you here in Greece, year-round.' Penelope exhaled deeply. With another sigh, she started to serve the chocolate and vanilla ice-cream. 'Two scoops each. Tonight, I will be cooking my specialty. Chicken, golden roast potatoes and my boy's favorite, pastitsio! Oh, my Andreas loved his pastitsio. Didn't you, my son?'

Andrew nodded and walked up to his mother. He rubbed her shoulders and bowed to lay a loud kiss on her right cheek.

'No cooking? No cleaning? If she doesn't interfere much, this just might be the best vacation ever.' Susan looked around. Her interior designer skills had an easy chore on their hands. The place seemed recently renovated. It was the outside that needed all the work. Enough work to keep Andrew busy. Enough time for her mind to escape London. Susan began to have high hopes for the summer.

'Finished!' Christopher's voice interrupted her thoughts once again. 'Can I go choose my room, now?'

Sophia's eyes sparkled. 'How many rooms are in the house, Yiayia? Please tell me we get our own bedroom!'

'Nice play with the yiayia touch!' Christopher whispered.

Penelope laughed. 'You will both...'

'Yes?' they asked in unison.

'Get your own room!'

'Happy dance time,' Christopher said and began to wave his hands while stomping his skinny legs. Deep down, Sophia wished she was not so uptight. The happy dance seemed fun, but she was no longer a silly child.

'My room is at the end of the hall. Your parents, with Maya, will be at the other end. Choose anyone of the remaining four. Go, get. Choose wisely!'

———

The rest of the evening featured an hour of unpacking, much-needed refreshing showers, much-more needed naps, and consuming Penelope's delicious Greek dishes.

'You sure you don't want to try the wine?' Penelope asked, her eyes fixed on the empty wine glass in front of her daughter-in-law.

'No, no. Thank you. Water is fine,' Susan replied, and she picked up her glass by her just-emptied plate. It had been a while since she last enjoyed such a meal.

'My, my! Look at the time,' Andrew said, looking down at his phone. The dark screen informed him that it was eleven o'clock. It also let him know that his battery was on the verge of dying. He tried to remember if he had seen his charger while unpacking.

'Come on, Maya,' Susan said reaching out her arms. 'Bedtime. I do believe this is the latest you have ever been up.'

'Go on, children! Upstairs with your mother.'

'Come on, Dad. It's summer...'

'Good night, Sophia.'

Sophia lowered her shoulders and trudged out of the kitchen. Their steps echoed through the vast hall as the four made their way up the spiral staircase, under the expensive chandelier. Christopher placed his reading glasses on, trying to figure out the carvings in the gold-plated pendant. '*The light is too strong.*'

Soon the house went quiet, and Andrew sat alone with his mother. 'I'll have some more wine,' he said, raising the bottle. 'Cheers,' he continued, raising his fine glass, sparkling in the candlelight. All the lights were switched on, yet Penelope always lit candles during meals. Always with exotic scents. Not that their aroma could compete with that departing from the honey-roasted chicken.

'Shouldn't you be joining your wife, my son?'

'I haven't seen you in years, Mama. I'd rather spend time with you.'

Penelope sniggered. 'And go down memory lane? In this place?'

'How is your memory, by the way?' he dared to ask.

'How is your marriage coping, by the way?'

Andrew tilted his head back and unleashed his trademark full-of-bass laughter.

'You haven't changed one bit,' he said and placed his hands upon hers. Her wrinkled hands were icy cold.

'Your wife has changed, though. Too much pain that one carries. It's your job to help lift the weight of incomprehensible loss. Go. Get to bed. Be where you're supposed to be.'

Chapter Seven

The first night

The lustrous moon sailed upon the somber night sky to find the Fotopoulos family fast asleep in the dark mansion. The wind howled outside, and the night animals joined in a cacophonous midnight symphony. Inside, in Sophia's newly-claimed bedroom, silence was queen of the room. Suddenly, Sophia's eyelids rapidly moved, her body sensing the tapping in the hallway outside her room. A light sleeper compared to her siblings, Sophia sleepily opened one eye. Faint light formed a line beneath her door. Someone had turned on the hallway lights.

Tap. Tap. Tap.

'Great! Every time Nan has to pee, she will wake me with her freaking cane!'

Tap. Tap. Tap.

Sophia placed her second pillow, the one with the gothic unicorn pillowcase, above her head and rolled her eyes. Just as she was about to close them and hope to be carried off to dreamland rather easily, she saw the shadow of the figure outside her door. No taps followed for a while. The shadow remained still for what seemed to Sophia for forever.

'Has she have forgotten where she was going? Should I get up and help her?'

Just then, her door handle journeyed downwards, and her door began to open. The lights in the hallway went out. Darkness spread and conquered once again. Sophia felt her heartbeats race into the hundreds. No tapping could be heard, yet she could vaguely see a hued figure coming into her room. Sophia closed her eyes shut.

Each hair on the back of her neck stood at attention as she sensed someone sitting down at the bottom of her bed. *'Holy shit.'*

She felt cold air under her dark sheet. A thick smell, a weird fragrance like burning leaves reached her nostrils. A hand touched her leg. Hard icy fingers crawled along her thigh. With cold sweat exiting nearly every pour of her startled skin, Sophia sat up.

'Nanny, you are in the wrong room...' she began to say as her right hand covered the surface of her bedside table in search for her lamp's switch. In a split second, light pushed the blackness away.

Sophia screamed at the top of her lungs.

She was alone in her room.

Minutes before her wail, Christopher awoke in his warm bed. The night breeze was not able to cool him from Greece's summer temperatures. His tongue ran along his dry lips. 'I'm not forgetting water again,' he whispered as he slid out of his sheets, and his feet landed upon the cool floor. He cracked his back, scratched his nose, and set off for the kitchen. He walked in the dark, following the clock's languid ticking to the tenebrous staircase. Step by step, Christopher hopped down to the ground floor. Moonlight shone in through the only window with its curtains drawn open. All light fell upon a large, majestic painting occupying the wall before him. At first, it was the naked black man that caught his attention. He giggled at the sight of his bare ass. He was, after all, a ten-year-old boy. Yet as he approached, it was the pain painted upon the various figures that engaged him. '*Are those bees or flies?*' His eyes gazed at the black river. Nothing but a small boat in it.

'The ve..vesti...vestibule,' he struggled to read the title below the painting. The next words had faded. Only a few words remained readable. 'Must... cross... Acheron.'

'Acheron,' he repeated. He had seen the peculiar word before. He was not awake enough though to remember where. The light hitting the painting faded and turned into shadow. 'A cloud must be covering the moon,' Christopher said as he turned around. His eyes opened wide. The curtains had been shut. Now, he was fully awake. He swallowed the lump in his throat and exhaled. 'Mum? Dad?'

His voice was drowned out by his sister's yells from above. Panting, he dashed up upstairs and switched on the hallway's lights. He stood outside his door and watched as his father and mother ran out from their room and into Sophia's.

Susan rushed to her panicking daughter and embraced her, while Andrew looked around the room. 'So, where's the cockroach?'

Sophia stopped her cries and looked straight at him; the corners of her feline eyes betrayed her anger. 'There's no insect. Grandma came into my room, and when I turned on the lights, she was gone.'

'There, there,' her mother said, stroking her hair, pulling

away hair stuck to her forehead's sweat. 'She probably lost her way...'

'No, you don't get it. She sat on my bed, and when I turned on the lights, she disappeared.'

'Like a ghost?' Christopher asked from the doorway.

'Go to bed, Son. Your sister had a nightmare. That's all.'

'It happened!'

Andrew walked out her room and down the long corridor. He stood outside his mother's door for a second and quietly pulled down the handle. He popped his head into her room. She was asleep in her bed, a serene look upon her face. Andrew sighed and closed the door.

'Let's all try and get back to bed,' he said and headed back to his comfortable king-sized bed.

Susan stayed with Sophia for a while, making sure her daughter managed to fall back to sleep. Her hands were restless. She let her hands play with each other, her fingers intertwined. She desired a glass of wine. Her lips craved the flavor. Her throat demanded to feel the alcohol flowing down it. Her mind visualized the bottles in the kitchen below.

Just one glass,' she lied to herself and stood up. She tiptoed out of the room and headed downstairs.

Chapter Eight

MESOPOTAMOS

1914

Menacing red eyes pierced through the darkness of the woods. Smoke plundered to Iphigenia's bare feet. Footsteps grew louder behind her. Iphigenia did not turn around. She sprinted forward feeling the rough ground dig into her skin. The wind around her carried eerie whispers. Words were spoken, yet none understood. Iphigenia felt as if she was hearing a strange foreign language. Suddenly, everything around her turned red as if the sun had just crept up from the East or as if a forest fire was heading her way. Her foot hit a dead tree trunk bathing in the leafy grounds. She stumbled forward and fell on all fours. As she raised her head, she saw three skinny figures approaching from the bright red light. Two men and a woman. All sickly looking. All with deep scars. All underfed. Toothless. Nearly hairless. Yellowy skin. They opened their mouths. Iphigenia could not hear a word. She tried to read their thin lips.

'Iphigenia? Effie?' she heard Gregory's drowsy voice. 'Effie, wake up!'

Iphigenia opened her eyes and looked at the chandelier above her head. Her fingers could feel the woven quilt covering her body. She turned to her side, and her trembling eyes saw Gregory staring at her. 'You keep talking in your sleep. You're driving me mad.'

Iphigenia tried to catch her elusive breath. 'Sorry,' she whispered. '*What an awful dream.*'

By the time she apologized, Gregory's breathing informed her that he had fallen back to sleep. Iphigenia pushed the heavy cover from her overheating body. 'Three figures...'

Her bare feet touched down on the new expensive rug by the side of her bed. She took one look at Gregory. '*Why can't I be so peaceful?*'

Iphigenia crept out from their bedroom door and lit a thick beige candle that nestled in a golden holder – a 'gift' she had taken from the church. The light danced upon the corridor walls as the flame swayed under her breath. Iphigenia took careful steps as she counted the steps of the spiral staircase during her descent to the ground floor. A grin appeared along her pale face as she walked into the room she was shaping as the house's library. She had always been an avid reader. She had always been a poor village girl. The latter fact devoured her dreams of reading and owning many books. Now, with more riches than she thought possible, she fed her undernourished passion. Rows of empty oak-carved shelves welcomed her into the room. She longed to fill them. Two bookcases filled with books stood opposite her. She used her candle to light the three standing on a round table in the center of the room. Her eyes embraced the stronger light and ran along the books' spines. Iphigenia picked up a rather heavy book about Greek Mythology and laid it upon the table. She smiled at the sight of the only two books, Gregory ever read. Over and over again, he read the Bible and the Iliad. Homer was the only author worth reading besides the prophets and the saints. At least, that was Gregory's opinion.

Her fingers turned the pages carefully as she sought the image imprinted in her mind. She was sure she had seen the three figures before.

Page two hundred and thirty.

There they were. Staring back at her in all their sickly glory. 'Nosoi,' she read the title.

She sat back in the burgundy armchair with the tall back. 'Nosoi, the diseases that plague mankind live at the entrance of the Underworld,' she continued reading. 'With Death, Grief, Hunger ...'

She stopped reading and looked at the open door. Did she hear footsteps?

'... together they usher in the souls of the dead, showing them their new home,' her smooth voice read on.

Tap. Tap. Tap.

Now, she was certain. She left the book opened and stood up. 'Gregory, I'm in here.'

A door slammed and the sharp thud travelled through the mansion. 'Gregory?' She picked up her candle holder and stepped outside. 'Gregory?' The kitchen door was shut. They never closed that door unless they were cooking with onions and spices. As she approached the door, scratching sounds reached her ears. It reminded her of a wicked lady, a teacher she had in primary school that ran her ruined nails upon the chalkboard whenever a whisper was heard in her classroom.

Iphigenia knelt slowly. She peeked through the keyhole.

Darkness. Pitch-black. Iphigenia bit her bottom lip. '*Am I still dreaming?*'

Scratch. Scratch. Scratch.

'*Get a grip, Effie. You left the window open. It's just a stray cat.*'

Her sweaty hand sat upon the cool doorknob for a good minute before turning it. Iphigenia took one step into the room. Her right arm circled the room, spreading faint candlelight around the empty kitchen. All windows were sealed. Her heartbeat reached speeds never reached before. She took two more steps into the kitchen and lowered her light to look under the table. Nothing.

Bang. The door slammed behind her. Iphigenia fell forward, shaking all over. Drops of wax fell to the marble floor and dried up into neat little hills. Hectically breathing, Iphigenia swung around to face the door. She gasped at the sight. The candle fell from her hand as she covered her mouth. She remained alone in the room, yet opposite her a huge red 'A' had been written upon the door. '*Is that blood?*'

'Gregory! Gregory!' she yelled. She hated the expression at the top of her lungs. Her mother used to say that often. Her yells were at the top of her lungs. She continued calling out his name, loud words into the night.

She exhaled in relief as she heard his footsteps as he ran down the stairs calling out her name.

'Kitchen!' she yelled.

He found her curled up by the table's leg. His large arms formed a hoop around her trembling body. His eyes stared at her hollow look. She was pointing at something. He looked behind him. 'What in God's name?'

'That is not a Godly deed,' she replied. 'I heard someone in here. I swear.'

Gregory stood up and checked the windows. He then

opened the top kitchen draw and picked up his butcher's knife. 'Follow me with the candle.'

Room by room they went. Room by room they checked. Silence. Empty rooms. Locked doors. They were alone.

Chapter Nine

MESOPOTAMOS

2010

'Beware of Greeks bearing gifts!' Christopher read the sign above the library door. '*That's a funny thing to have written in a Greek home,*' he thought as he entered the room and closed the wooden door behind him. Strong light stormed the room as he pulled back the thick curtains allowing the morning sun to sail in. '*Where is she off to?*'

Sophia jogged by in the distance. She looked as if Adidas Sportswear had sponsored her morning run. Trainers, shorts, T-shirt, cap. Headphones nested in her ears as she made her way out of his view.

In front of the house, Andrew stood with his eyes fixed on the old building. That was where Susan found him. She read his expression well. 'Smug bastard,' she whispered the words prisoned behind closed teeth. She could see the dollar signs in his shiny eyes. She could picture him accepting the seven-digit check from an elderly American couple. She stood in the shade, an inch away from the sun's rays. She placed her rather large straw hat on and stepped into the kingdom of light. Her freckles stood out on her bare shoulders as the sun illuminated her snow-white skin. Multiple layers of sunscreen covered every inch of her unprotected body.

'Gloating already?'

Andrew did not turn to see her. 'All it needs is fixing up the outside. The pipes which were my main concern seem to be working great. And outside all it needs is a good clean and a coat of paint. A couple of cheap-labor Albanians to cut out the weeds...'

'That's borderline racist.'

Andrew sighed. 'You know what I mean. I thought the place was in ruins. My retirement plan is more fixed than I thought.'

'Shame your mother is still alive, huh?'

A dark shadow spread across his chiselled face. 'What the fuck, Susan? Got out of the wrong side of the bed, have we?'

Susan gazed at the clear sky. 'You look at this place as money. Not like it's your home. Your mother's home. You haven't even started work on it nor discussed with your rather lucid mother about your future plans...'

'This was never nobody's home,' he said without emotion, without moving a single body muscle.

Susan turned to face him. With their height difference, Andrew always found it easy to ignore her and steer away from her detective eyes. He forced a flat smile and walked off, seemingly inspecting the ground and heading to the gardens surrounding the manor.

Susan stuck her tongue out behind his back. Just then, a tingling sensation arrived at the back of her neck. She wiped her skin in fear of a Greek *creepy-crawly* scavenging upon her. Dry leaves sprinted past her, yet she felt no wind gathering strength. She twitched her neck. Maya standing in the shadow by the open front door caught her attention. She held a drawing in her right hand. Susan smiled and walked toward her, preparing herself for an attack of words provided by her chatty daughter. Listening to her describe her drawings was often her day's highlight. A hand lay on Maya's shoulder, yet Susan could not see Penelope's figure in the shadows. With each step, Susan felt colder and unsafe. The hand remained still. Too still. Susan fastened her pace. The hand was small. The hand looked young. Susan found herself running toward her daughter who giggled and stepped outside to hug her mother. Susan picked her up. 'Penelope? Penelope?' she asked loudly as she entered the house.

'Yes, my dear?' her mother-in-laws voice came from upstairs. 'I'm tidying up. Maya and I have been painting.'

'What's wrong, Mummy? You're blowing air like the big bad wolf. Come. Come,' she encouraged her mother while pulling on her sweaty hand. 'Kitchen. Sit down. Look at all my paintings!'

Susan sat down and held her head. She took in a deep breath, shook her head to release stray hair that had stuck to her skin, and turned her attention to her eager daughter.

'This is us and Granny,' Maya said and placed the first drawing in front of her mother.

Susan smiled at the squiggly figures dotted on the white paper. Two things separated the males from the females. Long hair and skirts. *'At what age to we teach sexism?'* The flowers stood at the same height as the humans. 'Lovely! Bravo, my darling.'

'And this is the house.'

Susan bit her lower lip. Something about the drawing

was off. The same bright flowers. The yellow sun. The blue sky. And the dark gloomy house. 'No colors for the house, baby?' Maya did not reply. Just as Susan was ready to push it aside and make room for Maya's third and final creation, her eye noticed a round circle at the attic's window. She took a close look. It had eyes. 'Maya? Is this you?'

Maya shook her head.

'Has Christopher or Sophia been up there? It's unsafe up there...'

'No, no,' the young child interrupted her. 'That's the Looker.'

Susan sat up straight. 'The Looker?'

'Yes, the man with the big eyes. He's the manager here.'

Susan ran her nails along the table. She felt drunk. Tired, dizzy and not truly comprehending the conversation. The hum of the fridge grew louder in her ears. 'What's your third drawing of?' she finally spoke, louder than usual.

'My friends.'

Susan took the paper into her hands and raised it to eye level. 'Aww, are these your best friends from school?'

Maya giggled. 'No, silly. That's Limos, the skinny one. This is Curae. She doesn't talk to me. And these are the kids that follow them around. I mostly play with Limos. He's funny.'

A mile away, Sophia slowed her pace. She had never run before in such scorching heat. She placed her hands on her strong knees, and just then she realized her music had stopped playing. She looked back. The mansion stood at a distance. Small. Like one of Maya's Playmobil houses. *'I wish I could just keep running. To the edge of the world. Away ...'*

She closed her eyes, unsure of her next step. *What's that?*

She raised her eyelids and yelled. The largest lizard she had ever seen had placed its front legs on her foot. She violently shook her leg and kicked it away. The bushes next to her rattled. Lizard after lizard came out of the cavernous bushes and into the sunlight. All facing her. Sophia took a step back and tripped on a pointy rock. She lost her balance and fell backward. Off the dirt path and down the side of the hill she went. Tumbling down like her emotions. Her body reached the bottom within seconds. She immediately stood up and looked to see if any of the long-tail reptiles had followed her. Only dust ran down the hill. She dusted herself off and gazed upon the deep scratch on her right arm.

'Was that there before?'

Opposite her, amongst the tall wheat and wild grass, was a church no bigger than their shed back in the UK. Weeds and countryside flowers grew out of its bricks. The wooden door had seen better days and groaned slightly as the wind passed by. Sophia approached it out of curiosity. She did not know if it was a teenage phase, but she never did care much for religion. Her mum was an Anglican, her father an Orthodox. She believed neither. No Santa, no Tooth Fairy, no heaven, and no hell. She sniggered at the engraving above the church. 'Holy shit.' She laughed as she read the sign. 'Saint Sophia's Church. May she offer you Hope, Faith and Charity.' Sophia pushed the door back and peeped inside. The air lingered inside cool and fresh. Multiple cracks in the windows allowed the breeze to roam the low-ceiling building of worship. Her eyes went from icon to icon. All female saints besides Jesus and John. Sophia did not enter. She walked around the church and froze at the sight of the marble crosses sticking out of the wheat behind the church. 'A graveyard?' Sophia stepped on the grass forcing it to crack and bend. 'Ilias Fotopoulos! Age, 41. Died 1972.' She pushed down more grass with her hands, clearing the cross to her left. 'Helena Fotopoulos. Age, 37. Died 1972. Fuck. This is the family cemetery...'

Back at the manor, Christopher had finally settled on a book for his recreational reading. 'Zorba, the Greek. Let's see what all the fuss is about,' Christopher mumbled as he carried the book in one hand, a bag of crisps in the other, and skipped out of the house. He had his eye on a wooden bench resting in the shade of a great fig tree since their arrival. Behind the house he went and down the stone-brick path to his new-found reading oasis. Loving to play the role of a sophisticated human, Christopher gazed at the vast meadows around him, took in a silent deep breath, and opened his book. He had not reached page two, when whistling pulled him out of the coffee shop in Piraeus and back to Mesopotamos. A man, not older than his father, dressed in black and wearing thick beige gloves was on his knees pulling out weeds from a row of rose bushes. A watering can and a pair of shears stood by his feet.

Christopher took a couple of steps toward the man and remained still. He formed greeting sentences in Greek inside his head. Just as he opened his mouth, the stranger turned toward his direction. 'Don't worry. I speak perfect English, Master Christopher.'

Christopher frowned. 'How do you know my name?'

A wide smile spread upon the bearded man's face. 'I take care of the gardens around here. Penelope told us that you were coming,' he replied, standing and dusting off his muddy trousers. 'I see you're a reader. My wife reads a lot, too. What book have you got there?'

'Err, Zorba the Greek.'

The man laughed. 'When in Rome, act like the Romans. When in Greece, read Greek books, huh?'

Christopher scratched the back of his head. 'Something like that.'

'So?'

'Sooo, what?'

'How are you finding the book? Does it live up to its glorious reviews?' the man asked and walked up to him, entering the heavenly shade of the mighty blossoming fig tree. He wiped his forehead and sat down on the bench.

'I just started it. It is really well written. I think I will like the lead character. I can't comment on the story yet.'

'All good stories need a likable lead. Someone who we can journey along with. Remember that when you are writing, Master Christopher,' the man said and stood up. 'Keep reading, boy. I better get back to work. Poor roses are thirsty.'

Chapter Ten

'Surprise! Surprise!' Andrew yelled, and his voice sailed through the open doors and floated upstairs.

Christopher sat up on his bed with his book in his grip. His eyes rushed over the last three sentences. End of paragraph. End of chapter. With his Batman bookmark in position, he placed the book with care, as if something breakable, on his bedside table. He walked the long hallway and felt his sisters' heavy steps as they ran down to the kitchen and their eagerly awaiting father.

Christopher's room back in England was beside his parents. If it was one thing Christopher could recognize with ease it was a whispery heated argument. The tone of voice used by his mother caught his attention. Christopher let his curiosity get the better of him and tiptoed to his grandmother's slightly ajar door.

'Penelope, she is three. You can't go filling in her head with weird stories!'

'My dear, I'm sure you're right, but as I keep telling you,

I can't remember telling Maya anything! She was drawing, and I was knitting. We hardly talked...'

The floorboards squeaked louder than the mouse his father once caught in a sticky trap in their old basement. His mother was walking toward the door.

'Anyway, let's go down. Andrew has cooked us a surprise dinner.'

'Who's Andrew, my dear?'

'Andrea. Your son,' his mother replied, four of her fingers appearing on the side of the door. Christopher took two steps back and slid into a hallway closet. The dark modest space featured a bucket, a mop and two brooms. One modern, and one made with hay. Christopher heard the two women walk by. He decided to count to ten.

'Ena, dyo, tria, tessera...' He practiced his Greek. He had not reached eight when he felt it. Right there on his shoulder. He froze on the spot. He could not bear to turn his head. As soon as he felt it touch his bare neck, he shivered violently, hoping it would fall off. He jumped back out to the hallway with the fitted Persian carpets and looked straight at the mirror opposite him. No spider on his shoulder. *'It must have been huuuuge. Its legs felt as large as fingers.'* Just then, he saw the closet door slowly close behind him.

'What the...? Was that eyes?'

Christopher remained still. He looked down at his green T-shirt, sure that he would be able to see his heart beating up against his skinny chest.

'Christopher! What you doing up there? We are all waiting for you,' his father's voice pulled him away from the closet door. Christopher ran downstairs. *'Did the set of glowing eyes belong to his vivid imagination? The gigantic spider? A cat or maybe, just maybe, something else?'* He never opened the door. His questions would never be answered. Considering how the following days played out, Christopher wished he had opened the door. Between proper knowledge and blissful ignorance, not knowing for sure was a bitch.

That night's meal was the last time they all had fun together. From beginning to end. From their father's special pastitsio to his lava cake dessert to jokes, board games, and a promise of the beach in the morning, that night offered only elation to the members of the Fotopoulos family.

'That's right, my little ones. To the beach!' Andrew had declared as he poured himself another Mythos beer, a glass of sweet-smelling red wine for his mother, and filled four different-height cups with orange juice.

Susan frowned. 'I thought we were expecting a group of expert builders tomorrow.'

'They called and cancelled...'

'Cancelled?'

He raised his palms. 'Wrong word. Raincheck. They can't tomorrow. Something came up, and they will be here the following day. No biggie.'

'What beach?' Sophia asked.

'Ammoudia,' both her parents replied. Andrew threw a side look toward his wife. 'You have looked it up? I was expecting Chris to say it...'

'An old lady on the bus told me about it.'

Penelope lowered her empty wine glass. 'I miss the sea.'

There was a certain sadness wrapped around her words. The kids giggled at Maya's fruitless attempts to drink her juice without a straw, but both adults kept their eyes on Penelope.

'The soul needs to be free.'

Andrew placed his hand upon his mother's. 'You know, there's not a day that goes by that I don't feel guilty for putting you in that place. I had no choice. We both work and our kids are small...'

Penelope looked straight into his eyes and stroked his unshaved cheek. 'We all exist in our own prisons. We all have bars and limitations. Yet, death awaits us all...'

'Mother! Come on...'

Penelope chuckled. 'Do not fear death, my boy. He is not a destroyer. He is a liberator,' she said in a steady voice. Then, she looked down at the two drops of crimson wine swimming at the bottom of her fine wine glass. 'Now, now. When did I drink that?' she asked in a shaky voice. 'What were we saying? Oh, yes. The beach. Oh, I can't wait.'

Chapter Eleven

The young grasshopper leaped from the fence to the nearest rose bush. A charcoal cloud above covered the crescent moon and darkened its way. It dared another leap. It would be his last. Susan watched from her bedroom window as a swift bat made a meal of the night-travelling bug. Andrew's weak snoring blended with the ticking of the hallway clock, creating a vexatious and tiresome soundtrack to Susan's inability to sleep. Her hands ran through her red hair and gathered it up into a ponytail. She blinked rapidly and exhaled a loud sigh.

'Fuck it...'

She kicked off her pink slippers and took quiet steps out of the master bedroom. She did not risk turning on any lights. She raised her cell phone and held it in front of her, forming a greenish fluorescent rectangle on the floor. Round and round the spiral she went. The house watched: dark, silent, still. Susan closed the kitchen door behind her, happy to not have made a sound. She placed her phone on the counter by the row of dirty dinner plates and pushed open its flashlight. A strong ray of light came from its camera lenses and fell upon the glasses on the table. Susan approached. She took another look toward the closed door and bent forward. Her nose stopped an inch away from Penelope's glass. Susan's tongue dived out of her mouth and licked the glass, journeying down, savoring the lone drop of wine lingering on the bottom.

A shiver of ecstasy like bolts of electricity shook every nerve in her skinny body. Her skin pores opened, and warm sweat exited her body. She looked around. Nervous. Guilty even. She swallowed the lump inhabiting her throat and steadily took the four steps needed to reach the cupboard where Penelope kept her wines.

Susan's eyes opened wide. Amongst the row of bottles, there it was. Standing proudly in the center. Nemea Agiorgitiko. Her favorite Greek red. She gently licked her lips. As the tip of her tongue sailed between her dry lips, her mind journeyed years back to when she first tasted the complex wine with notes of dark fruit, tar, leather and spice. Back when it was just her, Andrew, and their carefree love honeymooning the majestic Greek Isles. The cliffs of Santorini, the narrow streets of Paros, the windmills of Myconos, and the port of Syros. Her fingers worked faster than her brain. As the movie theatre of her brain flashed images of turquoise beaches and plates of marinated octopus, her hands had found the wine-opener and soon the cork fell to the beige counter.

Susan did not bother with a glass. Like a lost soul in a desert, she had found water. Maybe even enough to extinguish her thirst. It flowed like a river into a dark cave. Soon, the bottle was placed on the counter beside the half-red cork. Empty. A devilish smile revealed reddish teeth and a satisfaction long lost -contentment from a bygone era.

Footsteps outside of the kitchen brought her back down. She quickly opened the dustbin and pushed in the bottle and its little companion. Her hands ran through her hair, she wiped her lips, and Susan prepared to greet whoever was approaching the door. The footsteps were light. Susan exhaled happily. *'At least it isn't Andrew. Andrew and his incredible sense of smell.'*

Step. Step. Step.

The door remained still. Untouched.

Susan took a step forward. Could Maya have come down all by herself? She looked at the bottom of the door. No light. In the dark?

'Christopher? Sophia?'

Silence.

Her arm extended, and she placed her hand upon the cool handle.

That's when she heard it.

That's when she froze.

A giggle. A familiar giggle. So unique; so distinct.

She could hear her heart crack. Her eyes watered up. She shook her head in disbelief.

More giggling. A toddler's giggle.

Susan wiped her nose. 'Eugene?' she asked with a shaky voice.

'Mummy!'

Step, step, step. Their sound fading in the distance. Susan opened the door and desperately searched for the switch. Click. Light spread around. She stood alone.

She shook her head. 'I'm not that drunk.'

Susan spent the next half-an-hour searching the entire ground floor of the mansion. When her heart finally listened to her brain, she gave up and sat down on the lower steps of the spiral staircase. 'Oh, dear sanity...'

And then she heard it loud and clear. A nursery rhyme. *His* nursery rhyme.

'The itsy-bitsy spider went up the waterspout...'

He always sang it wrong. She always corrected him. She mouthed the words. 'Climbed up...'

'Down came the rain and washed...'

Pause. Susan stood up and followed the echo. It came from the kitchen.

'...the liar out!'

Susan stepped into the kitchen. Alone again. She held her head and wished she could scream at the top of her capable lungs. That's when she saw it. Red, bloody, heartless, taunting.

The letter A was written on the wine cupboard's door.

Susan gazed in disbelief. She shook her head. She even closed her eyes, counted to three slowly, and then reopened them. The A was still there. *'Get a grip, Susan.'* She walked toward it. Her eyes swayed side-to-side, exploring the kitchen's lush surroundings, searching in dark corners for whoever was responsible for the A. She raised her shaking arm, and her index finger landed upon the right leg of the A. In slow motion she turned her finger and brought it to eye level. Her finger was colored red. The paint -she hoped it was paint- was fresh. Breathing heavily, she picked up the orange kitchen sponge and attacked the letter. Pieces of scrunched-up kitchen roll followed, and soon, a shiny clean cupboard was before her. With her head heavier than a dead donkey, she pulled out a kitchen chair and collapsed, physically and emotionally. *A good cry cures the soul,* her granny used to say. Susan was not sure if her silent cry was a good one or not, but her guilty soul was not up for curing.

Chapter Twelve

Ferocious.

The only appropriate word for the Greek sun.

From early morning, the heat-wave showed its glowing teeth.

Susan awoke as the first ray invaded through the thin white curtains that decorated the rail above the main kitchen window -the one with the view of the grounds' massive gardens. Sophia had stood there on their first day and quoted the Lion King, much to her father's pleasing. 'Everything the light touches is our kingdom.' Susan felt anything but a queen. The only thing ruling was her majestic hangover. A familiar balloon inflating inside her head started to vibrate. Yesterday's meal swam up and settled in her throat. The scent of sweet wine, once luring, now was the cause of intense, mocking nausea. Her sweaty forehead was glued to the kitchen table's surface. She stood up in shock. She had spent the entire night on the hard wooden chair. Her bones clicked and clucked as her body retaliated to her tiptoeing back upstairs, hoping that

Andrew had not noticed her missing. She had no desire to get into any sort of conversation with him, where he took on his *serious face* and *lectured* her -her words.

The bedroom was dark and cool. Even better, Andrew was in his deep-sleep, fetal position. Sneaking back to his side brought back memories. Bad memories, but Susan had no more tears left to shed.

Christopher, the Fotopoulos early bird, was up next. Christopher never ate breakfast with his family on weekends and bank holidays. His tummy never had the patience to wait the sometimes up to two hours until his parents rose from the deep slumber. He headed first to the bathroom and then downstairs for cereal. As always in front of him stood a book.

Christopher was not the only one reading those days. Sophia had googled multiple articles about Greek foods and their nutritional values.

What to eat and what to avoid while on holiday in Greece.
Eat healthier! Eat Greek!
The Greek secret to long life.

Sophia read them all. Sophia was at war with eating. Not that anyone noticed much. She did not blame her parents. She did not blame them for anything since Eugene died. She did not want them to notice the weight she had lost. She did this for herself. For her to finally love her body. She did not want them involved, turning her dieting into a teenage cry for attention.

Words and words passed by Christopher's and Sophia's eyes. Maya had only one word on her mind: beach. Maya had never been to the beach before. She had seen it only through YouTube videos made by fame-seeking parents with photogenic children. Maya came down the spiral staircase that morning with a wide smile. She stopped in the middle, and her violet eyes looked to their left. She remained still for a while, before opening her mouth and sticking out her tongue. Then, she continued her descent, happily anxious for her meeting with the blue sea.

Yet another day was going to be born and die with Maya not going to the beach.

The doorbell changed their plans that day.

Maya stared outside at the three tall, muscular men talking with Daddy and Mummy. Maya saw Mummy return inside to announce that beach day was going to have to wait.

'Not cancelled, postponed. Will we go tomorrow,' Mummy said strictly to Sophia who said a bad word upon hearing their cancelled/delayed/postponed plans.

The builders from the firm Daddy had spoken with the previous day had come a day earlier. Or rather, they came on their proper day. She did not catch the reason why. Maya was confused.

'Don't worry, dear. I promise you, we will go tomorrow,' Granny Penelope said as she stroked her strawberry-smelling hair. 'Come on; let's go do some more painting. And how about I teach you to knit?'

'Knit?'

Penelope laughed. 'Oh, my sweet one. New word for you, huh?'

Christopher took it better than everyone else. He picked up his book and headed out to the bench. His bench. As he made his way through the rose bushes, he hoped to see the kind gardener again. He seemed to know his Greek heroes and Gods.

Susan sat down on the tall-back armchair under the freaky river painting. She took small sips from her apple juice and knocked back two painkillers as she watched

Andrew discuss things with the three men. He waved his hands as he explained *his vision*.

'*Blah, blah, blah. Money, money, money.*' Susan smiled as the words echoed in her mind. She was glad... no... she was relieved that the house did not need her. The interior was more than fine. She was free from having to work with Andrew. She finished her apple juice and stood up, stroking her floral short dress. '*Time for some Susan time.*'

She headed outside, her faithful straw hat protecting her sensitive skin from the fierce sun. Susan took a stroll down the stone path-way and headed to the rows of lemon, orange, and olive trees in the lands to her west. She let her senses take in the place. 'You're surely not in Kansas, anymore,' she whispered as she thought of the contrast with the streets she walked in London.

A shed at the edge of the rows of aged trees caught her eyes. It stood dark under two twisted carob trees. Susan found herself drawn to it. She followed the crumbled road that led to it. It surely had not aged well, yet Susan could picture it as a beauty from an era long past. Its door had been eaten away; the weather and the wild bugs had won. Susan tried to look inside, while avoiding shiny, silvery spider webs glowing in the sun. Its roof was no longer able to repel neither rain nor snow, and nature's elements had invaded the single room.

Multiple loud baas pulled her out of her daydreaming about the insides of the dead shed. Susan walked around the building and watched as dozens of freshly shaved sheep made their way just meters from her. Two dogs barked in the distance.

That is when she saw him. *Him*. The magnificent Greek male specimen. The shirtless specimen. The man with a body ancient Greek statues would envy.

Water sprang out of his raised bottle and fell like a miniature waterfall upon his lips. The water shone and sparkled as he drank; drops formed rivulets on his high cheekbones, rushing down to his strong jaw and free diving to his sweaty bare chest. He wore black boots and a pair of old, worn-in army trousers. He threw his empty bottle next to his bag by the trunk of a twisted olive tree and picked up his long, wooden stick. He rhythmically whistled to his two border collies —one black and white, one brown and white, both happy and lively, signalling them to relax and let the herd graze the grassland.

As he entered the shade provided by the lone tree in the meadow, his eye caught a glimpse of the woman watching him from a distance.

'Kalimera!' he said with his deep bass voice. A welcoming, genuine, Greek-village good morning.

Susan looked down and smiled. 'Kalimera.'

The man raised his hand and waved to her to come and join him. Due to their distance, and her rather limited knowledge of Greek, Susan did not catch all of his sentences. '*Is he really inviting me over to share his breakfast?*' The urge to wave a *no, thanks* and leave and the urge to walk down to the handsome man, fought inside her head. It was a short, uneven fight. In a matter of seconds, Susan found herself cat walking toward the man. She stopped at the edge of the cloud-shaped shade, explaining in broken Greek that she did not speak the language well.

'That won't be a problem. My English is excellent,' the shepherd replied and smiled, revealing a row of shiny teeth. Like a formation of tic-tacs.

'Wow. Your English is indeed excellent,' she replied and immediately felt guilty for sounding so amazed. She wished it did not sound like she was implying that a shepherd could not be educated in the English language.

'I spent my summers in New York growing up. My parents used to ship me off to my aunt's. But, my place is here, with my people and my animals,' he said and theatrically took in a deep breath of fresh summer air. 'May I ask what a lady from the UK, I presume from the accent, is doing out in the middle of nowhere in a field in Greece?'

Susan smiled, took a step into the shade, and removed her hat. She ran her hands through her hair, quickly making it presentable —or so she hoped. 'I think I might own this land,' she said and let loose a controlled laugh. 'My husband's family owns the mansion,' she continued and pointed to the direction of the house. 'I don't know where our land ends...'

'Right there,' he said pointing to a small cottage in the far away distance and laughed back. 'I am your closest neighbor. Jimmy,' he said and extended his arm.

Susan's pale hand slid into his. She admired his healthy olive skin. 'Susan.'

'Come sit with me. You have to try my bread. I made it this morning. A gift for my pretty new neighbor.' His dark green eyes sparkled as he kept them on her and knelt by his bluish backpack with the diagonal silvery zippers that sat on a rather square rock. She felt his gaze piercing through her. She controlled the shiver well. '*Why am I feeling this way?*'

She stood still, glad that the gentle breeze had enough strength to cool her palms and neck, as the muscular man set up his version of a picnic. A checkered tablecloth covered the short newborn grass and upon it bread, broken into slices by hand, lay on two white napkins. A bottle of tsipouro followed, straight out of his ice cooler. He then placed two shot glasses on the flat rock by his side.

WELCOME TO MESOPOTAMOS was printed on their side.

Susan found herself searching for the right words to turn down his kind offer. Yet, as if out of her body, she witnessed herself nest cozily on the red and white covering. She heard her *logic* departure and disappear. Its last words being *the best medicine to a hangover, is to keep on drinking*. Susan would be the worst AA counsellor.

Her teeth cut through the soft fresh bread with the thin crunchy exterior and awoke her senses. 'It's divine.' There it was again. His perfect smile. 'Thank you. My mama's recipe.'

'Give her my compliments.'

'I live alone.'

Susan knocked back her served tsipouro and felt the alcohol journeying down. *'Alone? Was that a hint of flirting?'*

'Do you eat olives?' he asked and opened a round, green-lid Tupperware in front of her. Her favorite. Salty olives. Savory with alcohol.

Olive. Shot. Olive. Shot. Small talk.

Two olives. Three shots. Laughing. *'Oh, that smile again.'*

His hand landed on hers. He caressed her arm. Susan loved watching the veins in his arm. She felt turned-on.

Shot. Shot. Shot.

Walking behind the man, admiring his broad back and shaped butt cheeks, Susan waved goodbye to the empty bottle. Even behind her designer shades, her eyes struggled with the bright light. Her hands were raised, like Eugene's when he pretended he was an airplane. The tips of golden wheat ran along her palms. The fresh air invaded her nostrils and filled her intoxicated lungs. She felt high. She felt loose. She felt willing.

The unlocking of his house's back door brought her back down.

'*Where are you going, Susan? What are you going to do?*'

It was her mother's voice. It always was. Susan was sweet sixteen when she lost her mother. Nothing sweet about that. Susan kept her alive. Not just with memories, but with giving her mama's voice to her inner thoughts.

'*I'm not sure ...*'

'*Yes, you are, dear.*'

'*So? Andrew hasn't touched me since Eugene died ...*'

'*Go touch him then.*'

'*He cheated, too.*'

'*An eye for an eye? Is that how I raised you?*'

Susan did not reply. Two hands grabbed her by the waist and pulled her close. Her breast squeezed up against his naked torso. She felt his erection push up against her. His hands travelled along her thighs, pulling up her dress. Soon, she stood before him in her black bra and beige knickers. Jimmy unbuttoned his trousers and let them fall to his boots. He wore no underwear. Susan's eyes widened. She only had one lover before Andrew. She was not what you would call experienced. However, the long, thick penis before her amazed her. It was even bigger than the ones she had seen in that one porn film Andrew had played for her. Susan sighed as his full lips landed on her tensed neck. She felt juvenile in her thoughts about his package. She was a grown woman. A woman with needs. A woman lost in more ways than one. She wanted to be carried away. Lifted in his strong arms. Taken to bed. Ravaged by him.

She fell back on his soft mattress. Bare. Body and soul. Thirsty for attention. Drowsy to think straight. His tongue circled her nipples while his fingers played around between her thighs.

'We are alone,' he whispered in her ear, his hot breath warming her.

'Reading my thoughts?' Susan began to sigh loudly. Sighs that transformed into pleasure's moaning. Moaning that was elevated to screams as he entered her and thrust away. Susan let go of her tight hold on the emerald green sheets and dug her nails into his sweaty back.

A logical thought in her drunken mind. '*I cut him.*'

She raised her hands. Small pieces of reddish skin tangled from three of her violet fingernails. She turned her eyes to his face. He did not seem to mind –or notice. He pulled out of her and flipped her over, laying on top of her. Fireworks were set off in her tsipouro-filled stomach, and with her head deep in his pillow, Susan exhaled in delight. Wave after wave, her orgasms kept coming.

Another logical thought. Scarier. '*Is he wearing a condom?*'

She twisted her body, signalling for a switch in position. '*Thank God. He is.*'

A minute later, he grunted. Susan smiled at his *sex face*. The tough macho Alpha reduced to a cute serene face of pure delight. He fell to her side, his chest revealing his quiet heavy breathing. With her head pillowed on him, Susan let her mind go blank.

She remained blank, until smoke reached her French nose. She opened her right eye, slightly, slowly. Jimmy was smoking.

Then, the pain attacked her, shaking her up from blissful oblivion. Susan yelled out, sat up and in disbelief looked down at her left thigh. A small round black circle where he had put out his cigarette.

Susan drowned her urge to scream at the man. More logic. '*He is a strong stranger. We are alone in his room. He could kill me ...*'

'Hey. You dropped your cigarette,' she began to say as she made her way to the edge of the bed, ready to make a run for the door. Her clothes were all on the living room floor. *'Grab them and get out!'*

There was something about his laughter. Croaky. Cold. Distant. Eerie.

Susan's feet reached the floor and she turned to see him.

Susan never thought she could ever scream as loud as she did at that very moment. An old man lay on the bed. Yellowy skin hung from his arms as he masturbated. Susan could see his bones though wounds on his legs. His dark laughter came out of a toothless mouth. His skull featured no more than a dozen grey hairs that failed to hide the many deep crimson scratches on the top of his dispropor-tion head. *'Jesus Christ, he has no eyes!'* Susan fell back. Drunk. Scared. Shocked.

On all fours, she sped for the door. She grabbed the cool handle and stood up. The floor boards creaked behind her. The old man's laughter grew louder, echoing in her drunken mind. Susan fell forward, tumbling down the stairs. Her hands reached out yet found no hold. Each step she fell upon offered new pain, a new bruise. Down and down, round and round, she went. She flew off the last few steps. Her head met the ground. Hard. Bang.

Susan awoke back upstairs in Jimmy's bed. Her pupils cornered and saw naked, normal Jimmy, alive Jimmy, young Jimmy sleeping happily and satisfied beside her. Susan covered her mouth with both her trembling hands. She swallowed the scream rising, ready to escape.

'No, it wasn't a dream. It was real. Too real.'

Susan moved like *a thief in the night*. For some weird reason, Susan loved that expression. On her tiptoes, she escaped the dim-lit room and made her way downstairs.

She hooked her underwear and floral dress from the floor. That's when she noticed it. The burnt mark on her thigh. With eyes screaming, she ran. She ran barefoot through the wild fields, dressing clumsily as she went. Every few seconds, she would look behind her. The house's door remained closed. Soon, it was smaller than a matchbox in the far distance.

Meanwhile, back at the house, Andrew was still explaining his vision for the mansion to the three similar-looking builders. The tallest of the three nodded, but Andrew sensed that he was not really paying him attention, at least, the focused attention that Andrew desired. An attentive audience to feed his ego was not what he got. The tall man's eyes were lowered and ran along the row of small square windows under the porch.

When Andrew finished with his ideas on how he pictured the exterior of the house, the man finally spoke.

'What about the basement?'

Andrew locked his tongue between his teeth. He even squeezed down, hoping the pain would kill his shiver.

'What about it?' He avoided the noun.

'Have you seen it?'

All three men took a step closer and stared at him, their eyes fixed on his lips.

'Err, no. Not yet. I don't see what it has to do with...'

'I never take on a job without seeing the complete structure. Safety first.'

'Safety first,' the other two said in unison.

'How can we build and knock things down above without checking the foundations ...' the tall man continued.

Andrew extended his arms. 'Alright, alright. The door is behind the staircase. It's eighteen steps down. The light switch is on your right.'

Andrew exhaled and smiled as he watched the three men walk in a line and disappear into the house, none questioning why he did not accompany them. His joy was short-lived.

'Mr. Fotopoulos?' the muscular voice found his ears. 'The door is locked.'

With his head slightly lowered, Andrew entered the mansion and took the twenty-three steps needed toward the basement's door. When he was younger, smaller, shorter it took more than thirty. And he never walked them. He ran them. Away from it. Them. Him.

Chapter Thirteen

MESOPOTAMOS

1972

Eight-year-old Andrew's face darkened as his father announced the news and raised his nearly-empty beer glass in the air.

'That's wonderful,' a young Penelope replied as she brought out cut watermelon to the garden table. She kissed her husband on his neck as she placed the porcelain, fruit-carrying dish by the tall candle holders.

On sweet summer nights, their love managed to reach new heights. Penelope felt she had nothing to be jealous of from the ladies in her romantic movies. She had her handsome protagonist, an exceptional son, and a mansion placed in paradise. 'So when is your brother arriving?'

'Next week. Friday morning. Just him and Helena.'

'The twins not coming?'

'The girls are twenty. They are going to Myconos with their friends from Uni.'

Penelope giggled. 'And they didn't invite their cool aunt?'

Jason Fotopoulos joined in her laughing. 'Wanna go clubbing with some young lads, huh?'

Neither noticed Andrew shaking opposite them. His eyes watered up. His heart danced upon a trampoline inside his little chest. He stood up and turned toward the house.

'Where you off to? I just brought watermelon aaaaaand... surprise! Cherries. Your favorite.'

'I need to use the toilet. I'll be right back,' he replied breathlessly, without stopping or slowing his fast pace. Andrew ran by the sleeping rose bushes and caught his blue shorts on their pointy thorns. The bush shook, startling the two love-making fireflies that found refuge from night frogs and sleepless spiders.

'I wish I could light up and fly away.'

Andrew stopped in the middle of the living room and set his eyes upon the fainted round circles on the tiles. That's where the statues used to be. All six of them. Penelope had moved them down to the basement as he had so many nightmares about them, he suffered from insomnia. A couple of pots changed place, a new-bought side table went above another, but their markings were still visible. The statues had stood in their home long before Penelope's family bought the place. Andrew slammed the bathroom door behind him and covered his mouth with both hands. At last, he could release the scream born in his guts upon hearing his uncle Ilias would be visiting this summer, again.

His sadist uncle. The one with the grey eyes. The one everyone loved and he feared. The one that loved to pinch him all over, even between the legs. The one that pushed him down the hillside, rushed after him, and knelt by his side. 'If you don't say you fell, I will strangle you in your sleep, you little fucker,' he had hissed in his ear as he licked the deep cut on his forehead.

His uncle was the reason he feared the statues.

Andrew was only four and a half at the time. Once again, his uncle had come to stay with them for a few very dreadful -for Andrew- weeks in a very humid summer. One hot August night, the adults wished to continue their after-dinner drinking while talking about all and nothing. The kids, Andrew and his uncle's twin girls, had dessert -apple pie and ice-cream- and were sent to bed. The teenage girls went their way. They did not need or care for any type of assistance. Andrew remained by his mother's side.

'I wanna story,' he whined.

'Tomorrow I will read you two. I promise,' Penelope said, interrupting her gossip with his aunt, Helena.

'Please, Mum. A short one. Anyone you want.'

Penelope frowned and opened her mouth, yet it was his uncle's voice that was heard. 'Stay, finish your wine, Penelope. I'll take him. I'm good with stories,' he said and pushed back his chair. 'Wasn't I, love?' he asked his wife as he stood up and stretched. 'Come on, lad.' Penelope whispered a thank you and watched the man and child walk into the house.

Andrew smiled. Andrew felt happy. Andrew held his uncle's hand.

Regret does not cover it. Looking back Andrew wished he never ask for a *fucking* story.

Andrew jumped upon his bed and picked up the *very hungry caterpillar* and *green eggs and ham*. 'Choose.'

A grin came across his uncle's sharp-corner face. It brought his beady eyes closer together. 'A man like you reads kid shit like this?'

Andrew's eyes widened. *Shit* was not a good word.

'Let me tell you a story. A *real* story.'

'A real story?'

Ilias nodded his head dramatically. 'Some say it's a legend, but it's real. It happened right here in this very village. Have you been to the Necromanteio before?'

Andrew shook his head.

'Dark forces live there. They escort the dead who like zombies walk around the place,' he said and raised his arms, mimicking a zombie-like walk. 'It is there where a young sixteen-year-old from this village was raped. Gang-raped.' He paused and stared at the kid. No reaction. 'Do you know what rape is, Andrew?'

Andrew shook his head.

'Well, sex is when a man, like you and me, puts his penis,' Ilias said and placed his right hand between Andrew's legs for a long second, 'in a girl's vagina. Her pussy. Rape is when she does not want the boy to do so, but he does it anyway. OK, so far?'

Andrew nodded. He was four. He had no clue how to reply. Too many unknown words. Too many naughty words.

'So, this young girl was raped by three men many, many years ago and she got pregnant. She wasn't married and this was a very bad thing back then. This is like sixty, seventy years ago. Turn of the century. That old. Where was I? Oh, yes. Pregnant. So, her father kicked her out. She lived out here, in these fields. Eating from the trees and killing rats and eating bugs. She lived wild, and her mind went crazy. She gave birth to a little boy like you. And guess where?' In the Necromanteio! Right on the spot where the men put their cocks in her. The boy had no chance to be normal. Demons roaming the site, the dead lost and wandering, a crazy mother... The boy grew up a psycho. His mind was not right.' Ilias rolled his index finger round-and-around by the side of his right temple. 'You must be wondering why I am telling you all this, right?'

Andrew raised his little shoulders.

'You know the statues in your living room? They have dead bodies in them!'

Andrew gasped in fear.

'Notice how real they look? Notice how they are the right size for a human? The details of their faces? The young boy that grew up a psycho made them. He prayed on the people of these streets. If he saw someone alone, he kidnapped them and took them back to the Necromanteio. He tortured them. Cut them. Bit them.'

Andrew shivered and pulled up his blue sheet to his neck. Ilias seemed satisfied to see the boy scared.

'Terrified, are you? Not as much as his victims. He murdered them and placed them on metal spears. Right up their bums,' Ilias said and laughed. 'And then, he covered them in cement. He sold them to the owners of this house. You have dead bodies in your house. And their souls come out at night to play...'

'Ilias?' Andrew's father's voice was heard in a loud yet whispery manner. 'What you doing up there?'

'Finishing the story. I'll be right down. Get me a nice cold one, bro.'

Ilias turned toward Andrew and grabbed his neck tightly -yet not too tight to leave a mark. 'Now, listen here, you little fucker. You do not say a word to your parents about my story. Got it? Or I will break the statues and let the zombies eat your mother.'

Andrew never forgot a single word his uncle told him that night. He never told anyone either. Now, he was eight and once again, his uncle was coming to stay.

The first two days under the same roof with Ilias went

by uneventfully. Andrew hoped that as he was older, his uncle would leave him alone. He was far from right.

The tragic night came on the third night of his uncle's stay.

A moonless night. A quiet night.

Penelope kissed her eight-year-old boy good night and stroked his shampoo-smelling hair. She turned off his light and closed his bedroom door behind her. Downstairs her husband, Ilias and Helena waited for her. She wore her good black dress and her prized necklace, white gold given to her by her love on their anniversary. Helena wore a colorful dress that kissed her curves while Jason Fotopoulos was in jeans and a smart blue shirt with small brown buttons. Ilias, on the other hand, stood topless. Only an old pair of sandals and black shorts were on his body.

'Look at you lucky three,' he said. 'Out to conquer all three taverns and two bars of the area!'

His brother laughed. 'Jealous little man. You picked the small straw. Now, suffer.'

'Stop teasing,' Penelope said and gently smacked her husband on his beer belly. 'Ilias, if you want me to stay home with Andreas, that's fine by me...'

'No, no, no. I lost fair and square. We can't all go out partying. Someone has to stay home with the boy. I really don't mind. I've been feeling a bit under the weather lately. An early night will do me good. Go, take my wife and have fun!'

Helena twirled and danced toward him. 'My man,' she said and granted him with a full lip kiss. 'I promise I won't be late, daddy!'

Ilias could still hear her cachinnation as they climbed into Jason's Ford and set off into the night. Ilias closed the front door and turned his attention to the spiral staircase.

His mind fixed on the young boy sleeping upstairs. The boy who was unaware that he was willingly left alone with the one man he would never choose to be alone with.

Twelve minutes past ten, Andrew's door opened.

Andrew felt his feet being tickled and drowsily opened his eyes. His sheet was gone. Now, a pile on the floor beside him.

'What are you doing here? I'm sleeping.'

Ilias smiled. 'Come, I want to show you something.'

The events that followed were never spoken about by Andrew. Not even in therapy. A kind psychologist suggested he wrote things down. He did. And he was better since then. He placed a full stop at the end of his three-page account and moved on with his new life in London. Penelope read the three pages alone. She cried for an hour and hid the notebook up in a locked box in the attic.

Andrew wrote how angry he was that his mother did not reply to his cries for help as his uncle pulled him out of bed and took him to the basement. Ilias forced Andrew to take off his pajamas and sit naked on the cold ground. All six statues were placed around him.

'Dance for them!' his uncle ordered from a dark corner.

Andrew knew well to not disobey his violent uncle.

'Touch them!' The next order came, and Andrew noticed that his uncle had lowered his pants and was playing with himself.

'Lick the balls of the statue to your left. That's right. Let me see your tongue.'

Andrew felt that he must have been doing something wrong as his uncle approached from behind, yanked his hair and pushed his face hard against the statue's genitals. 'Suck it. Like a lollipop. Go on!' he yelled. Andrew obeyed. He trembled all over. He was naked, performing sexual acts on a statue while his uncle masturbated behind him. 'Good, you're getting the hang of it. You're a natural,' Ilias said and pulled him back by the hair again. 'Close your eyes and open your mouth. As wide as you can. Like the dentist.' On his knees, Andrew felt his uncle's cock upon his lips.

Andrew's entire ordeal lasted just twelve minutes, but it seemed longer.

Andrew did not sleep that night. After puking in the toilet, he put on his pajamas, ran to his room, closed his door and pretended to be asleep. He heard his father's car pull up outside, hours after midnight. He heard the drunken horde stumble to their rooms.

Andrew was alone with his wild thoughts. Dark whispers in his ears, in his mind. He wrote that he felt the house was talking to him. He felt out of his body, out of himself. He described that the kitchen knife felt good in his small hand. Empowering. Andrew opened the guest bedroom in the middle of the moonless night and stabbed his sleeping uncle six times, one piercing his heart. His drunken auntie's screams interrupted the quiet of the night. He stabbed her in the head and watched as fresh, warm blood sprayed up like the geysers he saw once in a documentary about Yellowstone. It did not mention Yogi Bear, unfortunately.

Lights were switched on.

Both his parents stood in the doorway. Pure shock. Disbelief.

Andrew witnessed his father fall to his knees. His hand upon his chest.

Knife: 2. Heart attack: 1.

Penelope checked her husband's pulse. She felt nothing. She looked at the two butchered bodies on the bed she proudly bought last year. And in the middle, her blood-painted son. She knew she was calling no ambulance.

'Go to your room, now!'

Once again, Andrew obeyed. He obeyed his uncle, he obeyed the voices, he obeyed his mother.

Penelope did not talk to him that night. She did not utter a word as she washed him, scrubbed him and put him to sleep. Penelope did not sleep that night. She rolled all three bodies in three separate sheets and drugged them out of the house. In total darkness, and amazed by her new-found strength, she took the bodies to the small cottage her husband used as a workplace.

The next day, neither Penelope nor Andrew spoke. Penelope prepared the day's three meals and sent her son to bed early. The next thing Andrew remembered hearing was the wailing of the fire truck.

The local newspapers wrote about the tragic fire.

Four adults playing strip poker in the shed. Drinking. Smoking. Getting stoned. Three died, one survived.

Three days later, Penelope said goodbye to her husband, to her house, and to her country. With her husband's life insurance money, she set off to relatives in England for a new start.

Chapter Fourteen

MESOPOTAMOS

2010

Andrew crunched his knuckles. He wished he could crunch his mind. Squeeze hard on the memories of the basement. Erase his uncle, just like he erased him from life. He held the basement's key in his shaking right hand. It was in the draw where he left it. In that ugly piece of furniture -ugly according to him, Penelope loved her bargain antic cabinet, under the painting of the river. He placed the key in its fitting hole and looked behind him. The three men waited silently. Andrew could swear that their faces seemed familiar to him. He looked back at the painting. He shook his head and controlled his laughter. *'Don't be stupid, Andrea. No, the builders aren't from the painting'* Yet, Andrew knew that when he was younger, there were more figures in that painting. *'Faded. That's all. Just like the letters below it.'*

'Is there a problem?' Boss the Builder asked with his thick, bushy eyebrows arching toward the top of his thin Byzantine nose.

Andrew turned the key. 'No, no. None at all. Andrew pushed the door and closed his eyes as dust plummeted and ganged up to form a short-lived dust cloud. 'Call me when you're done,' he said, and with his palm, he urged the men to enter.

'You first. Turn on the lights for us and show us around,' Boss Man said and hugged him around the shoulders, ushering him into the darkness.

Andrew took a deep breath and stepped on the first wooden step. Just the creak of it sent shivers down his spine. With the builder's hands on his shoulder, he felt like a young boy again, being lured down by his filthy uncle. The builder was too close to him. Andrew could feel the man's bulge against him.

'Take a step back!' he yelled.

'Sorry. It's just so dark down here. I thought you were turning on the lights. No need to shout, sir.'

Andrew exhaled and shook his head. Neither act calmed his raging anger or his growing fear. He reached out and flicked on the lights.

One. Two. Three. Four.

Andrew counted the light bulbs that came to life to reveal the dust that had settled on them. Anything to keep his eyesight from the statues in the center of the low-ceiling room.

Step. Creak. Step. Creak.

Soon, all four stood by the dusty statues.

'Such art, and you have it down here?'

'Wow, they are so lifelike.'

'Look at these perfect round breasts.'

Andrew ignored their comments. 'As you can see, the house has strong foundations. The six main pillars run along...'

'*Was the statue always in the pose? Concentrate, Andrew.*'

'...and as you can see, the brick here is...'

'*Wait, is a statue missing? How many were there? Concentrate, Andrew.*'

'...the old wall was reinforced in the sixties...'

'*Why are the statues staring at me? Concentrate for fuck's sake!*'

But his eyes travelled down the statues naked body. The one he was forced to lick. Cold sweat swam upon his boiling skin.

'The rest you can see for yourself. I need to use the bathroom,' he quickly said and rushed up the squeaking steps.

Yet again, he found himself running from that room.

'Dad, can you...'

He did not stop. 'Not now, Sophia!'

'Typical,' Sophia muttered.

Now, he did stop. He did not turn to face her. 'What was that?'

Sophia was old enough to remember his anger phase. *All* of his anger phases. Her eyes were locked on his clenched fists. He never hit anyone. His victims were limited to walls, furniture and the room's air. Dogs that bark...

'Nothing. I understand you're busy,' she quickly replied and took lengthy steps toward the stairs.

Later that day, down the hallway, in the renovated bathroom, the water came out strong. Susan let the cold water hit her face and run down her body. She smiled slightly as she stood under the showerhead. Her second shower that day. She had managed to survive the day. She had managed to creep back home, clean the shepherd off her, devour six crunchy crackers dipped in honey (Susan's witchcraft against hangovers), avoid conversations with the rest of her family members (something easier than she expected as everyone seemed lost in their own little projects, their own little worlds), cook for all (lemon garlic chicken and eggplants with feta cheese), feed and bathe Maya, pace up and down her room as a quieter-than-usual Andrew showered, and finally, undress and lock the bathroom door behind her. 'What a day...'

As she whispered the three words, she noticed the shower curtain had somehow moved up along the bath, and she was splashing water *all over the place! Fuck!* She turned the shiny faucet and watched the waterfall diminish to a drip. Her arm journeyed north, and her hand searched for her green towel. The one with the grey line and the silver owl imprinted on it. It was nowhere to be seen.

Had she forgotten to bring it in with her? It wouldn't be the first time.

'Andrew?' she called out. Loud enough to be heard in the next room, yet not loud enough to awake Maya. 'Andrew?' she repeated as she opened the bathroom door. No reply. His heavy breathing informed her off his heavy slumber.

Ah, the towel dilemma. To dry with the not-big-enough hand towel or to dash for the desired towel even though dripping from every part of your naked body?

Susan decided on a combination of both. She stood by the toilet, on its welcoming mat, and picked up the small hand towel. She wiped her arms and leaned forward to dry her feet. That is when she heard the door click closed behind her. Susan stood up straight. Water began to fall once again. Hot, boiling water if she judged by the steam clouds filling up the room. Susan turned around and her hand landed on her mouth, suffocating down what would have been a loud gasp. The bath's curtain was closed. Splashing could be heard behind it. The shadow of a small figure was visible. Little arms waving around, playing with the water.

Then, the giggle pierced her soul.

'Eugene?'

'Mama!'

Susan wiped her eyes and tried to take a step forward. Her logic forbade her, yet her heart wished to leap into the bath and see her son. Touch him. Play with him. *'Who cares if it's just an illusion?'*

Two reluctant steps followed. Her arm flew through the misty air and grabbed the wet curtain.

'One, two...'

Three was never uttered. Her countdown to the reveal was stopped by the sound of fingers rubbing against glass. Susan bit her lower lip and turned to face the small mirror glued to the wall above the dripping sink.

A line was forming on its surface, cutting the fog residing upon it. The line then began to curve. Soon, a clear letter faced her. D. Susan lowered her eyes in disbelief. That's when she noticed her lost towel laying on the floor; shaped as the letter D. Susan looked up and screamed.

In the mirror, she saw the curtain open slowly. The small boy gradually revealed. A shadow in the fog. The light above her flickered. The water suddenly stopped. The mist cleared.

The skeleton of a child was waving to her.

'What the...?' Andrew said as he opened the door and saw his wife sitting on the wet floor, naked and curled up. 'Did you fall? Are you okay? I heard you scream. Please tell me that you didn't wake us all up for a bloody cockroach?'

Susan always hated his ability to speak so much as soon as he opened his eyes. After sleep, she wished for silence and a strong coffee. Now, she was more annoyed by his lack of empathy.

'I could be dying, and you would be like, is it a cockroach, a spider to kill? Could you die a little more quietly, the children are asleep, blah, blah, fucking blah!'

Andrew rolled his eyes. 'Great. You've been drinking. You lying bitch...'

'Fuck you!' she said and pushed herself up from the ground.

'I doubt you remember how,' he snickered.

Susan wrapped her towel around her. Her trembling soul watered her eyes as they looked around the bathroom. All seemed *normal*.

Maya's voice calling out to her gave strength to her feet. Andrew stood in front of her. Towering over her. His shoulders up and straight. He loved looking big in front of her. 'Move it, Andrew. The baby needs me.'

He took a step sideways and bowed as he showed her the way. 'Run along, your majesty.'

'You're a real ass when you want to be.'

'Said the *drunk*.'

Hate was too light to describe how Susan felt about *that* word. Despised. That was closer. Abhorred. That was even closer when she heard it from his lips.

'*Silence is golden.*' Another one of her granny's favorite sayings. '*Fuck you, you smug prick.*' One of her own favorites.

Susan left the room. 'There, there, baby,' she said as she picked up Maya and laid her upon her. 'Ssshh. Close your eyes. Go back to sleep. Hush little baby, don't you cry...'

A.

D.

Two letters kept her awake that night.

Chapter Fifteen

August had the reputation, yet July *almost* always welcomed more heat waves. Notch by notch that morning, the blood-resembling mercury conquered its glass prison and rose to forty-two degrees Celsius.

'Well, well. We have chosen a hot day for the beach, that's for sure,' Granny Penelope said, staring up at the strong sun perched on a cloudless light-blue sky. Her thick-framed designer shades offered style to the seven-decade-old woman. The sparkling red sunglasses ran into her silver hair while a pink bikini tried to cover her elderly body. Pink sandals with flamingos printed on their sides covered her feet yet revealed her purple toe nails. 'Let's get baking!' she yelled and gave Sophia a nudge before rushing as much as her legs would permit to the *overstuffed with beach toys, colorful lilos and donut swim rings* car.

'Nana thinks she is a teenager again,' Sophia joked and followed her grandmother.

Susan exchanged a worried look with Andrew. He

raised his shoulders. 'Doctors say you go back to your youthful days,' he whispered.

'I'm worried about the heat. I don't need to worry about your mother as well.'

'Just because you are unable to have fun, doesn't mean the rest of us can't. Let me do the worrying about my own mother, thank you very much.'

Susan straightened her beige straw hat. 'Oh, you're still in *that* mood.'

Andrew took a step closer. 'You promised no more drinking. *Ever*.'

Susan raised her gaze and locked onto his eyes. 'We can't all be as perfect as you dear. We humans tend to fail and fuck up from time to time,' she said and strolled off.

Andrew watched her make her way to the car and then turned toward the house.

'Christopher!' he yelled. 'Come on, Son.'

No reply came, but in the matter of half a minute, Christopher came through the door, hand-in-hand with Maya.

'Your daughter remembered to pee. Last-minute as always!'

Andrew shuffled the kid's hair and offered him a sincere smile and a wink.

Just then, the floorboard behind him creaked. Cronus, AKA Boss the Builder, once again stood behind him making him feel uneasy. Was he going to rub himself against him again? Andrew did not wait to find out and turned to face the tall man.

'You all seem set for a fun day,' the builder said.

'Best idea to keep out your way. You and your men have plenty to do today. Thanks for lending us your car by the way. We were planning on taking a taxi...'

Cronus waved his hand. 'Nonsense. This is not faceless, unfriendly London. We help out whenever we can out here. Besides, it's just a ten-minute ride.'

Andrew nodded in agreement. 'It is very kind of you.'

The man smiled widely and placed his hand on Andrew's shoulder. 'Anything for you.'

Andrew stood lost for words. His lips parted twice, yet no sounds created any words. Finally, he nodded nervously and took a step back. 'I better be off. They are all waiting for me in the car, in this heat...'

'The car is running, and the air-con is on full. I'm a very considerate man, too. Caring. Tender even.'

Andrew found himself nodding and on edge again. He replied with an awkward half-smile and dashed for the vehicle bathing under the scorching sun.

Christopher dominated the car conversations with his knowledge about the myths and legends surrounding the area, its village, and the river.

'...Acherontas River wasn't for fun and rafting like it is today. For the ancient Greeks, it was a place of worship and a place of fear!'

'Fear?' Sophia asked as she inspected her pink and black painted nails. After the beach, they would surely need a re-do.

Christopher sat up straight, glowing, glad his sister for once was paying attention to his monologues. 'Well, it did belong to Hades.'

'Hades?' Andrew asked as he sat in the vehicle and quickly put his foot on the gas. He looked in the rear-view mirror. A thick cloud of dust was created by his speedy getaway. He watched as Cronus vanished from his sight. 'What joyful talk are you lot having about the God of the Dead?'

'The dead?' Sophia asked. 'And *we lot* aren't having any talk. Chris is talking. Again. Non-stop!'

Christopher sighed. 'God of the Underworld,' he corrected his father.

'Where the dead lived,' his father replied, turning onto the main road.

'Lived, Dad? Really?'

Penelope chuckled. 'Continue, my sweet boy. You were telling your sister about the river.'

'Oh, yes. The ancients believed the river flowed to the underworld, to their version of hell, really.'

Penelope patted the boy on his shoulder. 'That's why, my smart boy, Dante mentions the Acheron River in Inferno. He said that the river was the border of Hell.'

'Sounds delightful. This little river by our side?' Sophia said and sniggered.

Christopher nodded. 'Just wait until you see the ferryman and his skeleton hand ready to take you to the other side!'

Susan finally turned her attention to her family sitting behind her. 'And you learned all this in your new book?'

Christopher shook his head. 'Nah, from our gardener.'

'We have a gardener?' Susan and Andrew asked in unison.

Christopher shrugged.

'Mum?' Andrew looked back at Penelope with deep thought lines gathering above his nose.

Penelope gave a side look to Christopher sitting beside her. 'Err, yes. Of course. He comes and goes. Helps around when he can. A bearded man, right?'

Christopher nodded. 'Yes. He talks so quietly and smoothly, and he knows so much about Greece and its mythology and religion...'

'Blah, blah, blah. Enough. We are here,' Sophia said and pointed ahead at the thin line of dark blue filling their entire horizon.

'Ammoudia beach, here come the Fotopoulos,' Andrew said and stepped further down on the pedal.

The little coastal village settled well in its lush green surroundings. In front of it was a bay of fine golden sand. One end of the bay was a fifty-meter rock filled with ever-greens, while the other end homed the delta of the Acheron River. Its cool turquoise waters flushed into the warm blue sea. A few scattered fishing boats bounced on the tranquil, slow-travelling waves; their shadows were visible due to the clear, pure waters that lingered in the scenic, picturesque cove.

Susan stepped out of the vehicle and let her eyes embrace the view. She took in a deep breath and held it. The salt of the sea tickled her nostrils. 'Breathe in the sea air, kids. Nature's best medicine.'

If it was not for last night's argument, Andrew would have hugged his wife at that very moment. He wanted to. He nearly did out of custom. Yet, his ego was always the winner. He stayed on his side of the car and gazed around as the three kids unloaded the car trunk.

Penelope remained in the car.

Andrew walked around the car and knelt by her. 'Need help, Mum?'

'Huh? Where are we?' she asked, her eyes jumping side-to-side.

'Ammoudia beach. We left home just ten minutes ago...'

She stroked his hair. 'I know you,' she proudly declared.

'I'm your son. Andreas.'

Her pupils sat still. Her chest relaxed. She managed a smile. 'Yes, yes. Andreas. My one and only. My love.'

'Come on, Mama,' he said and gave her a helping hand out of the car.

Behind him, under a twisted old olive tree the kind that was so old, they were dead and hollow inside, Susan ordered her offspring to stand still. 'What's the rule?'

'Sunscreen is placed in the shade,' all three said as if in an unrehearsed school play.

'That's right,' Susan said and approached them, fifty-plus sunscreen in hand, the blue one with the spray head and the little kids drawn on its side.

'And this is when she turns us into Casper, the friendly ghost,' Christopher said and earned his big sister's laughter. Maya began to sing the tune from the hit cartoon show. '...the friendliest ghost you know...'

'Better safe than sorry.'

Christopher closed his eyes as his mother sprayed her fingers and began to spread the lotion on his cheeks, burying his row of freckles.

'Look at all the other kids, Mum,' Sophia said.

'They are Greek and used to the sun. Look at their tanned skin. You lot will frizzle out there!'

'...ten fat sausages sizzling in a pan...' Maya change her tune as she waited for her turn to become white paste. Even under shade, the children were sweating. Not even a single leaf moved. The wind had taken the hot day off. Soon, three half-Greek yet full-British skinned kids followed their father and grandmother down to the beach. Susan stayed behind, safe in her shade, and applied sun lotion to all her non-covered parts. Extra care was given to her nose and forehead. She knew the state she would be in if burnt by the sun.

'Just pray to Apollo, Mum,' Christopher joked. 'He is

the god in charge of the fireball being carried across his great grandfather, Uranus.'

'Daaad. Christopher said anus.'

Andrew let out a loud laugh. A genuine burst of joy. His dentist's proud work shone under the sun. A row of pearls parted and laughter escaped. 'Jesus Christ, Sophia. He said Uranus. It's the Greek word for sky....'

'The name of the god of the sky. There's even a planet!' Christopher added.

'Geeks,' Sophia mumbled and pulled out her cell phone to take yet another selfie. She was getting nervous. No social media action from her friends or her crush. She had started to believe that there was no internet in this god-forsaken village and that her father and her phone were lying to her. Yet the internet box in her grandmother's living room seemed fully functional. Sophia put it down to jealously as neither of her close mates replied to her messages. Maybe she was doing something wrong. She tried both with the country code and without. Everything seemed to be working as it should. Everything but her social status. Her ego needed attention. It had not fed for days.

Christopher continued laughing at her -not with her, which was usually the case. Andrew had stopped. His mother's blank expression during the entire commotion dampened his spirits. She had seemed fine during the last few days. *'Maybe I shouldn't have taken her away from the house? Maybe the familiar surroundings help her? Is this too much for her?'*

The long stretch of sandy beach welcomed them by burning their feet as they took off their bright-colored flip flops.

'I think we should keep them on until we reach the water,' Susan advised from behind them as she caught up.

There were sunbeds and umbrellas for hire in the center,

while the two edges of the croissant bay of Ammoudia were free for everyone to lay down a towel. Andrew- to Susan's delight as she longed for shade -opted for the sunbeds. The front row of roughly a dozen blue-mat beds were all occupied, either by a person or a colorful towel.

'Four beds is well enough, right, hun?' Andrew asked, looking back at Susan. She controlled her facial expressions well. '*Hun? Really, dipshit?*' She had learned the curse word from Sophia who had a craze for anything teen American. Susan preferred her drama shows offered by ITV and the BBC. She replied with a nod.

'Come, Mama. Come relax here,' Andrew said, helping his mother sit down. Penelope sat down, kicked off her sandals, and buried her feet in the sand. She gazed around at her heavenly setting and smiled with her eyes closed. Her face seemed calmer.

'Can we go in the water, now?' Sophia's questions sounded more like a moan than a question since she hit puberty. Christopher thought she was a living, talking, whining cliché. A cliché that was his sister, and he loved her to bits. Not that he ever admitted such a fact. 'Yeah, can we go, now? Please?' he asked with his puppy eyes and dragging the vowels in his *please*. He wanted to make sure the answer would be positive.

'Just the two of you,' Andrew finally replied. The two-second wait for his response seemed longer to them. 'I'll bring Maya. Don't go too far in. Check to see how deep it is based on the people around you.'

Christopher ran the fourteen-meter distance in a time that would qualify as a record in his school. The water rushing toward him, caressing his toes did not slow him down. He took long steps, conquering the short puny waves, and in a matter of seconds, he dived into the clear waters of the Ionian Sea. Sophia stopped inches from the short-lived line created by the sea on the golden sand. Her toe took off and lingered in the air as the next waved died upon the shore and pushed water her way. Her toe dipped in the sea. 'It's cold,' she mumbled.

'Mia xara einai.'

'Excuse me?' she asked as she turned to the direction of the voice.

A tanned teen with carefree curls, a long Roman nose, and deep green eyes was smiling at her.

'I said it is okay,' he said in broken English. 'It is because you are hot, from the sun I mean, and the sea seems cold. Go in and you will see. Go full in. Escape the heat.' He spoke slowly, having to process the words inside his head. When he finished his sentence, he beamed proudly. His father's money on private lessons paid off.

Sophia replied with a quick smile and proceeded forward with steady steps. She wanted to gaze at the handsome youth more but knew well that boys *stick better when ignored*. The boy watched her make her way into the water, huffing and puffing as new parts of her body descended into the cool waters. He scratched the back of his head and turned to walk toward the sunbeds.

'Good morning, sir,' he said to Andrew as he opened his black belt back and took out his block of receipts. 'Four beds, two umbrellas?'

'That's right.'

'Twelve Euro, please,' he said and cut six pieces of paper.

'And what's the discount for the man whose daughter you were just flirting with and goggling at?'

The boy's cheeks flushed, and swallowed hard. 'Err, I would say ten?'

'Sounds like a deal,' Andrew said, passing him the note and taking a hopping Maya by the hand.

'Keep an eye on them,' Susan said as she laid down her Scooby-Doo towel on the only sunbed fully in the protective shade. 'You're not coming in?' Andrew placed his hand above his eyes to provide his pupils with a shield from the sun.

'Maybe later. Now, go. Enjoy your kids.'

Susan had no desire for small talk. Penelope not being herself suited her just fine on that sun-attacking, Susan-white-skin-sizzling day. She also had no desire of joining her family, splashing each other and giggling in the sea. Not so much to avoid and bitter Andrew. She never punished her kids from her company whenever he was a dickhead (her word, not Sophia's). She was not feeling herself inside her own skin. She felt dirty. Guilty. Slutty. She could still feel the shepherd's skilful hands moving upon her naked body... her naked soul. Worse, every time she closed her eyes, she pictured herself having sex with the monster she saw on the bed. She had been way passed simple drunk before, but hallucinations were something entirely new. '*He must have slipped something in my drink... But why? I was already willing. What was the point?*'

A chill ran down her spine. '*Maybe he wanted to torture me... or murder me... he did burn me after all... Susan, you stupid cow. Going off with a stranger in a strange land. You have a family...*'

'Isws itan daimonas. Ellinikos oxi xristianikes vlakeies.'

Penelope's voice interrupting her thoughts startled her. She did not catch every word. She did not know every word.

'Excuse me, Penelope. You were saying?' she asked, sitting up straight.

'I'm thirsty, dear. I do believe we brought some lemonade with us, right?'

Susan nodded and leaned to her side in search of the green and yellow cool box. She was sure that was not Penelope's first sentence. She knew the Greek words for thirsty and lemonade. She passed the bottle to her mother-in-law and fell back into the bed and her thoughts.

'And what the hell do A and D mean?! God, I'm driving myself mad.'

Meanwhile, in the Ionian waters, Andrew acted out his bad wolf persona as he blew up Maya's Dora the Explorer swimming vest. The little one screeched in laughter.

'I hope her laughter changes as she grows up. It's way too high-pitched.'

Christopher shook his head. 'Do you always have to complain about something?' he asked his sister.

'Don't start!' Andrew said between puffs.

'Come on, Dad. When can we go in the deep? The water isn't even up to our waist. Can I go alone? You know I am an expert swimmer.'

'Give me a sec, Chris. I'll come with you. As good as a swimmer you are, these are unknown waters.' Soon, Andrew placed a fully inflated life jacket on his youngest daughter. 'You wanna go to the deep, Sophia?'

Sophia shook her head. She was enjoying the attention from the Greek boy working the sunbeds.

'Good. Keep an eye on Maya as I go for a swim with your brother.'

Sophia took Maya by her hands. 'Come on, Maya. Kick your legs. I'll teach you how to swim in no time.'

Andrew smiled, patted Christopher on the back, and said, 'First one to that rock. One, two, go!' Instantaneously, both disappeared beneath the waves, only to pop out meters away. They swam side by side. Andrew was impressed by his son's speed. The lessons were paying off well. *'He is getting older. They grow up so fast. Or maybe I am just growing old...'* His last thought slowed him down, and he lost his concentration. Christopher climbed up onto the two square meters of rock with the two dying bushes and broke into his victory dance. His father breathlessly clapped below him.

'And back!' Andrew declared and turned around, swimming as fast as he could. He anticipated sensing his son diving in beside him. He was expecting to see his young boy challenging him. He kept on swimming alone. He stopped and turned around. Christopher was nowhere to be seen. Andrew looked around; his eyes falling on each head popping in the water. None were his son. 'Christopher?'

Andrew swam back to the rock. 'Christopher?' he asked again, expecting his son to jump out from behind the rocky islet and try to scare him. Andrew swam around. The emptiness of the rock and the sea around it were daunting. Andrew climbed up and stood on the rather smooth surface. He turned 360 degrees. 'Christopher?' he yelled.

Christopher could not hear him, six feet under the water's surface. A strong underwater current had suddenly grabbed him as he leaped into the sea to catch up to his father. Christopher knew to keep his mouth closed, to save in his last good breath. He kicked his legs ferociously and tried to rise above the current pulling him away. Nothing. He was going under. He began to panic. His limps were stretched out, yet there was nothing to hold, to step on. *'So, this is it...'*

A hand suddenly grabbed his. A figure of a woman swimming by him. He recognized the colors of her swimsuit. *'Am I dreaming? Grandma?'*

Penelope pulled him out of the current and together

they kicked toward the shiny, magical surface. Christopher gasped for air, having escaped the hell of the cold sea depth. His little chest shook as it welcomed in fresh again once again. 'Thank you, Grandma.'

Penelope smiled widely. 'A soul for a soul,' she said and stopped swimming. The current quickly pulled her under, and Christopher watched her vanish from his sight. He took a deep breath and ducked under. She was gone.

Christopher remained in the same spot, unsure of his next move. He had no strength to dive back under, and the shore was a thin yellow line on the horizon. He was surprised on how far out the water had taken him. He used minimum effort to stay afloat.

'You'll float too,' he whispered his favorite line from his favorite horror book.

He heard his name being called. It was that of his father's. Soon, his dad's arms were wrapped around him. 'Thank God. What the hell are you doing out here?'

One sentence painted with relief. One sentence sprayed with anger.

'The current pulled me out here. Grandma pulled me out. I was drowning...'

'Grandma? Chris, Nana is out on her sunbed with your mother. She probably hasn't swum in years.'

Christopher did not reply. He wished his father was right. As the shore expanded on the horizon and his toes felt sand again, Christopher's desire to see his grandmother safe and sound grew.

In the shallows, his sisters played oblivious to his ordeal.

'You two look exhausted,' Sophia commented. Sophia had to comment on everything. Christopher walked straight past her. His eyes tried to find a spot, a gap between the front row beds. He finally caught a glimpse of his mother.

Step by step his heartbeat elevated. Empty bed, empty bed, empty bed. His mother sat alone.

'Where's grandma?'

Susan raised her head. 'Oh, hi, sweetie. How was your swim? Here, let me find your towel...'

'Where is grandma?'

Hit tone froze her search for his blue towel. 'What's wrong, Christopher?'

'Shit, Mum. Just answer the freaking question.'

Susan's jaw dropped. She would have expected language from Sophia on a bad day, but never from her son. Her articulate, kind, educated spirit of a boy. She was just about to reply, having decided between the dilemma of telling him off or enquiring what caused this outburst of bad behavior, when Andrew showed up behind Christopher.

'Where's my mum?'

Same tone, same worried face.

'She was just here minutes ago. I closed my eyes and laid back. I think I heard her bed rattle. I guessed she was changing side or maybe coming to the water to see you guys,' she said in one-second sentences. 'What the hell is going on?'

Christopher ran off back to the edge of the sea and scanned around the waters.

'Great going, Susan. You had one job. Only you could lose an old lady...'

Susan bit her tongue. 'She couldn't have gone far...'

'According to Christopher, she swam out to the deep and saved him from an underwater current.'

Susan stood up. 'Saved him?'

'He says it pulled him under.'

Susan took a step toward him. 'And where were you? What about your one job to take care of the kids?'

Andrew clenched his fists. 'I was there. Looking for him. And I brought him back. Where is my mother?'

'She can hardly walk. I doubt she swam all the way out there. Maybe Christopher pictured it out of fear, or another old lady helped him out and he couldn't see well UNDERWATER!'

Andrew raised his hands. 'Great time to pull a Susan. Yeap. Start shouting. Make a scene. Make this about you.'

Just then, Sophia appeared behind her father, Maya in her arms. 'Erm, guys? Christopher is acting weird, well weirder than usual. He's with the lifeguard running up and down the beach calling grandma's name.'

Susan exhaled. 'Let's go find Penelope.'

The search for Penelope began with a lifeguard, a family of five, and a couple of caring bystanders. In an hour, it had grown into a search party of two coastguards upon their vessel, two lifeguards, a worried, teary family of five and more than a couple of dozen bystanders.

Penelope was nowhere to be seen.

Hours later, the family ate at the restaurant nestled among the tall trees in the right corner of the bay. They ate fish and calamari, courtesy of the kind owner with the thick mustache. That is where the police man with the thin mustache took their statements. Andrew and Christopher's that is.

The return home could not have been gloomier. In total contrast with the ecstatic joy of the morning route, the evening route home was driven in silence. Six set off, but only five returned.

Andrew bit his lower lip at the sight of his family mansion. He had no strength or will in him to explain himself to Cronus. He had promised the car back hours ago. He checked his cell phone. Zero calls. *'They must still be at the house...'*

Down the driveway they went, and the house waited for them, dark and alone.

'The builders must have finished up and left together,' Susan commented as if reading his thoughts. Her voice was quieter than usual. It came from a tired soul. Weak words tinted with melancholy. He recognized that voice well. He lived with it for months after Eugene's death.

'Thankfully, they came in two cars. I feel bad for keeping his car...' Andrew began to say as he parked by the entrance.

'Who cares? Grandma is gone!' Christopher shouted as he exited the car. He slammed the door behind him and rushed off. The four watched him as he vanished behind the rock-made garden wall.

'Should I go after him?' Andrew asked. Susan shook her head. 'Let him be. He will go blow off steam out at his reading spot.'

'Is Granny really lost?'

Both turned to face Maya sitting still in the back with watery violet eyes. In all the searching and worrying, both had forgotten that they had a three-year-old to comfort. A small child unable to fully understand what was going on. Their daughter who since coming to the Mesopotamos spent most of her day with her grandmother.

'She met her just to lose her...' Andrew whispered.

'Stop being pessimistic,' Susan replied in the same whispery manner. 'Now, listen dear,' she said, raising her voice. 'I'm sure granny is just fine,' she lied. 'She is just old and forgetful, you know? Remember when your friend Lily's cat wandered off and returned days later and Lily's mum said that it lost its way home?'

Maya nodded while Sophia scoffed and got out of the vehicle. Strangely enough, a black cat like the one just mentioned sat on the wall to her left and was starring straight at her. Sophia was ready to walk to the house when the cat raised its front paw.

'*Are you waving at me?*' Sophia took a few steps forward, sure that the stray would sprint away at the sight of the approaching human. The cat remained in its spot. As Sophia drew closer, it even stood up and lowered its head, begging her for a render stroke. Sophia reached out and let her fingers ran through its fur. 'You're too friendly and clean to be homeless,' she spoke to it and searched for a collar. 'Wow, your fur is so soft.' She continued stroking it, enjoying its loud, smoothing purring. She gently picked up its front paws, helping the feline stand on both its back legs. 'Now, are you a boy cat or a girl cat?' she asked as she ducked to check. 'Yes! You're a girl.' The cat rubbed its head against her pink T-shirt with dried sea patches of stubborn and sticky golden sand. With a small sprint, it leaped into her arms and settled like a newborn baby. 'Well, aren't you a friendly one.' Sophia tickled the cat's belly much to the animal's enjoyment. Sophia gazed back at the house. 'You know what cat? I sure do need a friend, right about now.' With the cat happily nestled in her embrace, Sophia was first to enter the empty mansion. It would feel strange for all without Penelope wandering around, her walking stick banging along her side, her whistling of old tunes, and her mumbling of lyrics from songs unfortunately long forgotten by the general public. There was her fine cooking and the way she could sit for hours drawing and playing with Maya without getting bored of the repetitive tea parties the three-year-old threw.

'...and this is my room, cat,' Sophia finished her tour. 'I

think we need to come up with a name for you. I can't continue calling you cat.'

The silky black cat jumped out of her arms and landed effortlessly on the ground. She went straight for the bed and sat down by Sophia's dairy. Sophia looked at her purple diary with the Black Eyed Peas stickers on its cover and the small silver lock on the side. The cat placed its right paw on the diary. Sophia giggled awkwardly. 'Seriously? Are you really showing me my diary?' Sophia said as she sat down by the cat and opened her treasured papers of secrets. The cat seemed to be interested in what Sophia was doing as she flicked through the pages. She stopped on the page with Gary's name written on top. Written in bold, splashed with glitter and underlined. Beneath various hearts and song lyrics, Sophia had written her name with Gary's surname. Sophia Johnson. On the line under that were names she had written for the imaginary future offspring. Noah if a boy, Olivia if a girl. 'Olivia. How about we call you Olivia? It suits you well. You're as black as a Greek olive.' The feline with the emerald eyes had been christened. Olivia rubbed her entire body along Sophia's back, purring loudly as she went. She laid down by the open diary and pushed it forward with her paws, tapping the top of the page.

'Who is Gary you ask. Oh, Olivia, he has the dreamiest of eyes and his hair? Shiny as yours.' The teen laughed and continued her tale with Gary's football accomplishments and how plain Gary's sort-of girlfriend was. '...I mean, she doesn't even have her ears pierced. I bet her parents are like some sort of religious nuts. That would explain her lousy taste in clothes...'

Sophia was not the only one lost in conversation. Christopher paced up and down under his beloved reading tree, stopping at the border between shade and light. The gardener sat on a rock opposite him and listened to the youth's retelling of the day. He did not interrupt once. He took off his thick dirty garden gloves and dropped his cutters on the ground. He sat leaned forward; his entire focus on the angry boy talking loudly and waving his arms around.

'... I should have swum after her.'

Christopher finally stood still. His chest rose and fell. His fingers met and intertwined to shape two small fists. His watery eyes let gathered tears run down his sun-kissed reddish cheeks.

'We can't save everyone. From what I understand, you didn't have the power to save her. Just like Orpheus who hopelessly tried to save Eurydice.'

'At least he tried...' Christopher said and let out a strong cry. 'What if she's dead?' he asked after his animal-like wail, turning toward the bearded man.

The man played with his long beard and looked straight at the boy. 'Does anything ever really die?'

Christopher rolled his eyes. 'Wrong time to get philosophical with me.'

'You're angry about something that has not been confirmed yet. Anger is a very dangerous emotion, my young friend. Angry people do angry acts. Artemis, Poseidon, Achilles, Hephaestus, Orestes, all performed acts of violence and death out of anger. Out of character. You are a gentle soul, my boy. A reader, a writer, a dreamer. Don't let the deaths in your life change you. You are going to witness horrible things in your future, but you have to remain you.'

Christopher wiped his eyes and nodded in agreement. He took his first step out of the shade and approached the gardener. 'Thank you,' he said and then raised his arms and took another step forward, leaning in for a hug. The man was startled by this and nearly fell back off his flat sitting rock. He stood up and took a few steps back, avoiding the boy's touch.

'You're welcome, young master. Glad to be of assistance. That is why I am here...'

'I was only going to give you a hug,' Christopher interrupted, slightly puzzled by the man's reaction -overreaction in Christopher's eyes. *'Maybe it's a cultural thing? Men don't touch and all. But they do kiss on the cheek twice...'*

A genuine Greek soothing smile spread upon the gardener's face, and his deep wrinkles around his kind eyes moved upward. 'Control your thoughts, my boy. I appreciate the gesture, but I can't be touched,' he said and picked up his cutters. 'Now, you better ran back home. They have enough to worry about. No need for extra stress thinking about your whereabouts. Go. Fly like Hermes,' he said and turned his attention to his blossoming rose bushes.

Back at the mansion, Susan sat quietly by a sleeping Maya. It had been a long day. Andrew was downstairs on the phone with the local police. She could hear him speak and feel his heavy footsteps. Since Eugene's death, Andrew always put Maya to sleep. Susan would burst into tears every time she saw Maya sleeping. She looked so much like her younger brother. They even slept in the same pose. They even sounded the same. The same rhythmic breathing. Susan would panic if her breathing would settle and check for a pulse. Sometimes she would wake the child just to be sure.

'No drinking tonight, Suzie. No visions. No Eugene. No letters!'

Chapter Sixteen

Susan sleepily swatted her nose with her palm.

The blow made her gasp and awake fully. She had missed the pesky fly, the large ones that the villagers called donkey flies, yet she was happy. Happy to be awake with the sun up and about. She had slept through the night. No drinking, no visions, no Eugene, and no letters. The plan worked. Seven full uneventful hours of restful slumber.

Andrew, on the other hand, did not get much sleep. *Much* being an understatement.

As someone who avoided showing emotions most of the time, he found himself confused on how to feel. Maybe he was entitled to feel it all at the same time.

Worry. His sick mother was lost.

Sadness. She could be dead, swallowed and drowned by the merciless sea.

Confused. How the hell did she swim out to Christopher?

He was also secretly enjoying a weird version of happy.

The house and land would pass to him to sell as soon as possible. Early retirement plans flooded his brain.

Tired. Sleepy. Hungry.

All mixed up and blended with a raving migraine.

He had walked up and down the hallway more times than he could count, before heading down to the kitchen for two beers and a jar of Nutella. Thoughts and thoughts. His inner Erinyes taunting him, bringing up images of a long-forgotten childhood. His mother did everything for him. Always by his side. Always on his team. A lonely tear quickly ran down his cheek and got lost in his rough, two-day facial hairs. A shower followed in the guest room of the ground floor. He masturbated. Violently. The only minutes his mind went blank. Naked as he was, he wiped his wet feet on the white towel he had flung to the floor and walked steadily to the basement door. Two deep breaths and then he was ready to place his hand on the handle. Another breath, and then he closed his eyes, and his hand went down. The door creaked. Step by step, he descended into the room of his nightmares. The lights were still flickering as they came to life as he took the sledgehammer in his hands. He looked up at the closed door and hoped that the thick wooden floorboards and the size of the house would drown out the noise.

'*Drown! What a poor choice of words, dickhead.*'

He tried breathing in through his nose and out through his mouth (remembering his high school coach's advice) to calm his heart. He was close to *the* statue. *That* statue. He raised the hammer in the air.

No swing came. Just thoughts.

'*What if there are indeed dead bodies in them? Don't be stupid, Andrew. That was just your pervert uncle's tale to scare you. Why aren't you smashing them, then?*'

Defeated by his fears, he let go of the heavy sledgehammer. He spat at the statue and turned to leave. As he reached the steps, he heard the footsteps behind him. Naked and afraid, just like back then, he did not turn around. Once again, Andrew found himself running from that room. He locked the door behind him and headed up to bed. He tossed and turned for most of the night. As the first ray of light sailed in, he stood up and got dressed.

The fly forced Susan to open her eyes as he was about to leave the room, fully dressed and well-groomed.

Andrew stood by the open door. He watched her wake up slowly. He witnessed the faint smile on her pale face. Her happiness annoyed him, yet he did not speak. He just stood there. Susan finally noticed him.

'Where are you off to?' she asked in her morning voice.

'The police station. My mother is still missing, you know. She's probably dead but it's okay, you continue with your lovely dream. At least, you're smiling ...'

He swallowed and contained the next few words. Or did he whisper them? '...*you moody bitch.*' If he said them, he hoped they came out of his mouth after he closed the door.

Susan fell back on her pillow. *'Trust Andrew to not let you enjoy a second of a new day...'*

Susan had enjoyed excellent hearing since as back as she could remember. Memories from her childhood contained the phrase 'can you hear that?', to which she received the blunt reply 'no.' She heard the car coming round the corner first, the dustbin men woke her up whenever they passed her parent's house in Enfield, and the ticking of clocks drove her crazy. Even as she was snuggled up in bed with one ear buried in the soft pillow, she heard Andrew storm down the stairs. She heard him open the fridge; probably grabbing one of those awful (in her opinion, not his) ready-made coffees in a can. She heard him open and close the main door. She heard the borrowed car speed off.

What amazed her more was the silence from her children. Nothing from the room to her left where Christopher slept, and there was nothing from the room to her right where, for the first time, the girls had chosen to sleep together.

She decided to capitalize on the quietude and forced her eyelids back down. A rare feat for her to steal time for herself and manage to sleep more. She had not looked at the time. She had no idea how much more she had slept when Sophia opened her door.

'Err, Mum? You awake? Maya's getting hungry. Do you wanna join us downstairs for breakfast or should I take care of her?'

Susan fought back the tangled sheet and sat up, placing her hand on her heart. 'My sweet daughter! I remember you! Where have you been for the last few years?'

Sophia could not help it. Her soft laughter, just a level above a giggle, echoed through the room. 'No, need to be sarcastic, Mother. I'm not always a moody teenage bitch, you know.'

'Language, Sophia.'

'You get my point. I just thought that after yesterday, you might not be up for much today. Besides, I made a new friend, and I know that in the end, it will be up to you if I get to keep her,' Sophia said and quickly closed the bedroom door before her mother switched to *FBI-mode* and began her interrogation.

'Let's go downstairs. Mummy is coming,' Sophia continued, turning her attention to Maya who stood behind her, cat in hands. Olivia jumped to the carpet and sprinted to the stairs. 'She seems to know the way to the kitchen,' Sophia said, giggling. She took Maya by her hand and followed the feline. Maya smiled widely. It had been a while since her sister had been in high spirits. As the girls made their way to the ground floor, Sophia noticed the thin line of light below the library's door. This kept her from noticing Maya opening her violet eyes wide and then quickly shutting them. Maya descended the rest of the spiral staircase with her eyes forced shut.

'Christopher?'

'What?'

Sophia shook her head. *'How can this boy enjoy reading first thing in the morning?'*

'Breakfast!' Maya shouted in reply, relieved to be away from the stairs.

The noise of a book being slammed closed travelled to their ears followed by a 'Coming.'

When Susan made her way to the kitchen, she stood surprised in the doorway. All three of her children had a bowl of cereal in front of them. Her attention though was caught by the black cat sitting in Penelope's chair.

'You're new,' she said as she walked up to the counter to prepare her morning tea. Despite the high temperatures, Susan drank her tea boiling hot. Regardless of the season, a *good cuppa* was craved by her system. 'I'm guessing this is your new friend, huh?' she asked as she pushed the silver button on the kettle.

Sophia nodded. 'Her name is Olivia. She is very friendly and look how clean she is, Mum. She's a sweetheart. Aren't you, baby?'

Olivia meowed, and the girls laughed.

'Grandma is still missing, you know?' Christopher's voice dampened their spirits.

'When is Granny coming home? I wanna draw,' Maya added.

Susan googled her eyes at her son. 'Maybe later, dear,' she replied to her daughter. 'There's nothing we can do about it. Your father is with the police as we speak. Stop mentioning her around Maya, please,' she whispered into her son's ear. Susan waited for the loud whistling of the kettle to settle down. 'How about we do something fun today? Together.'

Christopher was never one to miss out on an opportunity.

'I've been reading about Mesopotamos, and its most visited sight is the Necromanteio. How about we go there for the day?'

Sophia bit down on her Frosties and digested them quickly. 'A: what's the Necraman thing, and b: how are we going to get there, genius?'

Once again, Christopher found himself rolling his eyes at his sister. 'A: it's called Necromanteio and it's the ruins of an ancient site where...'

'Blah, blah, mythology, blah, blah, ancient Greeks, blah...'

'And B' -he raised his voice over his sister's- 'it's nearby, and we have that taxi driver's number. I'll pay from my pocket money.'

Both turned toward their mother, puzzled by her silence. Susan paused sipping on her hot beverage. Goosebumps travelled along her arms and settled on the back of her neck. She was sure she heard that word before. '*The old woman on the bus. She warned me about that place...*'

'Mum!' Christopher shouted. 'Earth to mum?

Mesopotamos calling Mrs Susan. Can we go? My treat? Please? I can't stay here all day. Not today. Otherwise, take us to the p-o-l-i-c-e so we can help in the search for g-r-a-n-d-m-a.'

Susan exhaled and nodded in agreement. '*How dangerous can an archaeological site be? It's probably been fixed up since the old lady's time.*'

Chapter Seventeen

Cronus was still not answering his phone.

'*Who doesn't check their phone for fifteen hours?*' Andrew thought, followed by a row of descriptive adjectives and curse words. Andrew drove the builder's car into town and parked outside a small building that was begging for a splash of paint. The summer sun, the torrential rain, and the economic crisis had not been kind on the walls that housed the local police station. The village boasted two officers compared to most rural, small-population villages as Ammoudia beach fell under their jurisdiction.

Andrew pushed the glass door and entered the cold air-conditioned room. His skin pores stood at attention as they escaped the sticky heat outside and greeted the low temperature inside. A little bell above his head rang, catching the attention of the blonde lady playing Solitaire on the lone computer of the reception desk. She wished him a good morning in Greek and asked how she may help him.

Something about her tone, her high-pitched, child-like squeaky voice brought back memories. 'Err, I am Andreas

Fotopoulos. I reported my mother, Penelope, missing yesterday eveni ...'

'Oh, yes, yes. Of course,' the lady said, leaping out of her seat. 'Please sit down. Let me get you a strong Greek coffee.'

Andrew waved his hands. 'No, no that's fine,' he said, yet the woman in the red dress and the black high heels continued with her coffee-brewing preparations anyhow. Her hands were quite shaky. Maybe she needed to prepare the coffee to keep her hands busy. Maybe she was the one that needed to drink it. '*Oh, shit. My mother is dead.*'

'I was calling here for the last two hours or so and no one was answering...'

The woman stopped and looked straight at him, tilting her head to her right. She licked her lips. 'Sir, our two officers have been out searching for your mother since the first light of dawn ...'

Andrew placed his hand on his heart. 'I did not mean it as a complaint ...'

'But,' she raised her screechy voice, 'I have been here, by the phone, all morning. My husband told me to sit here and take the calls just in case any information was called in. He is one fine officer, and if anyone can find your mother, it is my Daniel.'

Andrew took in a deep breath of cold air. His mind travelled back to his London office where the majority of his female co-workers complained about the low temperatures that their male counterparts set the air-conditioning units to in the summer months. Not than any of them dealt with anything comparable to Greece's heat-waves. 'May I ask, do I know you? Your voice sounds awfully familiar ...'

The woman chuckled. 'Yes, I guess my voice is quite recognizable. For all the wrong reasons, unfortunately. We were in school together, Andrea. For a couple of years. Up until ...' She paused. She searched for the right words. In front of her was a man inquiring about a tragedy, and she was reminding him of a worse tragedy of the past. '... you moved to England.'

Andrew nodded. 'Don't tell me. Annita?'

Her drawn-on eyebrows moved upward forming a McDonald's arch. 'You remember.'

'Soooo, er, any news on my mother?'

Annita shook her head. 'Nothing so far. But you know what they say. No news is good news, right?' She forced a smile as she played with her thumbs. 'Weird that you say you were calling. I was right here. You probably have the wrong number. It would have saved you from driving down here...'

'I needed to get out the house,' he replied honestly. 'But it's the number the officers gave me yesterday. Here, look,' he said and pulled out the scrunched-up paper out of his blue shorts. Annita looked down. She squinted her eyes. More out of disbelief, than fixing her ability to see well. 'That's my Daniel's handwriting. The number is correct. You sure you were dialling it correctly? I don't mean to insult you, it's just at such times of worry and stress, our minds ...'

Andrew placed his iPhone 3GS on the counter in front of her.

'Oh, shoot. The coffee,' she said and turned to save the near-burnt beverage. The strong aroma filled the low-ceiling room as she placed two cups next to his phone. 'Now, let me see,' she said and took the cell phone in her hand.

'Check my calls. I've been calling here and my builder all morning.'

Once again, her head tilted, and she looked more puzzled than before. 'Andrew? Your phone's off.'

Andrew took the phone out of her thin fingers. 'What?' She was right. He pressed the turn-on button. Nothing. The phone was dead.

Annita pressed her thumbs together. Her eyes looked at her toes. 'As I said, times of stress...'

Andrew shook his head. 'It was on. I punched in the numbers. I'm not crazy.'

A flat-line smile appeared on Annita's now pale face. 'I haven't seen this type of phone before. I have a Nokia, and Daniel has a Samsung. I have our chargers ...'

'It's an Apple. It needs an Apple charger.' Andrew's tone had changed. Sorrow gave way to anger. 'Where are Daniel and his assistant now?'

'I believe they are in the woods by Ammoudia. The coastguard is going along the shore, so they thought to search the forest just in case your dear mother got disoriented and couldn't see any signs of civilization. She has Alzheimer's, right?'

A few miles away, Susan also held her phone in her hand. She pushed in the numbers that Christopher was reciting to her from the business card given to them by the taxi driver.

'Yes? Hello? This is Susan. Susan Fotopoulos?'

The three children watched as their mother talked with the taxi driver from when they arrived. 'Yeah, yeah. To the Necromanteio. The kids need to do some sightseeing to ... err ... have you heard the news?'

Susan nodded. 'Of course. Big news; small village. Just

as you said ... hmm ... yes, that would be great. See you soon.'

Susan pressed the red circle on her screen and faced her kids. 'No problem, he said. He will be here shortly. Go get ready. Quickly. Wear decent shoes. Sophia, help Maya. Shorts and any T-shirt. I'm going to text your father and let him know where we are heading ...'

Sophia moved air around in her cheeks before speaking. 'Do you think that's a good idea? Might just make him angry that we are having fun while...'

'Shorts and a T-shirt, Sophia. Go on.'

Sophia placed her top row of pearly teeth on her bottom lip. She stared at her mother for a few seconds. Then, without saying a word, she took her little sister by the hand and walked off to get ready. Christopher shouted 'I'm ready,' before they even reached their room.

In fifteen minutes, just like he said, Harry, the lanky taxi driver, honked outside. All four of the Fotopoulos gang were ready and exited the front door in order of age, from youngest to oldest.

Susan realized she would be riding shotgun as her three children climbed in the back and buckled up. The air blew at them even colder than they remembered. The difference with the hot air outside was tremendous. 'Good morning,' she said, noticing for the first time how thin the man truly was. '*There's more meat on a chicken bone, my nana used to say.*'

'Kalimera, good morning, bonjour, buongiorno, buenos dias!' he replied with a wide smile. The man hardly had lips. Two thin lines of pale pink. His teeth, however, were excellent. Magazine-type flashy and structured. 'Necromanteio, huh? What a place! Great choice, Christopher,' he cheerily said and placed his foot on the gas. Once again, the mansion accepted a large dust cloud. '*That road needs to be paved. People don't ride around on donkeys anymore,*' Susan thought before asking, 'How do you know it was Christopher's choice?'

'Didn't you say so on the phone?'

'I don't believe I did.'

Harry looked in the rear-view mirror and clicked his tongue. 'He seems the one interested in such places. I think during our first ride together, he spoke about mythology and such.'

'Sounds like Christopher,' Sophia commented and raised her eyebrows, titling toward her brother.

Christopher pushed her back in place. 'What he is trying to say, Mum, is that I look like the intellectual one out of the bunch!' He turned toward his sister and stuck his tongue out.

'Yeah, a real intellectual, looking like a twat.'

'Einstein's most famous photo is of him with his tongue out.'

Susan looked back at her children. Both recognized *that* look. The *be quiet* look their mother used in public spaces. Susan rubbed her arms. The icy air surrounded her, settling on her skin. '*At least it's a short ride.*' She gazed outside. In a matter of a few minutes, the last houses of Mesopotamos village were behind them and an old asphalt road welcomed them. Cracks were the norm of the country road, and holes had been filled in sloppily, resulting in the road featuring more shades of grey than the steamy novel Susan had regretted reading. She was more into murder/mysteries. She wanted a book to trigger her mind, not her lady parts.

'There it is. Up there, upon the hill.' Christopher's arm stretched out and pointed straight forward.

'Looks like a church,' Sophia said with her cheek glued to the window and her hand above her eyes to cover the bright rays of the sun. Sophia sat back and scoffed. 'I was expecting some fascinating Greek temple or something. Tombs of Kings. Anything.'

Christopher prepared a short yet elaborate reply in his mind and opened his mouth. He did not speak though as the taxi driver looked back at Sophia. 'Oh, my dear. Don't be disappointed by the small abandoned monastery. The greatness is below. The temple runs underground through majestic tunnels. It truly is a beauty. They don't make them like they used to,' he added and quickly turned his attention back to the road that began its uphill climb. Christopher smiled widely. Not because of the driver's answer, but also because of the shine he witnessed in his sister's eyes. She was intrigued.

VISITORS PARKING.

A blue arrow was drawn below the bold capital letters. An empty field with white lines of chalk to separate the twelve parking spots spread out before their eyes.

'Are we the only ones here? Is it open?' Susan asked as the vehicle came to a halt.

Harry chuckled. 'Of course. It is always open. The guide, she is... err, related to me. By wedding that is. I called ahead. She is waiting for you,' he answered to Susan's relief. 'They all are.'

'Excuse me?'

'Huh?'

'You said something at the end...'

Harry smiled. 'Just a cough.'

Susan was sure she heard those three words. She did not feel comfortable in the car; she did not feel comfortable getting out. The slamming of both the back doors made her jump. Her three kids were already heading toward the tall, dark-green Cypresses that proudly stood by the entrance. 'How much do I owe you?'

'Pay me when I take you back home.'

'Oh, my husband will pick us up. I've texted him where we are. So, how much will it be?' Susan asked eager to join her children.

'One obolos.'

'Excuse me?'

'Six Euro. As you saw, it's just a short ride here. Look. You can even see your house!'

Susan fiddled around in her burgundy designer purse and placed in the man's wrinkly hand three two Euro coins. She murmured a compulsory thank you and exited into the heat.

She remained still as the man reversed his taxi and vanished down the hill. Her gaze was fixed on the topography around her. The mansion was nearer to the Necromanteio than she knew or thought, the view blocked from the house's windows by the tall trees of the back garden. Wild fields filled up the space between their property and the sacred ground. No road connected the two. She looked around at the mansion's lands, the roads, and the village. The eight-minute drive was needed. If there was a road from their back garden it surely would have been a three-minute drive; close enough to even walk it, she thought.

'Come on, Mum!' Christopher's voice made her turn. She put on her motherly smile and expression and skipped toward them. 'Come on, my darlings. Let's go exploring!' She had to be cheery. She had to pretend. She had to lock away the sorrow and the darkness, if just for a while. She owed it to her children -her living children. Her children that most likely lost their grandmother and would be attending a funeral during their summer holiday in Greece.

A stone wall ran around the hilltop. Not like the walls down at the village —or any old village in Greece. These were large rocks. Large and dark, unlike the smaller, lighter-tone ones that homes and walls were normally made out of. The four walked through the large open gate and followed the rock-paved path toward the church. Broken columns were on both their sides, as were a dozen or so crosses.

'I guess the church has a cemetery, too...'

'Oh, no, my beautiful girl.' The voice came from the dark shade by the church's towering wall. Tick, tick. High heels echoed in the air. A tall woman came forward out of the shadows and into the vibrant light. Susan's eyes ran up from the red heels to a stunning pair of legs shinning in the sun. The woman had that smooth, healthy-white complexion Susan envied. A white skirt was held to the woman's small waist by a thin red belt. The lady's turquoise shirt had enough buttons unfastened to reveal much of her plentiful bosom. Curly, auburn hair fell to her neck and featured an array of real small flowers in them. Her green eyes were focused on the children, so Susan had enough time to check her out. Enough to feel jealous. Enough to feel under-dressed in her shorts and plain blouse. Enough to wish that she had placed more make-up on. The woman's red lips and high-cheek bones could have been featured in Cosmopolitan or Vogue.

'It's not a cemetery?' Sophia asked, stepping forward.

'Oh, that it is, my dear child. I was referring to the church part. It's a monastery actually. My name is Perse-phone, and I will be your guide for the day,' she said with an exotic voice and manner. 'And you three pretty things are?'

'Sophia...'

'Pleasure to meet you, Sophia,' the woman said and

shook her hand. The woman's hand was smooth and cool compared to their sweaty palms.

'Christopher.'

'Sir.' She shook his hand gently. 'And you, little one? Why, what extraordinary eyes you have, my mystical one,' she commented as she knelt in front of the girl.

Maya giggled and muttered her name. 'That you are. That you are. Simply magical,' she said standing up and turning toward Susan. 'And you must be the lucky mother. Must be a blessing to have many children. The more, the merrier, right?'

'I'm Susan. Nice to meet you. My son, Christopher, loves everything mythological. It was his idea. I hope there is much for him to see,' Susan said, avoiding commenting on the *many children*. She did not ask the beautiful woman if she had any. She would rather picture that she had not. That would explain her figure. And what if she answered that she had four? Susan's soul would shrivel up inside. Susan's pupils travelled to their corners as she spoke, only columns and rocks between wild bushes. '*I hope there's more. Christopher needs this. The driver did say something about underground.*'

Persephone's eyes lit up, and a dazzling smile spread out on her wrinkle-less face. 'Get ready for a feast of the eyes. The awe is downstairs.'

Chapter Eighteen

'This way!'

Christopher went first, following Persephone around the monastery walls. The color from the rocks had faded from the time spent under the sun.

'Watch your step.'

Christopher's jaw slowly journeyed south. Wooden steps led down to a huge tunnel built right under the monastery. A big black hole with no end visible took up half the space the holy building was built on.

'Is it safe?' Susan asked as she picked up Maya, and looking at her feet, made her way down the eight steps.

'We have had thousands of visitors so far. None have ever gotten hurt in the tunnels.'

Susan put Maya down and took her hand. 'I meant for the church. My husband and I are in the building business you may say, and it seems weird to build a monastery above such a large tunnel.'

Persephone urged them to join her in the shade. As they formed a half-cycle in front of her, she took on her guide voice. 'Welcome to the entrance of the Necromanteio. First, a gift from me.' Persephone took three small bright red flowers out of a straw basket behind her. 'Pomegranate flowers. Amazingly red, aren't they?' she asked as she placed a blossom in each of the girls' hair. 'And for the gentleman... a blue Iris. Not much hair, so I will place it on your ear.' Persephone's smile was mesmerizing. She moved among them elegantly and effortlessly. Her soft touch and care caught their full attention. 'Let the tour begin. To answer your question, Susan. The monastery was built in the eighteenth century. The entire hill was then, just dirt, bushes, and maybe a few scattered old stones from the columns. The monks had no idea what was beneath them or so they claimed.'

The mysterious tone she marinated the last sentence in sent Christopher's mind in overdrive. 'You believe they knew?'

'Well, I don't wish to ruin your tour, but let's say that this place had a significant meaning for the ancients and their beloved ones that passed away. Everyone knows about the oracle at Delfi, right?' Christopher nodded three times. 'This place was more famous than that during ancient times. I'm sure they knew about it and that is why they built Saint John above it. They feared this place. They wanted to cleanse it. John the Baptist is the cleanser of souls. Do you know what a cleanser is?'

Christopher smiled. 'Of course. But please, don't ask my sister. She thinks it's a product she uses on her face.' Persephone laughed at his joke and her subtle laughter echoed down the tunnel. It continued going, bouncing from wall to wall, lasting for seconds. 'Boys will be boys, my pretty one. You're a smart one, but we women love to take care of ourselves. You use your cleanser and anything your little heart pleases. None will stay young forever up here. Come on, follow me. Mind your step and stay together.' Lights flickered to life along the arches that held up the tunnel. Susan rubbed the back of her neck, trying to calm hairs standing at attention. She looked behind Persephone for a switch, yet did not see one. '*How did the lights come on?*'

'Wow,' Maya gushed and began to clap. Her three-year-old eyes opened wide and her pupils dilated at the long corridor. The paved grounds led slightly downward and split into three at the end.

'Welcome to the Necromanteio. The most important temple in ancient Greece...'

'Temple?'

'Yes, it is a Ziggurat-like temple,' Persephone replied and quickly explained the word. 'Ziggurat is a massive structure built in Mesopotamia, in the Middle East. Its name is used to describe temples that have tunnels or stairwells that lead to multiple levers below the building visible on top.'

Sophia wiped her forehead from the few droplets of sweat that the outside sun had offered her. Inside, a cool refreshing air roamed the tunnels. 'But there is no building on top.'

'There used to be. The Romans burned it when they shut down this place.'

'Why?' Christopher asked as he touched the first arch.

Persephone opened her hands and raised her palms. 'Some say they wished to subdue the Greeks and gradually change their traditions. Some say they feared this place.'

'Like the monks.'

'Exactly.'

Susan stood proudly, admiring her children. Locked up at home after Eugene's death, she had forgotten how strong, smart, and curious her children were. Always eager to try new things, to learn, to live. 'And where are the monks today? The monastery seems a bit run down, if you know what I mean.'

'None remain.'

Susan raised her eyebrows. 'They left?'

Persephone shrugged her shoulders. 'It never had much of a population. Not many signed up here. Most of the graves you saw outside are of the monks that once lived here.'

The clicks from Sophia's selfies caught their attention. 'Shall we move on?'

Persephone walked ahead, and her smooth voice filled the narrow space.

'The acoustics down here are excellent,' Sophia commented, her mind on recording a song in the tunnels to post on her MySpace.

Persephone stopped by the three gated tunnels before them. 'Necro means dead, and manteio means oracle, but this was not a place of prophecies by priests of the Gods. No Pythia here chewing on her magical leaves and telling half-truths and polysemic words. The ancient Greeks came here for one reason and one reason only: Nekyia.'

'I know that word,' Christopher gloated. 'I read it in the Odyssey. Odysseus wanted to see his dead mother again and poured wine and killed a goat.'

'That's barbaric.'

'All religions sacrificed animals, Sophia. Even Christians did it back in the day.'

'Nerd.'

'You two remind me of my kids. They are all grown up now,' Persephone said. 'Bravo on your knowledge, Christopher.'

Susan bit her lip to the point of pain. She was not sure which of the two sentences irritated her more. The perfect-figured woman had bore children. And, they were grown up now. Persephone did not look a day older than thirty.

'Nekyia is the rite by which the spirits -or ghosts if you prefer- are called upon. Most of the time, they are questioned about the future.'

'Ghosts!' Maya said and giggled. The only place she had ever heard the word before was in Scooby-Doo. And those ghosts, by the end of the episode, turned out to be ugly, angry men looking for revenge or businessmen with dollar signs in their eyes.

'And these ghosts did not appear if you didn't sacrifice a goat?' Sophia cringed at the thought. She was never much of a food person, and she loved animals more than most people, so the thought of turning full vegan had twirled around her mind since primary school.

'Well, it could have been a sheep or a ...'

'I meant did they always have to butcher an animal?'

Persephone beamed of compassion. The corner of her lips moved upward and her expression sweetened. 'Unfortunately, yes. It was a whole elaborate ceremony,' she said as she pushed the first iron gate back. Again, the lights in the tunnel came to life as Persephone walked down it. *'Must be a sensor.'* Susan could not see one, but it was the only logical explanation. 'The priests and priestesses here were very strict and meticulous,' Persephone continued as she picked up the pace. 'The person seeking to communicate with a dead relative of theirs had to oblige by their rules or it was a no show.' Multiple corridors were seen on their sides. Persephone turned left down one of them. Then, right.

'It's like a maze down here.'

'Yes, it is, my dear. And each corridor leads to a different room with a different purpose. Talking to the dead was complicated, but it also meant big business for the people that ran this place. The responsibility came with great wealth and power. I'm taking you to the main chambers. Stay close, but no need to worry. I know this place like the back of my palm.'

'What were the rules?' Christopher asked as the group turned once again.

'The guests were offered a meal before entering, and they had to consume it all. From records of the time, we know that the meal consisted of beans, pork, bread and oysters.'

Christopher scratched his nose. The air was getting a bit thicker, and he was sensitive to dust. The walls seemed ready to crumble and reveal the apple pie behind them. 'Why these particular foods?'

'It was food available in the area. It really had no value to the process. The main point was to get the guest to eat the narcotics in the meal.'

Christopher stopped on the spot. 'No way. Shit!'

'Christopher!'

Christopher lowered his ecstatic eyes. 'Sorry, Mum.'

Persephone chuckled. 'You see, the guests had to be willing to believe. So the priests gave them something to make them more receptive.'

'Or make them hallucinate,' Susan commented. 'They had to make them believe they saw something, right?'

Persephone looked straight at her. Her facial muscles swam around her still lips and motionless eyes. She coughed as if to clear her throat. Susan received no answer. The low-ceiling tunnel echoed with her Dido ringtone. 'It's your father,' she said and took a few steps back to answer her cell phone. 'Hello? Hello?' Susan looked down at her phone. It jumped from one line to no signal repeatedly. 'Andrew? Andrew, can you hear me?' All she picked up before the phone going dead was the word *emergency*. Susan exhaled deeply, and her sigh filled up the space. She looked at her kids. 'I'm so sorry. We have to go back. I need to call Dad ...'

'No. Not now. We are about to hear about the ceremony,' Christopher reacted, angrier than what she was used to from him. It caught her off guard. She even took a step back. *'Not his father's mean streak. Please, no.'* She moved her eyes over to Persephone. 'Are we coming outside, soon? My husband said it was an emergency, and there is no signal down here.'

Persephone shook her head. 'We are heading downward actually. But we haven't come too far. Leave the kids with me. They seem to be enjoying the tour.' All three nodded in agreement and put on their puppy eyes for their mother. 'They are safe with me. I work with kids all the time. Head back and call your husband. Remember, left, left, right and you will be back at the three gates. The sun will guide you from there.'

Susan's cheeks twitched. 'I'm not completely sure...' She dragged the last word, her eyes jumping from one smiling child to another. 'Oh, okay.' The children cheered. 'Err, where will I find you?'

'Stay at the entrance. Entrance, exit, all the same.' She waved her arm. 'Our return is through the second gate.'

Susan placed a kiss on each of her children and dashed back down the corridor. 'Love you. See you soon. Enjoy,' she mumbled as she went.

'What's down the third gate?'

'What's that, my pretty?'

Sophia's ego got a boost with every compliment she

received. 'We entered the first gate, and I guess we go full circle to exit the second gate at the same point. So, what's down the third gate?'

'I've never been down there.'

Christopher rolled his eyes in his boyish theatrical manner. 'Come on. As if. You work here. You're only making it sound more mysterious. What's down there?'

'I'm telling the truth. No one goes down there. Its passage is reserved only for the dead. It heads out to the entrance of Hades, the underworld realm of Pluto, God of the Dead.'

'Where is the entrance?'

'Where the deadly rivers used to meet.'

'Used to?'

'Oh, yes. Thousands of years and man's meddling can have that effect. Acherontas, Cocytus, and Pyriphlegethon met just a few miles away from here. That is why the Necromanteio was built here. To be close to the underworld. Close to the souls that the guests wished to contact.'

Sophia ground her teeth. 'Those are some hard names to pronounce. I thought Acherontas was tough. I can't even say the others.'

'Ancient Greek, my star. Anyway, it's much better with their old names. Their translations are just so grim.'

Christopher straightened his back and took a step forward. Sophia could picture him as a high-school professor. University even. Teaching boring mythology 101. 'I know Acherontas means joyless.'

'Correct, bright mind. And Cocotus means lament. Deep grief and sorrow.' Persephone stroked the flower in Sophia's hair. 'Pyriphlegethos,' she said, leaving breathing gaps between syllables, 'literally translates to burning coals. Basically, representing the fires and fumes of hell.'

'Sounds like a lovely place. Gate three is out of the question,' Sophia said and beam as she watched Persephone laugh at her sarcasm. Persephone gently clapped her hands. 'Now... back to our tour. Christopher is waiting to hear more about the ceremony of calling the dead. So, after the offered meal...'

'The drugged one.'

'That's right. The guests went through a cleansing process. A perfumed bath and something resembling confession, though it was the priests that asked the questions. You didn't just chat about your problems and sins like today,' she said and then placed her velvety hands upon Sophia's ears. 'After that came the slaughter of the offered animal.'

'I can still hear, you know.' Sophia giggled and pushed back a renegade streak of hair that plummeted before her eyes, somehow escaping her tight hair band.

'Then?' Christopher asked as he picked up his sister. Maya had her arms raised since her mother left. Persephone kept increasing her pace, and the corridors were getting longer and longer. Her tiny feet craved to escape the hardship of walking such distances, and she wished to be carried.

'The guests took the route we are on. Leaving offerings, oil and gold and such, all the way to the grand hall.'

As she said the last two words, the four passed under a large archway and entered a cavernous room. Statues of the Olympian Gods formed a circle around them below a massive dome. Time had taken its toll, yet a painted sun was still visible up high in the center of the cupola. Christopher stood in awe, letting his eyes take in the feast. Even Sophia was impressed. She held her phone with both hands and snapped away. She stayed by Aphrodite's statue the longest, admiring her bare breasts, perfect proportions, and her symmetrical face. Christopher placed Maya on the marble ground. 'Don't touch anything.' He wasn't sure if he was mimicking his mother's tone, or if that was just the natural tone that comes with any short order given to a toddler or young child. Persephone remained silent, observing the three children. Christopher cleared his throat, and an echo spread out through the rotunda. He whispered the names as he went, 'Hera, Artemis, Athena, Ares, Hermes, Zeus...'

He turned to Persephone.

'I know what it is that you are going to ask. You know the answer. The sun above is your clue.'

Christopher smiled awkwardly. How did she know what he was going to ask? He stood still and raised his eyes. 'Apollo, the sun god.'

Persephone fixed her hair and smiled. 'Correct. Go on.'

'He was also the god of oracles, of seeing into the future. The patron god of prophecies...'

Sophia swallowed the word nerd. Her curiosity brought out the best in her. 'That's interesting, Brother. But, what was the question?'

Persephone strolled toward her, her healthy hair flowing slightly in the breeze that seemed to live permanently in the tunnels. 'He wanted to know why Apollo's statue was placed nearest to the thrones, and why it is slightly larger than the rest. This is probably one of the few places with this many statues and without Zeus, the father of the gods, the king of the gods, being the larger central figure.' She turned her attention to Christopher. 'Come on, mythology expert, who is missing from the main gods? Who you would expect to see at a place like this?'

Christopher knew the answer, yet he still gazed around at the twelve statues. 'All Olympians are here. But Pluto is not. For a place dedicated to calling upon the dead, it is weird that there is no worship of the god of the underworld. Surely, they needed his blessing to release a soul. Just like with Orpheus.'

'Exactly.'

Christopher waited for her to say more. Seconds flew by, and Persephone preoccupied herself with rearranging Sophia's hair. 'So?'

'So what, my smart one?'

'Why didn't the priest here worship him?'

'Because he was here with them.'

Christopher whistled. He was not sure what to feel. The air felt colder all of a sudden. The echo from his whistle returned eerily to his ears. He giggled. 'Yeah, right. So, after ticking the ceremonial to-do list, the priests sat on the two thrones and...'

'No priest was allowed to sit on the thrones. The throne was for Pluto. Hades himself in all his darkful glory.'

'*Is there even such a word?*' Christopher walked up to the two thrones. Both made out of stone, and both lacking elaborate carvings usually found on artifacts from ancient Greece. He placed his hand on the tall back. 'And what did the priests do then?'

'Who cares? Who sat next to him?' Sophia asked while chasing after Maya who ventured off behind a large square rock in the back of the room.

Persephone smiled. 'One. One question, please.' She chuckled. 'Sophia, if you wish for a romance story about a king and a queen, this is not the place to find it.' Sophia turned around and raised her shoulders. 'I guess true romance doesn't even exist in fairy tales,' she said and dashed behind the rock in search of Maya. The little girl stood before a small tunnel. Small enough to make adults duck before entering. 'Maya, it's not safe to wander off in a place like this. Please, don't get me into trouble with mum.' She took the girl's petite hand into hers and tugged. Maya remained as still as Apollo's statue behind them. 'It's my friend from the house. Can I go play?' Sophia moved her shoulders around, closed her eyes, and knelt by her sister. She sighed and opened her eyes. Darkness. She saw nothing down the tunnel. 'Come on, Maya.' Sophia pulled her sister with a bit more force. Maya reluctantly turned to leave. 'But he said he knows where grandma is.'

An icy shiver shook Sophia's spine. 'Maya, cut it out.' She raised her voice as they re-entered the throne room. Persephone was answering Christopher's question. '...priests and guests chanted together and then boom, the main priest was raised from the ground and flew before their very eyes, leaving them in shock and awe!'

Christopher's face could not light up further. His pupils had reached their diluted limits. 'For real? Or was it a hallucination from the drugs?'

'For reals, of course! Well, they did have help. Greeks invented the theatrical cranes, you know?' Persephone winked at him.

'Gotcha! And what did they chant about?'

Persephone walked up the four steps and sat down on the smaller throne. 'Sit down, my young ones. Ὑμνεύσι ρα θεῶν δώρ' ἄμβροτα... ἠδ' ανθρώπων τλημοσύνας... ος έχοντες υπ' αθανάτοισι θεοίσι ζώουσ'... αφραδέες και αμήχανοι... θανάτοιο τ' άκος και γήραος άλκαρ...'

Her smooth voice travelled around the room. The kids had no idea what she was saying but were mesmerized by her melody.

Chapter Nineteen

Droplets of sweat exited her pores. Dizziness escalated the attack on her brain as she dashed through the tunnels with her eyes down, fixed on her phone's screen. Susan hoped to not have to exit the temple completely. With every step, she was farther and farther from her children. Her young children -that she left alone with a complete stranger.

'She's the freaking guide, Suz. She works here. The kids are fine,' she calmed herself in a whisper. 'Left, then right... right? Shit, still no reception.' She shook her phone and turned again. 'This better be important, Andrew!' Her mind travelled to her kids. 'They are fine!' She raised her voice and stressed all three words. '*At least, she's not a man ...*'

Susan froze on the spot. The spontaneous thought terrified her. 'Women can kill, too.' Tears fell from her eyes as she turned once again. The tunnel was narrow and dimly lit. 'Wait. This is not the way we came.' She paused again. The air was getting thicker. 'Wrong way, Suz.' She turned around and headed back to where she thought she came from. The tunnel came to some stairs. Susan gasped. Her pupils shook in her widened eyes. 'These were not here before...' She looked back. One by one, the lights in the tunnel flickered and died.

Desperation.

Susan knew the emotion well. They were old friends. Susan grew up too fast, her grandmother used to say. She said it like it was a good thing. Something to be proud of. A fine young lady. Mature beyond her years. For Susan, all it meant was that she found the girls her age too immature to play with. While her friends talked about how silly boys were and their love of children's television programs, she had thoughts about life and death. She searched for meaning and purpose in life during her teen years, and the lack of findings scared her. Her granny and her mother had both been housewives. Proud housewives. Susan could not imagine herself leading such a dull, hollow life. That's how she viewed it, and their happiness irritated her. It was her fear of being domesticated that helped cope with three part-time jobs to afford to go to university. The future though continued to terrify her. The unknown. Her mind could not relax and accept the natural flow of time and life. Her mind constantly reminded her that life had no meaning. It had no purpose. You existed by chance, and one day the switch would be pulled. She wished her mind had a switch. To be able to stop her depressing thoughts. And one day, she found the switch. It happened at Holly's birthday party. Holly was a Liverpool girl from class that invited everyone to her house party. She invited most boys to her bed too, but Susan never judged Holly's lack of morals or decent clothes. Susan was never the type of girl to show much flesh. Most of her skin remained safe and unseen under heavy clothes. She drifted through the two-story house, nodding, waving a few *hellos* to familiar faces from uni. Her mind came as a guest as well.

'*What's the point in dancing? What in hell is this awful music? Look at them, half-naked, kissing, touching...*'

'Who invited Holly's auntie to the party?'

She heard the boys behind her well. She clenched her cheeks and ground her teeth. They were not worthy of a reply.

'It's these spinster-looking girls that are freaks in the sheets,' another boy commented.

'Nah, she looks like a virgin.'

'Then, Jack should have her. He would deflower anything that moves. It would be an upgrade from his sheep back in Wales.'

'Fuck you, John. My sheep are better looking.'

Susan's eyes watered up as the boys laughed. She did not turn to face them but continued into the kitchen. A bottle of Vodka sat on the counter. Susan took one glass, one carton of orange juice and the Absolut bottle.

Outside, alone on a bench in the park facing the house, Susan found her switch. There, in the freezing midnight air, the dark silent trees and the neglected playground games, Susan found the way to turn off her thoughts -or at least settle them to sleep for a while.

Since then, whenever desperation attacked and pushed its fangs into her mind, Susan had the antidote. Vodka gave way to wine after her graduation, but the solution remained the same. Drink until dizziness mingled up and silenced the thoughts.

But as much as she drank, as many battles against hopelessness alcohol helped her win, desperation would always return.

'*Great job, you stupid idiot. You've gone and gotten yourself lost in catacombs with no reception on your phone. Shit! What am I supposed to do now? I want a drink. I want to lie down and die...'*

Susan sat down on the first step, and once again, she found herself holding back tears. *'No wonder everything is salty to you, you miserable cow. Too many tears held in...'*

'Hello?' she shouted into the darkness. Only echoes returned. 'Persephone?' she screamed. *'Where are you with your perfect body, hair, and voice, huh?'* Susan stood up. The carved-in-the-rock stairs were lit well. Pitch-black roamed the tunnel which she came from. She took a step into the darkness, her hand against the decaying wall. Another step. And another. 'When are the lights gonna come on?' Susan stopped and looked back at the stairs. 'They lead up. It must be an exit.'

She could not see the end. The steps curved as if forming a spiral. She thought of the stairs back at the mansion. *'Why didn't you just stay home today?'*

Strong light could be seen ahead. 'Yes! An exit.'

But it was not.

Susan found herself stepping into a large round room with twelve tunnel entrances around it.

'Fuck!'

And with that yelled curse, the lights died. Susan sat down in the middle of the room and finally let her gathered tears drop to freedom. *'I can hear something...'*

Someone was singing. Melodic chanting in a foreign language reached her ears. At first, it seized her sobbing. The music that followed was initially soothing. Then, it grew louder, harsher, angrier. New voices were added to the chanting. Susan covered her ears. *'What the hell is going on?'* Screaming voices and animal-like howling echoed from the tunnels. Susan was panting yet did not move. *'Run to where?'*

Suddenly, the voices stopped. The music continued

playing for a few seconds, then faded away. And in the silence, she heard him.

'Don't be scared, Mummy. They won't hurt you.'

Susan covered her mouth and released more tears than ever before. 'Don't be sad, Mummy. Aren't you happy to see me?'

Susan licked her lips and wiped her swollen eyes. '*Ok, Suz. You're not drunk. Eugene is not here. Which means you're insane. You are hallucinating.*'

'Why aren't you talking to me, Mummy? Aren't you my friend anymore? I miss you. Haven't you missed me? Why don't I live with you anymore?'

Susan's entire body shook as she cried. It was his voice surrounding her in the darkness. 'I miss you, too,' she managed to say.

'So, be happy to see me,' Eugene said, and she felt his tiny arms hug her from behind. Susan shivered and gasped. 'But I can't see you, baby. It's way too dark in here.'

Eugene giggled right next to her ear as he placed his head on her shoulder. 'Oh, mummy. I forgot the living can't see in the dark.'

Susan's eyes widened. Five wall lamps came to life above her, shedding abundant light into the cave. Susan closed her eyes and took in a deep breath -probably the deepest she had ever taken. She raised her eyelids slowly and turned her head. Her pupils ran to their corners. A small skeleton hand lay on her quivering shoulder.

'Eugene?'

'Yes, Mummy?'

Susan leaned forward and stood up. A woman's voice chanting came through the tunnels loud and clear. Susan placed both her hands upon her chest. 'One... Two...'

'Are we playing, Mummy?'

'Three!'

Susan swung around and laid eyes on the boy opposite her. A three-foot skeleton was waving at her. Patches of hair grew out of his skull. Dark, rotten skin failed to cover white bones while both eyes were missing from their sockets. Torn, dirty clothes rested on its torso. Their color had faded, but Susan recognized them. She had bought them herself. Thomas the Tank Engine pajamas from Marks and Spencer down on the high street. Susan shook her head, her shoulders heaving as she sobbed. 'No, no, no...'

'Hug me, Mummy,' Eugene shouted and ran toward her with his arms spread out wide. Not long ago, she would have knelt and opened hers, welcoming his warm, excited, and loving body into her embrace. Now, she closed her eyes and screamed uncontrollably. She fell to the ground and curled up. 'No, no, no,' she cried and hit the ground. The lights flicked on and off before dying out for good. One by one, the twelve tunnels lit up. Smoke began to come out of one. Red lights appeared along its path. Susan opened her eyes. Eugene never touched her. He was gone. And above the entrance, another letter was written in blood. M. The third letter, big and proud upon the rock. Susan pulled her hair, screaming and crying. She needed to feel pain. She dug her nails into her skin and ran down the smoky tunnel, coughing as she went.

'I'll see you when you're ready. Join me. Join me. Join me. Join me.'

Eugene's voice taunted her all the way up. The circle of light up ahead gave strength to her tired feet. With a loud gasp, Susan leaped out of the tunnel and fell to the ground outside.

'Mum, what's wrong?' A hand touched her. Susan screamed out and slapped the hand away. 'Mum!'

'Mrs. Susan, are you okay?'

Susan looked up to see Persephone standing above her. Her three children stood terrified behind her, Christopher holding his slapped hand.

Maya's eyes trembled as she saw her mother crawling in the dirt, her arms bleeding from scratches, streaks of hair stuck in her chipped nails, tears running freely down her pale cheeks. 'Why is mummy screaming, Sophia?'

Chapter Twenty

MESOPOTAMOS

1914

Iphigenia was no longer herself. She did not feel herself under her own skin. Madness and despair crept inside her like nasty parasites. Parasites whose only goal was to take over her mind. She no longer trusted neither her eyes nor her thoughts. She barely distinguished between reality and nightmares.

She gazed to the mirror on her left. She loved her antique mirror. The money she spent to acquire it was more than her farm back in Parga used to make in a month. Yet, she fell in love with its carved wooden legs and its white marble frame with hints of pink in its stone. And money was not an issue in her life since stealing the treasures from below the church.

The mirror remained the same: majestic, exquisite, elegant, expensive. Iphigenia did not. She had aged ten years since her nightmares and visions began two months ago. Iphigenia stroked her hair and pushed it around. It begged for a wash. It begged to be released from its knots. White hairs smiled tauntingly back at her. Her eyes spooked her. There were the eyes of a crazy woman. Never settling. Never peaceful. A purple bruise on her left cheek reminded her of the final letter two nights ago. The word lingered in her fragile mind since.

Naked and cold on the bathroom floor, she made her decision. What more did she have to lose? Gregory was drifting further away from her, daily. He found refuge in his garden and his cherished flowers. They were beautiful, and she was not. There were silent, and she yelled and cried. They were serene, and she was deranged.

How could she blame him for choosing them over her?

She placed her hands on the tiles. Two of her nails were chipped, and one was black. She pushed herself up and decided to bathe. The procedure sounded like just was she needed. Punishment: to carry bucket after bucket to fill up the porcelain enamel tub. Cleansing: to immerse in the cool waters.

Iphigenia counted the heavy buckets. Twenty. Twenty trips to the kitchen. The only tap with running water was there, and with the heavy wooden bucket lifted by both her hands, she crossed the living room, went down the hall, and into the bathroom. 'Couldn't have put a temporary tap in there, Effie, huh? No, you had to order one from Paris and wait months until it comes. But our guests will use it. It must represent us, blah, blah, blah,' she mumbled as she went.

The last time she had to carry such weight was two years ago during apple picking. During a time when she was still a mother. And still married to Giorgo. Just the thought of the dull man made her shiver. '*Boring talks, boring sex, boring life.*' She despised being his wife. As hard as she tried, when-ever her mind travelled back to her days with him, she could never find a happy moment. It was always a memory of mental anguish. When she was pregnant with the boys, Giorgo went to the local pub every night. When she asked him why he never stayed home with her, he replied that no bull fucks a knocked-up cow. His job was done. When the boys were young, her mother-in-law came to visit and stayed for a month. She judged her every move. Giorgo agreed with her. 'She has a mood swing on the front porch. She takes a swing and decides if she is up to cleaning or taking care of the kids. You gave me a lazy bride, Mama.' She remembered hearing them. She remembered how she thought of ripping off his mother's left arm and beating them both with the wet end.

She was glad he was out of her life. She was glad he was not still alive.

Twenty. The water flowed out of the last bucket. Iphigenia lit two candles and placed them on the floor by the tub's front legs. She loved the frizzling noise made by the matches. She gazed at the flame and let it burn down to her finger. She forced her body to subject to the burning feeling, to the pain of the heat. '*Feel something, anything*' She stepped into the waters and laid back with a loud sigh. Inch by inch, she slid down the tub's slippery back. The water reached her mouth. The letters flew around her mind. One by one they formed a word. Iphigenia slipped further down. Soon, she submerged into the water. An inner battle began. Her lungs fought for air, yet her will kept her under. With a tumultuous gasp, her head came up. Panting, she yelled. 'Confession time, Gregory!'

Chapter Twenty-One

Andrew reached the final T-junction before the beach. It was left to head down to Ammoudia. He looked across at the tranquil bay. The waters, like virgin olive oil, were floating still. Thick woods ran from the west to meet it. *'Could my mother be lost in those cypresses and kermes oaks? I hate the unknown. A body for closure, a body to bury, a body to get the will going...'*

The honking from the car behind made him jump. Eager tourists were waiting for him to turn. 'Fucking foreigners,' he cursed without his teeth departing. Even Andrew could sense the irony in his statement. With a grin upon his unshaven face, he placed his foot on the gas and sped away. He turned one more time down a dirt track that he saw snake-lined toward the forest. The sun opposite him invaded the vehicle. He closed his sore, sleepless eyes. With his right hand, he lowered the visor and reopened them. He could see the police car by the first row of trees. He was on the right track. *'What did she say his name was? Daniel, that's right...'* he thought as he raised his foot from the gas. The car did not slow down. The red arrow before him remained fixed on seventy miles per hour. 'What the...?' The car began to bump up and down on the uneven country road. Andrew lifted his foot. The car continued at the same speed. The trees were getting closer. Andrew stepped on the brakes. Nothing. Again and again. The trees were getting bigger. Andrew pulled the handbrake. No response. No change. 'Oh, shit.' Andrew held the stirring wheel and swirled. The car leaped upon rocks and tumbled over. It rolled violently, only to be stopped by a sizable pine tree. Bang.

Andrew gasped and opened his eyes. He was back at the beginning of the road. Just where he turned. The sun invaded the car. This time he did not close his eyes. He lowered the visor and exhaled deeply. *'Did I fall asleep? Can you dream in a split second?'* Andrew wiped his sweaty forehead and lifted his foot off the gas. The vehicle slowed down. He gently stepped on the brakes. Soon, he was cruising down the dirt road at a speed of ten miles per hour. He parked by the police car, pulled up the handbrake, and jumped out of the car. He ran toward the first tree and leaned forward. He hadn't puked since college.

He ran his arm across his face and wiped his mouth with his hand. He looked down. He hated the sight of puke. He coughed just hearing mention of it. He kicked dirt over his chewed breakfast and leaned back on a tall cypress, trying to catch his breath. *'In through the nose, and out through the mouth.'* He focused on the voice inside his head as he performed the task. Anything to take his mind of *it*.

He chuckled. He hit his head back on the trunk and grinned.

As much as he despised *it*, *it* brought back a lot of

memories. Happy memories. Andrew felt that compared to your average Joe, he had not had that many of those.

It was during his last year in Cambridge (you have to mention Cambridge, if you studied at Cambridge) when his best friend Lloyd pulled him back by his shoulders. 'Get your nose out of those books, man,' he said with his thick Jamaican accent. 'Go shower and get ready. There's a party going on at Atomic tonight. Winston says that they are girls coming up from other schools, too. Special event and all that. Come on, bro.' Andrew didn't even reply. He stood up and went straight for the shower. He wasn't one for partying, but he never said no to Lloyd. Lloyd had been with him through thick and thin. A best friend like no other. And cancer managed to take down that gentle giant with the huge heart and the contagious smile in just eight months. It was outside of Atomic club at 'fuck knows what time after midnight' that Andrew and Lloyd hid behind their car in the dark parking lot to enjoy a joint.

'This spliff is well strong...'

'Ssshhh,' Andrew said placing his finger on Lloyd's thick lips.

'Why you so scared, man? Are you getting paranoid on me, bruh?'

Andrew shook his head. 'Shut up. Listen.'

Heavy breathing and coughing came from the tall bushes by the pathway. Andrew leaned forward to catch a better look. Two fine legs were visible. A girl wearing jean shorts was bent over trying to control her long blonde hair. Andrew passed the joint back to Lloyd and rushed over.

'Err, can I help you? You seem to be having a hard time breathing...' he said and crunched his knuckles.

'Great. A doctor.'

'An architect, really...'

Susan stood up and looked behind her. Andrew gazed into her stunning blue eyes. 'I'm really, really, really drunk and you're cute, so can you please walk away.'

'I'm really, really, really good at holding back hair.'

Susan laughed. 'We really need to stop using the word really in every other sentence.'

Andrew had no time to think of a smart reply. Susan leaned forward and vomited on his cherished white Adidas trainers. With the sight of puke on him, Andrew turned sideways and began to upload his fish and chip dinner.

Lloyd's deep-bass laughter found them. 'Look at you two drunken twats.'

Two years later, he was the best man at their wedding.

And then, the kids came along. And more vomiting. Andrew banged his head again against the tree. Sophia, Christopher, Maya, Eugene. How many times did he have to run out the room to keep his stomach's contents in? Andrew shook his head. *'There's nothing worse than a parent having to bury a child.'* He clenched his fists, turned around, and punched the innocent cypress. 'Happy memories, my ass. Try to think of the day you met your wife, and life reminds you of your dead best friend. Try to think of funny moments with your kids, and life reminds you of that little body you lowered into the ground. That fucking tiny casket. Jesus! And where am I now? In a forest looking for my lost mother. Well, you know what? Screw you, life.' His voice scared two lizards that ran off in opposite directions, crunching up dried leaves as they went. Andrew snuffled and clicked his tongue. *'Get a move on, loser.'*

He walked into the woods, following a narrow dirt path that had more curves than the Monaco Grand Prix. Twigs and dead leaves snapped below his feet as he went. The forest to his right reminded him of animal stripes. Dark tree, sunlight. Dark tree, sunlight. Another long curve. Soon, he could hear the waves crashing down below. Under other circumstances, Andrew would have enjoyed the stroll in the peaceful woods. London was too grey for him. Yes, it had fine parks, but as a boy raised surrounded by nature and turquoise seas, London was cold to him. Un-human in a twisted sort of way. Too many living like ants in a dull colony, rather than like humans. Susan, of course, loved the city and all it had to offer. With each new birth, she would start again her tour of the great city. Museums, theme parks, sights. As if with each kid, she looked for meaning. For art, for fun, for life.

'*Voices up ahead.*'

Two police-men were walking side by side. The tall one with the dark shades looked to the left, while the other with the broad shoulders and thin mustache looked to the right.

Andrew shook his head. '*They are still looking. They have found nothing.*' The branch below his feet was too thick to snap. Andrew tripped. He waved out his arms and found his balance. Both officers turned, caution written upon their stern faces. The tall guy even had his hand near his holder.

'Oh, hi,' Andrew said holding out his hands. 'I'm Andreas Fotopoulos. It's my mother you're looking for. I was just at the station and... your wife? Right? She said you were here. I saw your vehicle...'

The two men smiled. 'Calm down. We're not trigger happy here in Greece,' the tall man said while the other approached him. He extended his hand, 'I'm Daniel. It's my wife, Annita, that you met.'

Andrew shook his hand. 'I see you haven't found her yet...'

The two men exchanged looks. Daniel placed his hands

on his sides and patted himself. 'I saw in your statement that your mother used a walking cane for support?'

Andrew blinked and nodded.

'Purple one, right? Sounds quite unique. Erm, you see, the reason we came here is that the coast guard found your mother's walking stick in the waters near here. Down below.'

Andrew placed his fingers upon his lips.

'They found nothing else in the water,' Daniel quickly added, having read his worried expression. 'She might have dropped it from here above. We want to explore every possibility.' Andrew smiled. Not from relief or from satisfaction that the police were doing a great job. He smiled because he thought that his missing mother was most likely the only case these guys had. He nodded and whispered, 'Thank you.'

Daniel scratched his jaw as the wind picked up strength. 'Have you spoken to the nursing home, Mr. Fotopoulos?'

'It's Andrew. Err, no. Why?'

Daniel pulled out from his right pocket a little black notebook. He opened it and flicked through the pages. 'You said in your statement that since your arrival, your mother had been living with you, right? Was she already at the house or did you pick her up from the nursing home? I guess you signed her out, right?'

Andrew squinted his eyes. 'Erm, no. She was already at the family home when we arrived. She even sent a taxi for us. She said she was feeling fine and that the nursing home allowed for her to be at home as she was going to have family to take care of her if she needed anything. Why do you ask?'

Daniel waved his hand. 'Just asking.'

The silence that followed felt awkward on all parties.

The two men in uniform had nothing more to say. They did not want to give him hope; they did not wish to offer him despair. Andrew was going to offer to help them during their search. However, something in the officer's last words kept him from stating the sentence of proposal.

Andrew scratched the back of his head and looked around. 'Err, I guess I should be letting you fine gentlemen carry on with your search. I appreciate everything you are doing. Thank you,' he said in one breath and speedily turned to leave.

The two officers watched as he stumbled back through the forest in the direction that he came from. As soon as his figure was the size of a lazy mantis, Daniel turned toward his colleague. 'Ten Euros says he is heading for the nursing home.'

The tall man spat to the leafy ground. 'That's one bet I would lose for sure.'

Andrew cursed from behind closed teeth as his toes went banging from tree root to rock. Breathless, he paused and gazed behind him. The restless leaves rattled around him, endlessly caressed by the northern winds. 'Shit, I should have exchanged mobile numbers...' He ground his dentist polished white teeth. He took his cell out of his pocket. Dead. He still could not comprehend how his phone had been drained of battery. An animal of routine and habit, he charged it every night. Better safe than sorry. He gave haste to his steps. Soon, the colors ahead signalled the end of the forest's domain and reminded him of a documentary he had watched months ago. Documentaries that helped him kill lonely, sleepless nights. The subject was how animals used their colors to blend into their environments. Tigers were black and orange as that's what prey saw as it moved inside the woods. The dark, shady trees and the illuminated orange gaps between them. Andrew felt like prey. Prey to life herself. A man hunted by misery. 'Or maybe you're just a sissy cry-baby, Andrew,' he said out loud as an answer to his thoughts. He beeped the borrowed vehicle open and jumped into the driver's seat. With his hands firmly on the steering wheel, he closed his eyes. His mind ventured back to the day of their arrival as the bus entered the quiet village. He remembered a crossroad sign. Hospital to your left, school up ahead, and Cozy Oak -retirement center and nursing home- to your right.

Chapter Twenty-Two

No one spoke on the ride home.

The three children sat in the back of the taxi, holding hands. Their eyes were fixed on the back of their mother's head as she rode shotgun. It was as if Susan was on vibrate-mode. Not a single hair lay still. Her shoulders went up and down and side to side. Christopher leaned forward slightly and watched as Susan's fingers moved around radically and intertwined with each other. Sophia swallowed the lump in her throat as she caught a glimpse of her mother's eyes in the rear-view mirror. Crazy eyes. Unsettling eyes. Sophia wrapped her hand around Maya and brought her closer. Even the usually-chatty taxi driver remained silent. Christopher did not hear what Mrs. Persephone said to the driver as she helped Susan into the vehicle, but he witnessed the change in the man's expression. A cloud settled upon his face. He drove with both hands on the wheel and both eyes on the road.

Susan knew she was a wreck.

'*Trainwreck, shipwreck, Susanwreck. A.A.A. Mad thoughts. D.D.D. A fragile mind pushed too far. M.M.M. Crack after crack, the glass reached its limit. Smash.*'

Her inner voice taunted her. She dug her nails into her thighs and scratched upward. The pain brought silence, if just for seconds.

'*What the hell are you doing now, Suz? Your kids are watching.*'

Even her mother's voice could not bring sense to her senseless thoughts.

'*I need help. I need pills. I need sleep. Maybe I am sleeping... Wake up, Suz.*'

Her nails journeyed deeper, leaving crimson lines behind. Blood surfaced and lingered in blobs. Susan gazed down at the red igloos on her trembling legs. '*This is reality. But what's real? Eugene is dead. Eugene is dead. Eugene is dead...*'

The driver's voice cut the loop. 'We are here, children,' he said and a smile transformed his stern face. Christopher and Sophia muttered, 'Thank you,' in unison and quickly exited the taxi. With Maya between them, hand in hand, they headed toward the house. Neither looked back. Sophia unlocked the heavy front door and all three entered, leaving it wide open. Upstairs they went and locked themselves in Sophia's room. 'Let's play a game,' Christopher said and smiled upon witnessing Maya's face light up.

'Anything to stop thinking,' Sophia said and headed to her side bed table. 'We are not spoilt for choice here, but I do have some UNO cards.'

Outside, the taxi sped away to the splendid horizon of the Greek countryside. Step by step, Susan walked in the cloud of dust offered by its getaway wheels. Drip by drip, droplets of her bleeding legs plummeted to the ground. Panting, Susan gazed around her with every step toward the house. Once the tranquil surroundings, now a fearsome hell. Birds chipping, lizards running, crickets calling out for mates. All noises scared her. They made her skin crawl.

'Eugene is dead, Eugene is dead, Eugene is dead...'

Susan made it to the creaking porch, entered the house, and pulled the front door behind her. She exhaled loudly three times.

Torn.

She had never felt more torn.

'If I don't drink, I am going to drive myself mad... further mad. If I do drink, I will hallucinate again. Picture Eugene. My sweet boy...'

That's when she felt it. Soft upon her skin. Her bare leg. A small cry escaped her dry cracked lips as she raised her leg and hopped backward. She sighed and relief calmed her twitching face. 'Oh, it's you,' she said, looking down at the stray cat that Sophia had decided to adopt. The feline meowed and continued its alluring dance around her feet. The black cat moved between her legs and made a dash to the kitchen door. It sat down on its back legs and gently scratched the door with its front paw.

'Okay, okay. Stop your meowing and begging. You're hungry, I get it.' Susan moved toward her and pushed the door open. The cat strolled into the kitchen and went straight for the last cabinet on the left. Again, it sat down and placed its paw on the cupboard door.

Susan wiped her forehead with both hands offering freedom to her red hair that had been captivated by her slight sweat, sweat provided by her anxiety, not the July weather. 'You seem to know your way around, Miss Stray. Please, don't be a dead cockroach or mouse that you are smelling.' Susan smiled at her acting normal. Just a minute ago, she was clawing at her own flesh, and here she was having a conversation with a cat, ready to feed it. Her fingers landed on the handle. Her eyes formed crescent moons as she opened the cupboard slowly. Susan laughed. A short, breathless laugh, yet still a laugh.

An open bag of Whiskas stood proudly on the shelf.

'Well, well, well. That's why you hang around the garden. Penelope, bless her soul, bought food for you. Susan picked up the bag, and her eyes spotted the bottle that was behind the cat biscuits. Susan unrolled the top of the bag and placed it by her side. The cat's head disappeared in the purple bag and crunching sounds soon echoed around the kitchen. Susan's trembling fingers travelled in the air and into the cupboard. Soon, they were wrapped around the red wine's neck.

'That's one dilemma solved. Company for my bath,' she said and took the prized alcohol into her embrace. She stroked the feline on its head and rushed out of the room. Up the spiral she went and off came her shoes on the last step. She crept along the corridor and placed her ear on Sophia's door.

Maya's giggling as she declared 'UNO!' brought a smile to her guilty, pale face. She didn't bother telling them she was heading for a bath. She continued down the hall, bottle in her bosom, all the way to the bathroom.

Click.

The sound of the key turning and locking the door was divine.

Alone. Alone with wine and scented candles.

Piece by piece, she removed her dirty clothes. She coughed as the dust from the Necromanteio invaded her sensitive nostrils. She sneezed loudly, spraying the oval mirror opposite her. Her eyes travelled upon her naked body. This time the mission was not to find scars of time nor to gloat at her fit (for her age) body. This time she was disgusted. Dirty nails, bags below her sleep-deprived eyes and scratched legs was the view offered by the reflecting glass.

She shook her head and moved her eyes away from the upsetting site. She took the box of matches in her hands and lit all three candles upon the white cupboard. She then turned her attention to the bottle of wine.

'Fuck! Give me a break!'

Susan approached the sink and opened the cabinet. Her eyes rolled along cotton buds, nail varnish remover, mouthwash, and new toothpaste. 'There you are,' she said and picked up the nail clippers. 'I pronounce you, wine opener.'

It took her over ten minutes, but Susan was persistent. Bit by bit she dug into the cork until a flow of wine was achieved. By then, the hot, steamy, running water had reached the middle of the spotless bathtub. Susan switched off the lights and let the candlelight caress the room. She brought the bottle to her lips. Half of the wine was devoured in one go. The rest vanished during her two-hour bath. She had no urge to return to the real world outside of her bathroom realm. Her mind longed for serenity. She numbed her body with hot water, she numbed her eyes with darkness, and she numbed her brain with wine.

She was, for now, calm.

———————————

The UNO game did not last for long. After letting Maya win the first round, her two competitive siblings fought for a second-round victory.

'Olivia!' Sophia yelled without anger in her voice. Her

cat leaped onto the soft bed and landed with feline skill on all four paws and all twenty playing cards. With a loud meow, she lay down and rolled around playfully among the red, blue, yellow and green cards.

'Well, that's one game that is over,' Christopher said, dropping his card. 'And, *I* was winning!'

'You wish!' Sophia stroked Olivia's belly, much to the cat's delight.

'I wanna draw.' Excitement was lacking from Maya's wish. Drawing was her passion. Maya drew daily. She drew at kindergarten, at home, on the underground, in the car. Blending colors and bringing to paper the world around her and the world in her mind. The last few days she drew with Penelope. She finally found a partner eager to draw with her, and now, Penelope was gone. Missing. Presumed dead, even. Christopher felt sadness overwhelm him as he heard his sister. Sophia had already laid back, cat on her tummy and phone in hand.

'I'm going to head out to read my book. Do you want to come with me, Maya? There's a beautiful bench under a big, big tree,' he said and waved his hands around to express the sheer size of the evergreen. 'Bring your papers and colors. There are tons of pretty flowers for you to draw!'

Her little face beamed brightly like the midday sun. With a wide smile upon her young face, she rushed out the room without saying a word. Christopher shook his head and followed her out of the room. He looked behind him. Olivia had her paw on the phone's screen.

'Want to listen to some music?' Sophia asked.

Christopher shook his head again and closed the door behind him. Water could be heard falling. Christopher turned his attention to the bathroom door. Steam ventured from its bottom. 'Poor mum,' he whispered. 'What the heck happened to her in the Necromanteio?' The boy found himself shaking his head once again and rushing to his bedside table for his book. He took Homer into his embrace and sprinted for the spiral stairs. He wanted to avoid his mother. It was something he did often the last few years when she wasn't herself. He missed Susan as she was when he was younger. When she was *just* his mother. His *normal* mother with normal expressions and ways. Before she metamorphosed into a woman who was either too happy or too sad or too tired or too dizzy.

Maya came after him seconds later. 'Let's go. Ladies first,' Christopher said and bowed, letting his sister lead the way. Round and round, they went. Halfway, Maya stopped and looked to her left. She pulled a couple of funny faces, opening her mouth and goggling. She then pulled out her tongue and skipped the remaining stairs.

'Maya, can I ask you something? I've seen you stop on the stairs before and wondered why.'

Maya's eyes travelled back to the staircase. She raised her shoulders. 'No reason.'

Christopher smiled and patted her head. 'You know you can tell me anything, right? I am, after all, your big brother! Psychologists now suggest that I am your main superhero figure and not dad.'

'Psy ko what?'

Christopher laughed at her fruitless attempt. 'Never mind. Come on, let's get out of here.'

Whistling, the two kids set forth for Christopher's reading bench. They roved through tall grass, moving carelessly, caressing the leaves with their palms. Soon, their small feet landed on the snake-like dirt path that led to the row of roses and the plethora of shade offered by the mighty tree that housed the wooden bench. The bench had taken its fair share of hits from nature's elements but still stood proudly. Its somber brown resembled their grandfather's old fishing boat in Whitstable Harbor. Christopher preferred to picture it as it surely was back in its prime. With fresh tones of vanish, glittering under the sun, before stretched out branches and thick leaves forced it to a sentence of eternal shade. Where others would see driftwood, Christopher saw a throne. A throne that gave him a nasty splinter once, yet still a royal reading seat.

'There,' Christopher said pointing ahead and picking up his pace. Maya followed, admiring the blossoming flowers around her. As Christopher settled on the welcoming bench with the heavy Iliad on his lap, Maya danced around the garden. Suddenly, she froze on the spot.

'Good day, Master Christopher!'

'Good day to you, too, sir.'

'Glad to see you are still reading the good book!' The gardener winked at him and offered his familiar, genuine smile.

Christopher carefully slid his bookmark in the book and placed it by his side.

'Oh, don't stop reading on my account. Please, continue. I just came to see if any of my friends needed trimming.

Christopher stood up with a hop to the ground. 'There's someone I would like you to meet. My sister, Maya.'

The man turned to the direction that the boy was pointing to.

Maya got a better look of his face. Her arms fell dead to her sides. Paintbrushes, colors, crayons. All fell to the ground. Pieces of paper scattered in the winds. Maya remained still. Christopher rushed to save as many white sheets as he could.

'Nice to meet you, Maya. Aren't you a delight for sore eyes? Christopher never mentioned such a beautiful and smart sister!' The gardener took a step forward. Maya took two back. The gardener extended his hand.

Christopher was puzzled by his chatty and sociable sister's behavior. 'Maya, what's wrong? Sir Gregory is my friend...'

Maya screamed as the man took another step closer to her. She turned around and ran, as fast as her tiny feet allowed her to.

'I'm so sorry. She isn't normally like this,' Christopher apologized and dashed after his sister.

'It's okay. Nothing to apologize for. I'm sorry if I scared her,' the gardener said, scratching his beard. 'What a strange little girl,' he muttered as he turned his attention to his rose garden.

Maya paid no attention to the heavenly-painted flowers around her this time. On her way back to the mansion, her teary eyes remained still, focused. Her hands resisted touching the soft hay dancing in the breeze. Her racing heartbeat told her to run. The man's face was imprinted in her mind.

'How can he be there? Walking around?'

Her eyes saw the mansion rising on the horizon. A small smile of relief unrolled on her ashen face. Just then, her little foot hit hard against the small, yet hard and pointy rock, camouflaged amongst the wild weeds. Maya lost her stepping; her body fell forward. Her small hands landed in the soft soil ahead, saving her face from impact at the very last second. Her leg wasn't as lucky. It scraped upon the rock, forming a rivulet of blood just below her knee. Maya hated the sight of it. She looked away and let her tears fall. She did not call out, neither from pain nor for help.

That is where Christopher found her, finally managing to catch up with her.

'Maya, you okay?' he asked, kneeling by her side.

'I'm fine. It doesn't hurt, really. Just can't look at it.'

Christopher pulled out a tissue from his right pocket and wiped the blood from her trembling leg. 'There you go. All gone. Keep your eyes up,' he said, helping her up.

'*Eyes up* is why I fell.' Maya giggled and placed her head upon her brother's body. She felt safe again. She looked behind them as they made their way back to the house. The bearded man was nowhere to be seen.

'Can we sit here?'

They had just stepped upon the mansion's first step. Christopher nodded and sat down. 'Why did you run off?'

'I know that man.'

Christopher looked straight at his sister. 'You know Mister Gregory, our gardener?'

Maya wiped her eyes. 'You know the stairs? You asked me why I pull funny faces...' The young girl looked away.

'Go on. I'm here for you. I'm listening.' Christopher rubbed her back.

'A man watches me. He pulls faces at me. But he never laughs.'

Christopher took a deep breath. 'And this man, where does he stand?'

Maya shook her head, golden locks swaying before her eyes. 'He does not stand. There is a rope around his neck. He hangs from the ceiling. He holds the rope and does this...'

Christopher's eyes widened as Maya mimicked a man chocking. It took him a minute to be able to form his next

166

question. 'And this man hanging by the stairs looks like Gregory?'

Maya shook her head again. 'You don't understand. He doesn't *look* like him. It *is* him. Same clothes, same beard, same face. It's him!' Christopher embraced his sister. 'Shall we go see if he is at the stairs, now?'

Just then, the door opened behind them, making them jump. 'What are you two doing out here?'

Both looked past Sophia; their eyes travelling to the staircase.

'He isn't there,' Maya whispered.

'Stay with Maya,' Christopher said, standing up. 'I left my book back at the bench. I'll be back soon,' he added as Maya held his hand strongly. 'Go play with Sophia and Olivia, and I'll be fine.'

'Be careful.'

The two girls watched as their brother, once again, made his way up to his reading spot. Christopher also ignored nature around him this time.

'Ah, you're still here.'

Gregory looked up, his garden shears blades stopping an inch away from a blossoming red rose. 'I was just going to cut your sister some flowers. She seemed upset. Is she okay?'

Christopher nodded. 'She will be fine. You reminded her of... of something bad.'

Gregory stared at the boy's eyes. 'Does Maya see things the rest of you don't?'

Christopher nodded again. 'Mum says she has a vivid imagination.'

'Or vivid insight. If I knew, I would have told her to look at me longer, deeper. She would see that there is nothing bad about me. Nothing to fear.'

Christopher walked into the shade and sat down. He

placed his hands upon his knees, exhaled and shot the question. 'Do you believe in ghosts?'

Gregory scratched his Greek nose. 'May I sit down with you, Master Christopher?'

'Are *you* a ghost?'

Gregory could not control his laughter. 'Don't be silly, Christopher. Do I look like a ghost? I'm not that weak. I'm as strong as a demon,' he said and continued laughing. 'I don't like the term ghosts, to be honest,' the man said, and he sat down by the boy. 'Modern languages ruin way too many proper meanings. There are no such things as ghosts, but there are plenty of souls. And, they leave the body and need to pass over.'

'Over to where?'

'Across the river. The souls have to muster the crossing of Acheron and make it to the vestibule of Hell.'

The difficult words sounded so familiar to him. He had heard them before or read them. 'The ancients believed that Acheron led to hell, right?'

'The moderns should believe, too, if you ask me.'

'Is Maya seeing ghosts?'

Gregory shrugged his shoulders. 'How should I know? I am not behind her eyes. I do not own them. I do not know what she sees with those weird purple eyes of hers.'

'Maybe she is seeing demons,' Christopher joked, using what he thought was a jest by Gregory.

'You say that as if it is a bad thing.'

'Isn't it? I mean, I can believe there is such a thing as a good ghost, but a good demon?'

Gregory stroked his hair. It was the first time the gardener had been so close to him. So friendly, so relaxed. 'My young boy, you have much still to learn. I thought we would have more time. You're a fast reader. I thought after

Homer, to teach you some Dante. And proper meaning to words. Ancient Greeks knew what they were talking about.' The man stared at the boy for a while. 'You will be fine.' He winked at the boy and stood up. 'Use your head. Always. The heart is overrated. Go now, your innocent sisters need you.'

Chapter Twenty-Three

'Cozy Oaks.' Andrew read the sign and sighed. The letters were burned into a thick oval chunk of oak that hung from the two oak trees that served as entrance posts. Andrew drove slowly up the narrow road, gazing around at the beautiful gardens that surrounded the nursing home. A plethora of Greek flowers and shrubs decorated the green lands. Marble benches, Greek statues, and a small fountain were the sugar coating of the huge yard in front of the turn of the previous century, twenty-bedroom building. A Turkish lord built the place as his summer home and had plans to expand it farther to be used as an inn to welcome important figures from the Ottoman dynasties that ruled Greece at the time. After the uprising and the spread of freedom, it was turned into a hospital by the local authorities. Budget cuts in health and a diminishing local population brought about the closing of the hospital. Years of abandonment followed until it was auctioned off during the eighties. The building was renovated and turned into a heaven for the elderly no longer capable of taking care of themselves.

'As if any of us can truly take care of ourselves,' Andrew whispered as he turned to park by an old truck that was occupying two spots. 'We are all just trying to survive...'

Stepping out of the vehicle, Andrew realized how serene the area was. The slamming of his car door was the only noise for miles. '*Where is everyone?*'

'One, two, three, four...' Andrew counted the steps up to the main entrance. He felt silly counting, but he had done it ever since he could remember. He knew the number of steps of his home, his relatives' homes, his old school, his uni, his office, the spiral staircase.

His index finger landed on the bell next to the intricately carved brass door that reminded him of the church door of Saint Nicholas back in London. The bell echoed loudly inside. With a sharp electrical screech, the piece of art of a door moved backward by itself.

'*Now, that's new.*'

Andrew stepped into the cavernous reception area. A tall lady in a red dress stood behind the counter. She was the only person in sight. With small steps and wary eyes, Andrew beelined toward her. 'Good morning, I am ...'

'Good morning, Mister Fotopoulos. I am so sorry to hear about your mother. Have the police informed you on any news?'

'*Small town; big news.*'

Andrew scratched the side of his forehead, smiled, and looked around. 'They are still out searching. Err, where is everyone?'

'Field trip today. Four villagers, six churches. Lunch by the river under the shade provided by grapevines. It's our residents' favorite,' the lady with the intense red lipstick said.

Andrew tried to focus away from the smudge of it on her front two teeth.

'And you are?'

She extended her hand. Her long nails made her fingers seem unnaturally long. 'Kate Ferraiou. Operations Manager.' Andrew shook her hand gently and quickly retrieved his. 'Great. You're not just a secretary. I am here to complain.'

Kate's fingers met and locked as she placed them on the greyish counter. She closed her eyes for two seconds and reopened them with a fake smile. 'Complain, sir?'

There was something about her smug face that irritated Andrew. Then again, it did not take much to irritate him. 'Why did you let my mother go without my permission? A woman in her state all alone in a house in the middle of nowhere...'

Kate raised her right palm. 'Sir, you are yelling at me...'

'I am not yelling, I am aggravated.'

'I will not pretend to understand how you may be feeling right now. Your mother is lost, but please, I am not the enemy here.'

Andrew exhaled loudly. 'Yet, I come to Greece to find my mother alone...'

'And you didn't immediately think of calling us?'

'She said you let her go.'

'Did we? Are we legally covered to do such a thing? You signed her in, sir and only you can sign her out.'

Andrew placed his hands on the counter. 'Are you saying that my mother escaped? And you never came looking for her?'

'Lord, give me strength!' Kate looked up at the ceiling.

'Lady, you are starting to really piss me off here.'

Kate's hands shuffled around in the top draw by her

side. She took out a black clipboard and dropped it in front of him.

'What's this?' Andrew asked, looking down at the sole paper held prisoner by the clip.

'Read it.'

Andrew ducked and focused on the title. 'Consent form for patient's removal...'

And on the bottom right was his name and his signature under it.

'Is this some sort of joke?'

'Is that your signature, sir?'

Andrew nodded. 'It was forged, though. I was in England on this date.'

Kate's brown eyes opened wide. 'Mister Fotopoulos, I was the one here when you came in and asked for your mother. I helped you pack. I advised against taking her out of here. I was worried about her. I called you every day since then to check up on poor Penelope, and you never answer once!'

Andrew took a step back and shook his head. 'You're lying. It's impossible. I was in England. Did my mother pay for a look-alike?'

Kate sniggered. 'It was you, sir. Spitting image. Same voice, too!'

Andrew continued shaking his head. 'You're covering your tracks. You know if something happens to my mother, I could sue. You lying bitch...'

'Bitch that cared enough to call every day. Twice a day. Phone calls on record. I have proof that I wanted to see if she was alright. You never answered since checking her out.'

Andrew banged his fist on the counter. The purple vase shook, and its roses trembled. 'I never checked her out. And you never called. I have no phone calls from you.'

'Check your phone, sir. Go on. Show me.'

Andrew shook his head, again. 'I can't. The battery is dead.'

'How convenient.'

Just then, his cell phone began to ring. Its standard tune echoed from his pocket. Kate laughed a short, sinister laugh. 'More lies, I see!'

Andrew pulled out his phone and stared at his ringing phone in amazement. 'Well, I'll be damned. Hello?'

'Mister Fotopoulos? This is police officer Daniel Maniatis. I am sorry, sir. I have bad news for you. No easy way to say these things. We have just located your mother's body.'

Andrew turned around, and even though the reception was fine, he squeezed his cell harder upon his ear. His dry throat cloaked up as his mind searched for words, for logic. 'Where?'

As soon as the conversation came to an end, Andrew found himself by the door. With his eyes closed, Andrew pushed his phone back into his pocket and with both hands upon the brass door, he exited to fresh air. Like a diver coming up for air, his mouth sucked in much-needed oxygen. His right shoulder ached and sent spikes of pain his way -an enemy from within. His heart pounded fast, and with each beat, the pain grew. He stumbled down the steps and wobbled to a tall pine tree. He placed his shaking hand upon the thick trunk and gazed down. He wanted to puke but couldn't. Just loud, dry, painful coughs came from his mouth. *Relax, old boy. Relax. You're gonna give yourself a heart attack.* He knelt and spat out to the ground, before sitting down with his back to the mighty tree. He disrupted a line of hard-working ants that quickly shifted around his black shoes and ventured off on a new route. The pieces of a forgotten cupcake had to be delivered.

Andrew had his eyes fixed on the nursing home's entrance. He did not wish that *awful woman* to see him like this. He hated forced sympathy. '*Breathe through your nose, exhale from your mouth. Breathe through your nose, exhale from your mouth. Breathe through your nose, exhale from your mouth...*' His body complied with his brain's commands. He soon tried to stand up. He wiped the cold sweat from his forehead and slowly made his way back to his borrowed vehicle.

He had never driven so slowly before. He drove like the people he cursed silently as he overtook them. He drove like his grandfather did. Andrew kept himself busy with thoughts. Simple thoughts like the speed he was travelling at, the dried-up countryside during the scorching summer months, and the shape of clouds lingering in the distance. 'That one looks like Santorini,' he whispered and let his mind drift to his favorite view. A winter sunset from Franco's bar, right on the edge of the caldera.

Anything but his mother.

Anything to deter him from acceptance.

Penelope was dead.

He turned onto the highway. E55 ran all along the Ionian Sea. His lips read the sign as he turned. No sound. General Hospital of Preveza. 40 kilometers away.

Thirty-seven minutes to amuse his mind. To keep his brain busy with songs, clouds, the sea, and the commenting on tourists walking carelessly and shirtless along village promenades.

Chapter Twenty-Four

Heather was known for her planning. Her friends feared and admired her set of skills equally.

Heather could suck the fun out of any activity by planning it down to the minute. 'So, eight-thirty we will be at the escape room's entrance. I have printed out the three teams. The game will begin at quarter to nine. It lasts for one hour. Fifteen minutes will be enough for photos and comparisons of games. If we set off at nine, we will be at the restaurant on time for our half-nine reservation. Club opens at eleven...'

Heather was also the mastermind behind every successful and legendary party their uni class held.

'Yes, this is Heather Moore. I spoke with you two days ago? I will be needing the bouncy castle delivered on Saturday, at eight o'clock sharp. Thank you, bye. Hello? Yes, this is Heather Moore, I am calling about an ad I saw of yours? About a foam machine maker?'

Her Southern American accent stood out amongst her

mostly European and Asian counterparts at the elite Swiss University.

But between her many plans and to-do lists, the unexpected crept and settled.

The group of eight twenty-year-olds rose from their white wooden chairs, leaving behind empty plates. With their youthful appetites, the four boys and four girls had devoured every single piece they had gathered from the lengthy breakfast buffet offered by Vrachos Beach Hotel, right on the mile-long sandy beach of Loutsas.

The group had chosen Greece as their summer destination, and Heather sorted out the rest. Heather googled the heck out of Greece's beaches and settled on one of the most picturesque, yet one of the most unknowns. 'Hidden gem,' she had called it when she began her PowerPoint presentation toward her friends.

Turquoise waters, green hills, dining by the pool, beach bars with handsome locals, and a strong sun or starry night above each image flashed before the young adults' eyes.

Heather took off her one-size-too-big T-shirt, folded it neatly into a perfect square and placed it on her blue sunbed. She took in a deep breath as she gazed around. 'Paradise,' she whispered as she took in her surroundings. Rows of palm trees grew out the thin golden sand and offered shade to the narrow road leading down to the cool waters. Heather stepped into the calm sea and walked until the waters reached her belly. The next step was always the hardest. She looked down and smiled at the clarity. She wiggled her feet and prepared for the next step and the plunge. Heather swam out to sea, leaving most tourists behind. Back home, in Oklahoma, she was the champion of her high school in every competitive swimming race.

And, there it was. The unplanned. Just as Heather

checked her watch to see if she was on time, the dark log appeared before her.

Panic.

Shark.

'Out of the water? It's floating?'

Heather's entire face screamed when she found the courage to swim closer.

A lifeless body was carried by the waters. The body looked ghostly. Too pale. Like a wax figure left outside to melt, the skin dangled from its bones. Heather looked back to shore. She was a mile out. No one could hear her.

So, Heather made a plan.

'You got this girl,' she said and placed her hand on the corpses rotting ankle. She gripped well and began to swim back to the beach.

'Every paradise contains a little bit of hell.'

The wind turned and blew her way, offering her speed, yet also a deadly stench that would take days to remove from her nostrils.

Her toes finally made contact with the sand below. Heather took in a deep salty breath and prepared for the commotion.

People screamed and covered children's eyes as the tall blonde swam by them tolling the old lady's body. Her face with widened eyes never to close again and opened mouth was the stuff nightmares were made of.

'Jesus Christ!' her friend Mark said as he quickly picked up his phone and dialled the European emergency number.

News reached police officer Daniel Maniatis quickly.

Penelope was dead. Dead and on her way to the morgue at Preveza's General Hospital. Daniel set off at once. He made two phone calls on the way. One to the coroner, and one to Andrew.

Chapter Twenty-Five

The heavy front door screeched as he kicked it closed behind him. It was not used to force. Christopher returned to the house confused. Words circled in the pool of wisdom located in the center of his mind.

'Your innocent sisters need you.'

Christopher walked forward and then counted the steps as he made his way to the top floor. 'One, two, three, four, five, six, seven, eight...' He paused and looked into the darkness to his right. 'Where are you, Maya's ghost?'

His two sisters' giggling journeyed toward him. Upbeat music followed. Chris knew well what they were doing. They were viewing funny video compilations. Christopher remained on the eighth step. He could picture them happily lying on the huge comfortable bed with their heads sunk in the tower created out of three pillows, and their hair spread out like a mythological sea beast, servant to the great Lord of the oceans, Poseidon.

'Gods, Greeks, demons...' Christopher whispered scattered words from the sentences he repeated in his head. He replayed his previous conversation with Gregory and began to make connections with sporadic mentions from other long conversations on long reading evenings.

He turned his attention lower, to the other side.

The library door was open. Christopher felt like he was being called in there. His sisters were fine. His father was away, and his mother was even more 'away.' He scratched his nails between them before taking a step down. And another. Then another, and with a capable leap, he jumped over the remaining steps, landing safely on the ground floor. He rushed into the dark room and switched on the lights. His eyes ran around the book-filled shelves like crazy. He spoke to himself. He spoke to the books. 'Bingo!' His hand landed on Dante. He placed the heavy book on the wooden desk. Two picture books of paintings followed and a thin book about ancient Greece before the twelve Olympian Gods joined them. Christopher had never felt such an adrenaline rush before. He blew dust away from yellowy pages and dug into his favorite world. That of words. Escaping to his happy place. People always thought of a holiday destination or the place they last felt joy, or they began reminiscing their childhood home when they had to do that. Christopher never escaped to reality. He had thousands of worlds to go to. Hundreds of timelines to explore. He read and read until his eyes felt heavy.

'Was that water always there? Did I bring it in with me? Could it be from yesterday?' The ten-year-old boy picked up the glass and looked at the water. Light lived in it, and rainbows shone toward him. He brought it to his dry lips and drank it down in one big gulp. He then stuck two fingers in the glass, wetting them with the remaining droplets. He washed his two eyes. 'It's too early in the day to feel so tired.' He thought of standing, but now he felt even weaker than before. Drowsiness conquered him, and he lay forward, closing his eyes.

Loud music and chanting woke him up.

Christopher sat up straight with such a force that the chair tilted back, and he fell to meet the floor. He opened his eyes slowly. Colors around him were too vivid, as if designed by a top Japanese videogame designer. Books dived off the top shelf and began to fly around the room as if birds carving the sky. More books joined in. Crow sounds echoed louder.

Deafening.

Christopher crawled back toward the wall and placed his hands above his ears in an ill attempt to drown out the sound that was rapidly climbing the Decibel scale. He stood up and dashed out of the library as each book flew around in a thick flock. Books started to collide with one another, and ripped pages fell like a rain of words to the ground. Christopher slammed the door behind him and ran to the spiral. 'Sophia? Maya?' he called out as he went.

'They are not here, young master.'

The creepy voice froze him on the spot. He gazed into the darkness. A black figure of a man was slightly visible. Christopher continued running up the stairs.

'And stop pulling faces at my sister!' he yelled, looking behind him. He had reached the top step as he turned his attention back around. He gasped in fear and fell to his knees. The entire floor was missing. He had climbed the spiral to the top of something that resembled of a volcano. With his fingers wrapped around the railing, he looked down into the lava. The figures from the living room painting were walking in a line. Their movements were weird, unnatural, frightening -as if their hands and legs had fewer bones in them. They swayed from side-to-side as a red entity followed them, howling out strange words in a harsh tone. The creature had two thick goat legs that shook the ground as he stomped up and down the line of weeping men and women. His chest was human and bare, while his tail was a snake that hissed as people passed it by. His face was dark, making it hard to distinguish features, yet his three eyes shone brightly. The beast looked up at Christopher and the boy could swear that it smiled at him. Christopher looked away. A sudden uproar from his right caught his attention. Massive waves of water rose like a tsunami and carved through the lava. Steam clouds filled up the atmosphere. A strong river floated by his eyes, and in the middle, he saw a boat carrying a cloaked figure holding a ferryman's pole. He also looked straight at the boy. His eyes were two pieces of gold coins. He nodded to Christopher as he sailed by, stopping at the shore by the line of sickly-looking people.

'All aboard!' the ferryman yelled, and each person in the line removed all the clothing. Christopher observed in shock. They looked like they hadn't eaten in days. As they took of their last piece of clothing, Christopher felt uneasy. He gazed around to see if anyone else was watching him. Christopher had never seen a naked woman before. His eyes fell to their vaginas. His pupils ran around their breasts. His breathing grew louder. 'That's right, you filthy pieces of shit. You take nothing!' The ferryman taunted them and let loose a sinister, cynical laugh. Suddenly, in unison, every single person raised their right hand and opened their palms. A coin laid on each of the palms. One by one they moved like zombies and fell into the wooden boat. The ferryman picked up each coin and dropped them into his brown sack by his side.

Cling. Cling. Cling.

'Twenty-eight souls today!' he declared as a blare of barks broke the silence from across the shore. A three-headed dog ran along the riverbank and disappeared into the darkness.

'Kerberos,' Christopher whispered and leaned forward to get a better look at the canine. Suddenly, the three-eyed demon grew wings. Christopher could hear its bones crack and break as feathers slashed out from below its skin. Resembling those of an eagle Chris once saw at Chessington World of Adventures, each wing was more than two meters wide. With ease, as if no effort was required, the goat-legged beast rose in the air. It only took him a few timid flaps and in a matter of seconds, he was opposite Christopher. The young boy fell back. Every facial muscle froze, and his pupils trembled inside their egg-shaped cages as the beast grew closer to him.

'Do not fear me, boy.'

His voice came out loud and clear, yet Christopher saw that the line on his dark face did not open.

'Stay back, demon.'

'Demon?' the beast repeated and chuckled as he landed beside him. 'And is that a bad thing? I guess you would prefer an appearance more to your modern, twisted ideas huh?'

A light bright came from the beast's chest. A light brighter than the morning sun. Christopher closed his eyes and covered them with his arm. His eyelids remained bright red for what seemed longer than the actual ten seconds that passed. 'It can't be real, it can't be real, it can't be real...' the boy repeated as he lowered his arm and reopened his eyes.

'Better now?'

The same disembodied voice, yet a different entity. A glorious, glowing angel stood before him. A handsome man with blonde curls and wings whiter than clouds on a fine spring day was smiling widely at him. 'I can look like whatever you want me to, young Christopher. Like you, I carry my own amount of wickedness and kindness.'

'Like me?'

'I mean, like humans.'

Christopher shook his head. 'We are taught that angels protect us and that demons are malevolent creatures...'

'That's quite some fancy words you know, kid. Yet, real knowledge escapes you. That's what Christianity taught you. We existed long before that. What did the ancient Greeks teach you?' the angel asked and snapped his fingers. A book fell out of thin air and landed in Christopher's hands.

'Cronus, Zeus, and the real daemons of ancient Greece,' Christopher read the title.

'I really do need a catchier title,' the angel said, and the book magically opened. The pages turned themselves until stopping on page twenty-six. Christopher looked down as letters ran along the white page and began grouping up to form words and sentences.

Christopher's eyes ran along the newborn text. A minute later, he looked up. 'Is this true?'

'Truer than true. So, what did you learn, young lord?'

Christopher stood up and the book vanished from his arms. 'Cronus created a golden race of men. When they died, they became demons. His helpers. Ever-present forces that watched mankind from the shadows were his eyes on Earth. They bestowed riches to the good people and suffering to the wicked.'

The angel winked at him. 'Told you I was good. And who changed all that?'

'Zeus.'

The angel rolled his eyes. 'History is written by the winners, right? Well, good old Zeus murdered his father and became King of the Gods...'

'Well, Cronus was eating all his children.'

'I never said he was perfect either,' the angel replied and laughed. It was a gentle, relaxed laugh. 'Now, where was I? Yes, Zeus. He did not care much about awarding the righteous. He wanted us only to spy on humans and report their unjust acts back to him. He made us punish them. Quite cruelly I may add. That's when the perspective humans had of us changed. We became kakodaimones. Evil, ugly, taunting. With the diminishment of the ancient gods, we found refuge in the Underworld and tried to go back to our norm. Some though were beyond help, beyond repair. Like my cousin Eurynomos.'

Christopher knew he would regret asking before even uttering the first word. 'What's wrong with Eurynomos?'

'Oh, he stays in the dark corners of Hades and eats any flesh left on the rotting corpses that linger down there.'

'And you?'

'Me? I like to believe I have returned to my righteous place. I look over the Necromanteio and its surroundings, playing my tricks on the sinners while doing my best to protect innocent children from the forces that reside around here. Persephone calls me the Looker, but I prefer my old name, Agathos.'

The angel placed his hand on Christopher's head, messed up his hair, and stroked his cheek. Christopher had never felt such warmth before. As if the heat left the body untouched yet lit the soul.

Suddenly, screeching female voices broke the silence, and ghostly spirits flew above them. 'The master is coming. The master is coming. All praise Hades.'

The angel looked down, straight into Christopher's eyes. He seemed worried. 'Time to go, kid. Wakey-wakey.' He taped Christopher on his forehead, and with a loud gasp, Christopher opened his eyes and fell off the library chair.

'Holy shit! Now, that's definitely topping my list of WTF dreams!'

Chapter Twenty-Six

Susan's nose touched the cool window. Her gaze travelled outside. Darkness and only darkness. The clock struck midnight, and Andrew had not returned home. 'Probably for the best.' She pulled on her bottom lip and tapped on the glass. She tapped out an old song, one she remembered from school assembly. 'All things bright and beautiful,' she whispered. A crazy laugh followed. 'All things dark and ugly, more like it.' She reopened her mouth as if ready to laugh again but quickly placed her hands upon her face. 'Sssh, you drunk bitch. The kids are sleeping.' She squinted her eyes as if thinking. Then, she nodded. 'Yes, yes. They are sleeping. They are fine. I heard them shower. Sophia cooked and put Maya to sleep. What a precious girl. I hope she doesn't turn into me, poor thing. The bookworm went to bed last. Reading till late. Always reading and reading...'

She brought her phone up to eye level. No missed calls. No messages. She had called Andrew three times. That was her limit. 'You better be looking for your senile mother and not be off fucking some young bimbo, you cheating cunt.'

The phone fell from her hand and landed with a thud on the floor. Susan paid no attention nor did any moves to pick it up.

'*Oh, don't use the C-word, Susie. It is so unladylike.*' Her mother's voice once again dominated her scattered thoughts. All silenced by the dominant voice.

'Cunt, cunt, cunt, cunt, cunt...' Susan sang as she clumsily made her way to her wardrobe. She opened the doors and knelt. Eleven bottles hid among her shoes and bags. All empty. 'Shit.'

She stood up and remained still as if contemplating if she had enough energy to make it downstairs. The comfortable king-sized bed with the heavenly mattress called out to her. 'Booze or dropping dead on the bed, Suz.' Her mother voted bed, and the rest voted wine.

With her hands upon the walls, Susan walked the dark, silent corridor. Step by step, she began to descend the spiral, finding it hard to maintain her balance. Her head was heavy, and her sight was blurred. What she did see clearly was the large spider that fell from above and landed on her shoulder. Susan did not have many phobias. Spiders, though, always creeped her out. It was not the legs as with most, it was something about their eyes. That unsettling, piercing, scary gaze.

Susan shrieked and with her eyes closed, she pushed the blackish/purple eight-legged creature off her. The sudden movement was enough. Enough for her to lose her step. Susan tumbled forward, first banging her head as her drunken mind did not manage to warn her hands in time. Her back received the next blow, three steps down. Round and round, her body went. Susan was unconscious when she reached the lower floor.

She remained *out* for minutes.

'The itchy bitchy spider fell down the spiral stairs. Out came the moon and dried up all the wine...'

Singing reached her ears.

Tick. Tock. Tick. Tock.

The front-room clock sounded right next to her. Louder than ever before.

Giggling followed.

'Eugene?'

She spoke, yet she could not move or open her eyes.

'Yes, Mummy?'

'Am I dead?'

More giggling. 'No! Silly Mummy.'

'Are *you* dead?'

She heard small footsteps coming from her right. She felt his tiny hand caress her red hair. 'I still exist. I exist here. Do you miss me, Mummy? Do you want to join me?'

Susan gathered all her strength and fought to forget the tremendous pain her body was in. Struggling, she reopened her eyes. And there, he was. Clear and colorful as a spring field. She missed his eyes. The way they smiled when he saw her. 'My prince. My angel,' she whispered.

The wide-smiling boy staring straight into her eyes, piercing her soul. She raised her arm, grinding her teeth in pain. She touched his rosy cheek. So real. So soft.

'You're bleeding, Mummy,' Eugene said and ran his little finger along her head wound. He lifted his hand, bringing his bloody index finger near his face. 'Mmm, you taste good, Mummy,' he said, sticking his finger into his mouth. 'I want more!' Susan screamed out in pain as the boy stuck all his fingers into her open wound. Her entire body shook violently as she felt his fingers dig deeper into her. Blood ran into her eyes, forcing her back to darkness.

'Enough!' Susan grappled with the pain, with her

thoughts, and with Eugene. She sat up. Panting, she looked behind her. She was alone. Small, red footsteps glowed on the floor. Her eyes followed them. And there it was. A clear *I*, written in blood (*her blood?*) upon the Acheron painting.

A cold tear ran down her cheek. 'How? To who? Andrew?'

The darkness did not reply.

'Eugene? Eugene?'

Click.

The lights came on.

'Mum?'

Susan turned her head toward the top of the stairs.

'Eugene?'

'Mum, it's Christopher.'

Susan trembled and scratched her tangled hair. 'Are you real?'

Christopher closed his eyes and rubbed his palms upon his bare thighs. 'Mum, splash some water on you and get to bed. You're scaring the girls. You're scaring me.'

Susan growled and raised her arms. 'And you fucking think that I am not shit scared?' she asked as she took twisted, painful steps toward the spiral. Christopher's eyes widened as he caught a clear view of his bloody mother. Susan began to conquer the steps, one by one, crawling on all fours.

Christopher turned and ran.

'Sophia, lock your door. Now!' he shouted as he passed by her room. Sophia had opened the door, just an inch, as she watched Christopher walk down the corridor to check on their mother. Sophia did not ask why. She slammed the door, locked it and climbed back into bed next to a sleeping Maya.

Christopher also turned his door's key and stayed behind it.

Waiting and waiting.

Their mother never came.

Soon, Susan's wailing broke the silence. She cried on the floor for an hour before crawling back to her room. She wiped off the dried blood and fainted from exhaustion, both physical and mental, on her bed.

Chapter Twenty-Seven

Beep. Beep. Beep.

The noise repeated itself after a pause of silence.

It hurt to open his eyes. The white fluorescent light invaded brightly from above and a stinging sensation settled around his eyelids. Andrew made an effort to raise his right arm. He was laying down, somewhere soft. Pain travelled from his arm, making his neck twitch. Something was piercing his skin.

'Mister Fotopoulos, please remain still.' A female voice. A calm voice. Soothing even.

'Who...?' A rough cough and a grunt -the ones that fool our frail minds that we can control the pain- did not allow him to say more. 'Where?' No strength for more. His throat was dry, his lips dryer.

'Relax, Andreas. I am Demetra. I am a nurse here at Preveza's hospital. Stay still. I will get the doctor for you.'

Andrew tried to focus, to adjust to the strong light. Blonde hair, slim figure. He watched as she strolled out of the room in search for a doctor. He looked around. He was alone in the room. He lay on a single bed with off-white linen. He hoped that was their original color. His back was raised. Thinking off how thin hospital pillows were, he figured he must have had more than three pillows behind him. The lone window was opened, so the air was fresh, yet it carried a slight hint of detergent in it. Logical. It could have been worse. Andrew hated *bad smells*. The sun near the horizon caught his eye. 'What? Is it rising? Is it morning?' He was not sure if he was speaking out loud or hearing the undertow of his thoughts. He shook his head. '*Come on, brain. Restart.*'

Two greyish shadows came into his vivid snowy surroundings. 'Focus, eyes, focus.' Lines began to form. White curtains. White walls. White coat on the short doctor. The room slowly came into focus. He recognized the man next to the doctor. It was the police officer he met in the woods.

'Mister Fotopoulos, I am Dr. Akis Kleanthis. You have been given quite strong medication, so do not be alarmed by your current state. It will take a while for you to truly wake up and feel better. Here, have some water,' the olive-skinned man said and passed him a glass from his bedside cabinet.

The refreshing water flowed like a river taking out a fire as it journeyed down his oesophagus.

'Why am I here?'

Andrew felt proud for forming an entire sentence. He even managed to sit up straight and face the two men.

'Andrew, you suffered a minor heart attack. It is a miracle that you drove nearly all the way here...'

'Nearly?'

Police officer Daniel Maniatis stepped forward. 'You crashed your car a few miles down. I had just left here and saw the whole scene. You just swirled off the road. Lucky for you, you were going slowly, and the vehicle came to a stand-still in the shallow ditch by the side of the road. If you were speeding, you would have kept on going, and the area is full of thickly trunked trees.'

Andrew pictured the crash. He had lived it in his dream. He placed his hand upon his chest. His heart was beating fast.

'Daniel brought you here safely in a matter of minutes...'

The good old doctor with the dyed black hair continued talking. Andrew picked up scattered words. ECG. Electrical impulses. Blood tests. Vessels. Echocardiogram. Coronary catheterization.

'*Blah. Blah. Fucking blah.*'

Andrew turned toward the police officer. '*What a smug face. One slap and that pitiful excuse of a mustache would fly off your fucking face...*'

'So, my mother is dead?'

The doctor stopped talking.

'Yes,' Daniel replied. 'Her body was found floating out at sea...'

Andrew chuckled. 'It seems my boy's story of his grand-mother swimming out to save him was true. Would not have thought that she had it in her. She always was a fighter. She died a hero.'

Daniel cleared his throat. 'Err, Andrew? You claim your mother was with you on the beach that day, right?'

Andrew tilted his head. His eyebrows set off on a march to meet at the root of his nose. 'Claim? What are you saying? Are you retarded or what?'

The doctor placed his hand on Daniel's chest. 'Maybe you should have this conversation later. Give the patient some time to relax. Andrew, please. You had a heart attack not many hours ago. Please. I understand this is a stressful time for you...'

'Claim? She was with us!'

Daniel ground his teeth. 'And, she was with you the entire week, right?'

'Yes!' Andrew raised his arms slightly. His ribs hurt.

Daniel shook his head and stormed out of the hospital room.

'What the hell is going on, doctor?'

The old man forced a smile and raised his right palm. 'Please, deep breaths. Relax. Try to sleep. I'll be back in a bit,' he quickly said and dashed out of the room.

The white curtains were pulled yet thin enough for Andrew to see the doctor go after the officer. *'What the heck is going on? I've been through enough shit!'* Andrew sat up straight ignoring the pain in his back. He slid his naked legs out from under the cover. A single hospital gown covered his body. Andrew stood up and gave himself a moment to regain his strength and senses. The cold floor cooled his bare feet. Andrew's anger had heated his entire body. He looked down at the tube entering his arm. 'Well, you're coming with me,' he mumbled and unclipped the hospital serum bottle. 'You're not!' Andrew ripped the blue cord that ended under a patch on his chest. He sighed loudly as the plaster took many hairs hostage. The monitor to his side began blaring. *Beep. Beep. Beep.* By the third beep, Andrew had left the room. The nurse with the blonde hair and the Cindy Crawford beauty spot ran into the room first. 'Where is he? Doctor! Doctor!'

Andrew called the elevator and read the sign quickly. 'Morgue, minus two.'

Chapter Twenty-Eight

Dr. Polina Christodoulou loved her peace and quiet. From a young age, she adored the silence. The calm that came when noises were muted. Even though she had always been a straight-A student, school was a nightmare for her. A loud hellish world where sounds came to reach their heights. Her father, a poor man that worked the land, had big dreams for his little girl. He raised her by himself on their farm on the outskirts of Larissa. A still-born son and a wife defeated by ovarian cancer meant it was just the two of them.

'You should be a teacher,' he said to her at the beginning of her senior year in high school. Her father towered her at six foot two against her five-foot-one figure.

'No way! Not in a million years. I'd cut open my head and throw my tormented brain in the gutter. And that would be just on the first day of school.'

Her father laughed and stroked her soft hair. 'You're a weird one, Polina. If you're so good at chopping heads maybe you should be a surgeon.' Her father continued laughing as he prepared her ham and cheese sandwich with four slices of cucumbers, yet only a single slice of tomato. Polina was not laughing. The notion intrigued her. Med school sounded serious, and even better, it sounded quiet.

Years later, she chose the quietest route available. Medical coroner.

Now, a mature woman of forty-two, married to her job and still in love with her silence, Polina stood in her morgue buried two floors down at Preveza's hospital.

'I am now proceeding with the autopsy of Panayiotis Castellano, age fifty-two,' Polina spoke into her small black recorder. Her low-pitched voice was the only noise in the vast morgue. Polina made sure her mask and gloves were firmly in place and picked up her shiny, sterilized scalpel.

Loud footsteps echoed from the narrow corridor outside. People yelling *stop* followed. Polina closed her eyes and swallowed her father's favorite curse word. The commotion grew louder. Polina exhaled quietly and looked behind her. The door handle on the first door of the morgue shook violently up and down.

'Hello? Is anybody in there? Open up! Open up, now!'

A man was shouting and banging on the door. The next door was unlocked. Polina ran to lock it. She was never the runner. Her father often joked how funny her short legs looked when she attempted to run. The door flew open and a tall man in a hospital gown entered. Polina took a step back and squeezed upon her scalpel, raising it in front of her.

'I'm not going to hurt you,' the man said and quickly slammed the door behind him. He turned the key, and Polina felt her heart pounding away under her Mediterranean breasts.

'I know exactly where to cut you,' she warned the man. 'You will bleed out in minutes. Stay back,' she added firmly.

She had heard that at a self-defense seminar a few years back. Talk at a steady pace and with confidence.

The man held out his palms. 'My name is Andrew. Andrew Fotopoulos.'

Banging and shouting from outside made Polina contemplate cutting herself and not the menacing stranger.

'My mother was brought in yesterday. Penelope Fotopoulos?'

Polina nodded. 'Yes? What is it that you want to know? What is going on, Andrew? Why are you dressed like a patient and being chased by what seems like half the personnel of this hospital?'

'Was there something unusual about my mother?' She drowned at sea, right?'

Polina lowered her arms. 'Andrew, your mother did not drown. I'm still waiting for test results to come in, but I see no signs of foul-play if that is what is going on. She seems to have died peacefully, most likely in her sleep, over a week ago.'

Andrew's mouth opened. No words came. He shook his head and sat down on the cold tiles. 'Penelope Fotopoulos?'

'Yes?'

'Died over a week ago?'

'That's right.'

Polina watched as the grown man sat down on the ground and began to rock back and forth while laughing.

'What the fuck is going on here? Am I dreaming?' His laughter turned sinister after the questions.

'Mister Fotopoulos? Andrew? Let me help you.'

Andrew shouted at her to stay away from him. 'My mother was alive during last week. Burn your medical degree, you dumb bitch. A week ago, my ass!'

Just then, the door behind them opened. Two muscular

men picked Andrew up by his shoulders and dragged him out of the morgue.

'Be gentle,' the doctor advised.

'So sorry,' the police officer said with a slight smile to Polina.

Minutes later, her lover returned. Cherished silence ruled the morgue once again.

Polina sighed and dropped her scalpel back into her silver tray. She pulled off her gloves and a small, short-lived cloud of white dust rose in the air. She walked over to her cabinet and took out a bottle of local Chardonnay. She poured herself a glass, filling it nearly to the brim. She slowly sat down behind her office and raised her glass while staring at her late father's photo. 'Still better than being a teacher!'

Chapter Twenty-Nine

The sedative wore off, and Andrew found himself back on the same hospital bed.

The window to his left remained a vibrant, colorful painting of a Greek summer's day. The only difference was that the sun had vanished from nature's work of art. The day had moved on. To his right, a guard stood outside of his door, a security man with a round baby face named George. The man's multiple white hairs though revealed his true age. Andrew never liked plump body shapes in certain occupations. Army, police, and security mainly. He felt it was their duty to keep fit.

'Excuse me? Mister security man?'

Slowly, wearing a bored expression, the short man in his late forties opened the door and poked his youthful face into the room.

'Do you need a doctor, sir?'

Andrew picked up his phone that sat on a plastic bedside table among his keys, his wallet and whatever else he was carrying in his jean pockets at the time of the crush. He waved the dark screen before the man.

'Any chance you have an iPhone and brought your charger to work?'

The man shook his head. But before Andrew could utter the word shit, the man spoke. 'My wife works here as a nurse. She always has her charger with her. She drains the battery more than she drains my spirit,' he said and let loose a croaky yet quiet laugh. 'Let me text her.'

'Thank you. Thank you so very much.'

Andrew tapped his fingers on his bed's scratched rail and wondered the stories that each abrasion could tell. Pain and death dug into a railing or just the marks of time and careless nurses crashing their medicine and food carts?

'Finally!' Andrew saw a petite woman dash up to the security guard. She placed a charger in his right hand, laid a kiss on his left cheek, and continued quickly down the long corridor.

'*He must squash her during sex.*' Andrew was never one to avoid immature thoughts. His inner filter had broken long ago.

The door screeched as the heavy man leaned on it to reopen it. 'Here you go.'

'Thanks a million.'

Andrew pushed the charger in one of the many sockets above his bed and connected it to his phone. The screen lit up. A battery symbol appeared with just one flashing light. Andrew pressed the side button and punched in his code. Sophia's birthday. A wide smile raised his ears. 'At last.' The cell began to vibrate. It continued vibrating for a whole minute as tens of messages and missed calls finally arrived at their destination. Most from days ago. It was as if his phone never came back to life after he switched it off during take-off from Heathrow Airport. 'What in the name of Mr. Blobby is going on?'

Farewell wishes from work.

Welcome to Greece messages from various networks.

Missed calls from the nursing home, the police station, Susan, the building company.

'How can this be?' Andrew mumbled as he scrolled along. 'I spoke with the builders many times.' He called Cronus's number. He had to inform him of the crash. 'The number you are dialling does not exist.' Andrew shook his head in disbelief. He called the building company's line number.

'Fast and Easy Restorations, how may I help you please?'

'Can I speak to Cronus, please?'

'Who, sir?'

'Cronus.'

'Sir, no one of that name works here.'

Andrew needed a moment. 'Lady, the guy showed up at my house in your uniform with another few builders.'

'When was this, sir? May I have your address?'

Andrew replied, and speechless, he listened to how no one from the company showed up as he never called to set up a date. Neither did he answer to any of their calls. They figured he had not arrived in Greece as planned.

Andrew ended the call and wiped the sweat from his forehead. He closed his eyes and breathed in deeply. 'Calm down, heart. Calm down.'

He dialled Susan's number. 'The number you are trying to reach is unavailable at the moment. Please try again later.'

'Shit.'

He dialled Sophia's number. The same voice. The same message.

'Give me a fucking break.' Andrew blew out loudly. He tapped his fingers on the phone before deciding to call the nursing home.

'Cozy Oaks.' Kate's voice was heard as if she stood at a distance from the speaker. Andrew could hear her flicking through papers.

'It's Andrew Fotopoulos...'

'Oh.'

Andrew controlled his rich cursing vocabulary. 'I'm calling from the hospital. My mother was found dead.'

A second oh. A different one. One covered in sadness.

'I am so sorry for your loss. Penelope was a lovely person. A marvellous soul. May God...'

'Skip the speech, Kate. I know you're up to something. You're covering your tracks. All this small town bullshit. You're all in on it. You, the police, the doctor. What is it you under-paid cunts want? Her estate? Make me sound mad, huh?'

'Sir, you sound mad just fine all by yourself. I have liter-ally no idea what the hell you are ranting on about!'

'The police and the coroner say that Penelope has been dead for over a week which is a downright lie. She has been with us at the house. You let her go and lied that I signed her out even though I was still in England. And now, you are going to make it seem like we killed her on our very first day in Greece. Lock me up. Send her sole heir to prison. I know her will. She made it before I had the kids. I'm listed first, and in case of my death, her estate goes to the village. She wanted to give back to her roots...'

'Sir, that doesn't even make sense. I understand you're in a state of shock and grief, but these accusations are ludicrous. Besides, even if you did go to prison, you're still alive. You would still inherit the place...'

'And what is stopping you lot from getting me killed in prison?'

'Good Lord, you're insane. Cut back on the Hollywood movies, sir. Goodbye.'

The phone went silent. Andrew screamed and threw it at the wall.

Chapter Thirty

Susan woke up sweating under the thin summer sheets. Two hours had passed since the first rays of the sun invaded the dark room and conquered the darkness. Well, nearly all the darkness. Susan had grunted and ducked for cover.

The air-conditioning unit was off -a necessity in Greece from May until late September. Under the flowery sheets, Susan gasped for fresh air, and with her still tired legs, she pushed the bed covers from her hot body. Her sweat had mingled with droplets of blood, and Susan stared at the sheets in despair. 'I should just burn this fucker down.' She rubbed her temples with considerable force. 'You, stupid brain, deserve the headaches,' she grumbled as she dragged her feet across the floor and headed to the bathroom for her morning routines. She needed to feel normal again. To feel human and not this unrecognizable excuse that stood before her, facing her from the mirror.

Her favorite day dress was chosen to fall upon her aching body. She loved her black dress with the red flowers that fell to the right length -an inch above her knee. She always smiled when she wore it. Mostly because she remembered how the possession was bought at half-price from a winter sale at Marks and Spencer. Thirty-five pounds and she adored it more than others worth multiple times more.

Susan pulled her red hair back in a tall ponytail. Her clear face in the mirror spread a smile from ear to ear. 'No more letters! No hallucinations today!'

Just then, as she spoke to herself in a whispery manner, she realized how quiet the house was. She slowly walked up to the door, opened it, and stepped outside to the corridor. All doors were open.

'Hello? Kids?'

Silence.

Susan walked past each room. Empty rooms welcomed her as she went.

Susan fastened her pace and headed downstairs. 'Sophia? Christopher? Maya?'

She had to pause as she was sure she was about to call out Eugene's name as well.

'Andrew?'

Silence.

Absolute silence. She hated it.

Susan scratched her shoulder and looked around. 'If I don't see anyone, how do I know I am not dreaming again?' She rushed for the front door. 'Kids? Good morning!' she shouted as she stepped outside to the bright world of the realm of the sun. A glorious Greek July day. Not a soul to be seen. Nor human nor any part of the animal kingdom. Susan bit her bottom lip and returned inside.

A door opening, gently squeaking on its old hinges, broke the mansion's abundance of silence. Susan watched as the basement's door moved along until it was wide open. Susan took in a deep breath and exhaled loudly. She took small steps ahead. Steps could be heard from the darkness below. Susan remained in the doorway. 'Eugene?'

Silence.

The lights came on.

Susan ground her teeth and down the creaking steps she went.

Outside, under the shade of Christopher's favorite tree, the Fotopoulos trio was enjoying their morning. A checkered tablecloth lay down above the short grass, and empty plastic plates bore witness to a breakfast picnic that had come to an end. With their tummies filled, the children indulged themselves in favorite activities. Anything to keep themselves busy. Anything to remain away from the house longer. Sophia sat on the edge of the reddish cloth, and with her cat curled up between her legs, she played on her phone, moving around furniture in her Sims's three-bedroom house. Maya, glad that the gardener with the familiar face had not yet appeared, ran around the field, chasing colorful butterflies and collecting wild flowers. 'I want one of each color,' she declared. 'I hope you mean the flowers,' Sophia joked without raising her eyes from her cell's screen.

'So that's what it truly means!' Christopher yelled happily as he stood up from his bench, Iliad in hand.

'What means what, bookworm?' Again, her eyes did not move.

'Φοβοῦ τοὺς Δαναοὺς καὶ δῶρα φέροντας.'

'You know I don't read Greek like you do, but I'm sure you're reading that wrong. You sound funny.'

Christopher could not resist an eye roll. This time Sophia had lowered her phone. She chuckled as she saw her brother. It felt like the old days. Happy days. Before Greece. Before Eugene.

'It's ancient Greek. It translates roughly into beware of the Greeks that bear gifts. A priest of Troy was warning the Trojans about the wooden horse the Greeks had left as a gift to their city.'

Sophia clicked her tongue with a raise of her right eyebrow and stroked Olivia. 'And why are you so excited about that?'

'Wow. You pay a lot of attention, huh? It is written above the library. I thought it was a weird thing to have written by Greeks in their own home.'

'And what does it mean?' Sophia said, returning to her game. A tone of boredom came back to her voice.

'It means that sometimes when we are presented with a gift, we should be wary. Dangers could be lurking. I love the idea that it is above the library door. Books are powerful, aren't they?'

Sophia nodded. 'Yes, they could put you to sleep or bore you to death. Especially the brick-sized ones you carry around.'

'Shallow and basic, as always.'

Sophia stuck out her tongue and raised her fist. 'Look a gift for you. Oh, no. What's this?' she asked as she raised her middle finger. 'Beware of my Greek screw-you finger! Beware!'

Their laughter spread out around the beautiful valley.

'Seven different colors,' Maya shouted and raised her bouquet in the air. Both of her siblings smiled and gave her a thumbs-up.

Happiness. Before Greece. Before Eugene.

Their brightness was in complete contrast to Susan's surroundings. As she approached the statues, amazed by how she had no knowledge of their existence, the lights went out.

Susan sniggered. 'Thank you, Lady Luck. Cheers, you bitch.' Susan reached out. Her fingers tapped against a statue's chest. She took a step forward. She had to get back to the stairs. Pitch-black ruled the basement. Nothing was visible as she took another step forward. Susan could not make out what caused her to trip, but she knew the blow to her already injured head was a heavy one. Disoriented and in anguish, she rolled on her back and remained on the dusty floor. Just as her heartbeats returned to normal, and she was willing to have another attempt for the savior switch by the stairs, she felt it. Him. Them. A touch on her hand, a man's heavy breath by her left ear, and two hands holding her ankles. Gasping, Susan sat up only to be forced back down.

'Let me go!'

She screamed like never before. Thunderous yells that did not stop the hands from holding her down. Strong hands holding down her head, her arms, her chest, her thighs, and her feet. She could hear them breathing. She sensed them moving around. She wished she wasn't in too much pain to struggle more. Her body swayed from side to side. Every time she tried to wiggle free, the hands used greater force. Her every twitch was drowned by their strength.

'What do you want from me? Let me go. My...'

She paused. The last thing she needed to mention to the intruders was her kids. '...my husband will be home soon.'

Just then, the hands grabbed a hold of her clothes. Piece by piece, they ripped off her dress. She wore no bra. The hands began to move across her chest. Susan felt helpless. Soon, a tongue journeyed upon her skin reaching her nipples. Two sets of teeth bit down gently. Susan felt dirty. Violated. She screamed for help. The group did not stop. Soon, many male voices began to chant. Weird, distorted sounds in an unrecognizable language. Sounds that were similar to those she had heard in the narrow tunnels below the Necromanteio. The men sang in complete unison. More tongues fell upon her body. One on her neck, and the other around her ear. Susan wept and trembled. '*How many are down here with me?*'

One by one, all pieces of clothing were removed from her body. Bare and in total darkness, she closed her eyes as she sensed the first fingers rush up her leg. 'Stop, please. Stop.' The fingers were now inside her. She tried begging in Greek. The chanting only grew louder. Then, she felt a naked man lay down upon her. He was heavy. Susan let out a small cry of pain as the man forced himself in her. She was completely dry. And utterly terrified.

'I have Aids.'

Susan had always stated that if she was ever going to be raped that would be her first line. Her mother's voice echoed in her mind. 'Stop going jogging in the park. It's not safe. Not safe for young girls. Rapist and killers lurk.' Susan would laugh. 'At six in the evening, Mum? I'm pretty sure the rapists are still having tea. Anyway, I will just shout that I have aids, and no one will rape me. Especially in this outfit and in the sweat I'm going to build up.'

The man grunted and shook. Susan could not believe that he came inside her. Now she did fear for STDs. It was the middle of her cycle. As the next man lay on top of her, she feared an unwanted pregnancy. The second man was rough. He slammed into her with force. He pulled her hair. He wanted to hear her cries. He fed off her pain.

A third man followed. Susan's mind escaped the dark room. It journeyed back in time. She remembered an article she had read about a young Chinese girl that was kept imprisoned in a basement by Japanese soldiers. The teenage girl was savaged by sixty-eight men. Sixty-eight! Susan wondered about her final number, and her mind came back to the room.

'Just one more to go, Mummy!'

'Eugene?'

'There are only four male statues. Oh, goodie. The third one is done. One more to go.'

Susan sobbed and wished she could see him. She did not care about the pain anymore. She did not know which pain was aching more. Her insides? Her cuts and bruises? Her soul? She no longer cared.

'Eugene?'

'Yes, Mummy?'

'This is the final letter, right?'

His giggle was gold. 'Aha! Clever mummy. Figured out the word, have you?'

'Admit.'

'And will you? Will you tell Daddy?'

Susan nodded even though she knew it was dark. 'I promise,' she said. 'Now, can you do something for me?'

'Anything and everything, Mummy dearest.'

'Sing to me until the men leave.'

The chanting stopped and Eugene's angelic voice filled the room.

Got a spark inside my soul,
Ignited flame, I'm losing all control

The speedometer is broken, see it soar
I'm knocking down every door, I'm ready for more

Don't wait for the break, no, I'm already there
My spirit's soaring high up in the atmosphere
This feeling's got me on the fast track, zero to bliss
Catch the rhythm, feel the magic, don't miss this!
I'm a comet in the darkness, tearing through the black
No turning 'round, no, I'm never looking back.

Forget the slow lane, the engine's gonna scream
Living out loud, living out the wildest dream.

The fourth man pulsed out of her and all hands let go.
Eugene's voice journeyed farther and farther away until she could hear him no more. The lights came back to life and so did Susan. She sat and stared down between her bruised legs. Blood and sperm were running out of her.

Her eyes looked up. On the statue closest to her, a bloody T was written upon his chest.

'Admit,' she whispered. 'Admit.'

Chapter Thirty-One

MESOPOTAMOS

1914

His fist ran straight through the weak wood. Multiple splinters entered his hand. Gregory growled in anger. It felt good to be able to express himself. To express any sort of emotion. He was alone in his self-built little shed on the outskirts of their property. He punched the wall again, leaving behind stains from his blood. There were years when praying would have had the same soothing and calming effect. Those years were gone.

He had been a happy child. Joyful in his mother's caring arms.

He had been a happy priest. Merry in the Lord's wide embrace.

He had been a happy man. Ecstatic next to Iphigenia's warm body.

His eyes remained still, focusing on the blood on the wood. It reminded him of a painting he had seen many years ago on a field trip with his theological school. He bit his lower lip and passed his bruised fingers through his hair. He was not used to misery. Unhappiness. He had left everything behind to be with the woman he loved. And more than anything, he desired to father children. But with the arrival of each month, his Effie would menstruate. And lately, intercourse had left the table completely. Iphigenia was unstable. Unable to concentrate, unable to hug him, kiss him, love him. A crazy woman roamed their palace, mumbling about visions and demons.

'We are cursed!'

Another punch. It wouldn't be his last.

He sighed and sat down on the bench he built to place under his favorite tree by his cherished rose bushes. He placed his bearded face in his hands and let the tears escape from his kind eyes. He breathed heavily. Too much gathered anger and despair. He pulled down his brown worn-in trousers. The ones he always wore when he worked with wood. He stroked the newly finished bench. He then pulled down his underwear and masturbated.

He masturbated violently.

Release did not take long to come. Naked as he was, he wept again.

Back at the house, Iphigenia had stepped out of the bathtub. She dressed quickly and went and sat on the second-to-last step of the spiral staircase.

'Where is he? Come on. Come on, priest. You're late for confession time.'

Iphigenia rocked back-and-forth and scraped her nails on the step. She tapped out tunes from her school years. Not that she had had many of those. Twelve years old was the last time she stepped into a schoolyard. Poor girls never stayed on longer.

Gregory heard her rattling around and mumbling, and

he stopped by the door. He took in a deep breath and held it in. The fresh country air carried the scent of blossoming citrus trees. It invaded his nostrils, and he could feel the orange flavor settle on his dry tongue. The door was unlocked, standing an inch away from its frame. Gregory placed his palm on it and pushed it open.

Iphigenia stood up, jumping up like a spring forced back. She played with her fingers and ran her teeth along her thin bottom lip.

'Effie, I've been thinking.' Gregory began pacing up and down, waving his hands around. 'It was a bad decision moving out here. We built a palace and filled it with expensive things. None filling our souls. We have loaded pockets and empty hearts. This life does not suit us, honey. My sweet girl, you are not yourself. We need to sell this place and head to an island. A small island like Spetses, Paros, or Santorini. Buy a cottage by the ocean. Let the endless blue ocean top up our eyes. Have little ones running around on the sand, throwing off their clothes and dashing for the waters...'

'I killed Giorgo.'

'And we can run after them, splashing around...' He stopped talking and turned toward her. He took four steady steps and towered her. 'What did you say?'

'I killed Giorgo!'

Gregory shook his head. 'I don't believe you. This is more of your mumble-jumbo crazy talk. How could you...'

'It was easier than I thought it would be. I poisoned him, you know? Watched him cough up his last supper and roll around on the floor. He called out for my help, and I just stood there. Satisfied, with a smile on my face through his whole ordeal. Happy to get rid of him. I was not sure if the poison killed him or not, so as soon as the streets were empty, I loaded him on the back of his carriage.' Iphigenia spoke quietly with a steady voice. She chuckled as she recalled pushing him out of the window onto the creaking carriage. 'Betrayed by his trusted donkey. He loved that beast more than me, I'll tell you that much. Yet, she carried him away. I took him out to the fields, passed the loop around his throat and tied the end to the donkey. And up and up, he went. That's when he woke up. I'm glad he did. Glad that he saw that it was me. The bitch he mistreated sent him to God...'

The word God was the trigger. Gregory raised his fist and punched her in the face. Iphigenia fell back and banged her head on the first step, coloring it crimson.

'Was he really suicidal, or did you make us all believe that? Make me believe that?'

Iphigenia did not reply. She touched her open wound and laughed hysterically at the sight of blood. Gregory picked up her feet and dragged her up the steps. Menacing voices awoke inside his head. 'Our whole life is a lie! You fouled me. Made me leave my church!' he shouted as her body left a red trail behind; a bloody carpet fitting for the spiral staircase. Iphigenia closed her eyes and welcomed the pain.

Punishment followed confession.

Gregory lifted her up and dropped her in the bathtub. Iphigenia opened her eyes and raised her head out of the cold water. Gregory grabbed her, his fingers squeezing into her neck. 'In the name of the Father, the Son, and the Holy Ghost, I banish your sins...'

'What are you doing?'

'Making sure we are not together in the next life.'

He pushed her under, watching as bubbles of air floated out of her. 'Heavenly Father, I, your humble servant, pray to you to ask for forgiveness for your tormented child. She did not know what she was doing. Save her. Take her into your loving arms.' Gregory opened his eyes and stared straight into hers. 'Iphigenia, you are forgiven of your sins by the light of our Lord, Jesus Christ, our savior.'

No more bubbles. No more struggling. He let go.

'Happy paradise.'

Iphigenia's lifeless body rose to the top of the now bloody waters. Gregory formed the sign of the cross on her forehead.

He slowly got off his knees and exited the room without looking back. 'Now, to make sure I go the other way.' Iphigenia's story inspired him to seek out the thickest rope they owned. He tied it to the grand chandelier by the spiral, passed the loop around his neck, and smiled. 'Satan takes in all murderers. Especially self-murderers...'

Gregory stood on the railing, closed his eyes, and stepped forward.

Chapter Thirty-Two

The sun approached the mountainous horizon and began its sky painting. Shades of pure orange spread out as the fiery ball started to hide. The three children gazed in silence. Not from amazement of Greek Nature's beauty, but with sorrow. Sadness of an obligational walk back home. They had stayed all hours of the sun outside. They ate, they played, they drank, they laughed, they drew, they chased, and they gathered. They were kids. Their despondency grew as the mansion appeared in their periphery, and they saw their mother pacing up and down outside, mumbling to herself.

Susan stopped her feet -and mouth- as she saw the three small figures come into view. If alcohol had taught her anything over the last few years, it was how to pretend to be normal when she was not. Susan controlled and tamed all her wild thoughts, pulled herself away from her plans, and calmed her twitching face. A widespread smile ran from ear to ear like a glowing pearl necklace, decorating her below her serene eyes. The kids were taken aback by the loving mother that rushed toward them, hugging them and kissing them. 'How was your day in the sun, my lovelies? Finished your book, my smart young man?'

The children murmured their replies.

'Where's Dad?' Sophia finally asked, raising her voice.

Susan had no clue. 'Helping the police with their investigation, my dear. Sweet Penelope has yet to be found. Fingers crossed; fingers crossed.' Susan's face hurt from the intense smiling. Her fingers twitched, and she felt the need to scratch, to go over things for the millionth time in her head. To yell. She could still feel the men's dirty hands upon her naked body.

Their tongues sliding on her shivering skin.

Their manhood inside her.

'*Focus. Control.*'

'Well, well, well. The sun is almost gone. Now, head inside. Wash your hands. Dinner is ready on the kitchen table. Enjoy. Roast chicken with golden potatoes, carrots and broccoli. Your favorite, Christopher.' She stroked the young boy's hair. She turned toward Sophia. 'I even found a jar of mint sauce.' She winked and shooed them inside.

'Aren't you eating with us?'

Susan remained outside. 'No, no, my dears. Mummy has a bit of a flu in her stomach. Go, go. Eat up, go up, shower, and off to bed. I want an early night from you lot tonight.'

The children stepped inside, and Christopher and Sophia exchange a worried look. 'Welcome to the twilight zone.'

'Don't joke, Sophia. She is mentally unstable. I saw her last night...'

'Cool it, Dr. Shrinkopoulos. Mentally unstable? Where did you read that?'

Christopher chuckled. 'Shrink-o-poulos. That's a good one, Sis.'

The divine aroma coming from the kitchen lured them in. Three sets of plates were already placed, while the food sat covered in tin foil in the center of the table. A bottle of lemonade stood at the end, surrounded by two glasses and one red plastic cup. A note lay by the covered glass tray of vegetables. ICE-CREAM IS IN THE FRIDGE. AS DESSERT THOUGH. EAT YOUR DINNER, AND **THEN** HAVE A SERVING.

It was written in all caps. It began with tidy letters but by the third sentence, the lines wobbled as they tried to form readable letters. The children did not read much into it. Their tummies grumbled as their nostrils and eyes were invaded with the uncovering.

None checked on their mother, though they obeyed her every word.

Eat.

Go up.

Shower.

Bed.

Susan's schedule was followed.

Soon, goodnights were exchanged as Christopher left the girls in Sophia's room and headed back to his. An hour later, the lights went out.

Susan still wandered around outside. 'Admit. Admit. Admit. I knew this time would come!'

The July night chill that roamed the valley spread out and fell upon her skin. Susan rubbed her arms. 'I'm a London girl, honey. I feel no cold.'

Yet, when Zephyrus, named after the god of the west wind, invaded, carrying with him the sharpness of the sea, Susan walked back into the house. She closed the door silently behind her and took steady steps toward the spiral staircase. She sat down on the second step and gazed at the door. 'Where is he? Come on.'

Susan looked down at her trembling fingers and quickly locked them in a fist of a prison. Calmness did not come. She started to tap out tunes from careless years. Nothing worked. '*I need a drink.*'

'Don't be stupid, Suzie. Don't blow it, now. This is the night your soul has been yearning for.'

'Mum, I need it.'

'No daughter of mine is a junkie.'

'Mum, don't say that. People with drinking problems are not junkies...'

She paused and looked upstairs. Darkness and silence. She was not sure if she was talking to herself inside her mind of talking out loud.'

'*Get a grip, Suz!*'

The hands on the ticking clock in the corner met at twelve. Susan gazed at it in dismay. She stood up and yelled without a sound. She mimicked every movement, yet produced no scream. She then sighed and declared defeat.

'He isn't coming.'

She turned and began to ascend the spiral.

Chapter Thirty-Three

The last night

Andrew often joked that he had an autistic memory.

Susan hated that joke. 'Just say photographic memory. It's offensive the way you say it.'

Yet, with a walk to the toilets going past the nurses' and doctors' board of routines and with a day's observation, Andrew had figured out the perfect time and perfect route to escape. He was no longer connected to any life-support machinery, and during the night, the guard locked him in his room and hardly stood outside. Snacks and cigarettes prevailed over his sense of proper duty.

Andrew crawled out of his bed at eleven o'clock sharp. Right after nurse Eleni's rounds. He quietly opened the window and stepped out onto the quite large ledge. '*The trick is not to look down.*' Words of wisdom provided by his father on an excursion to Vikos gorge on a fine spring day in 1970.

Andrew slid his feet across the dirty ledge, kicking mostly

pigeon droppings as he made his way to the window of the room next door. The patient checked out late that evening, and no other was due. The cleaner had it on her list for cleaning at ten o'clock. Mopping and opened windows went hand-in-hand. Soon, his filthy feet soiled the clean floor.

Nurse Eleni had not finished her night round yet. Andrew counted on that. He needed her car keys. She wouldn't be in need of her car till sunlight. Enough hours to head back to the house, get Susan and the kids, drive over the border to Albania, fly home, and get a lawyer to deal with the town's scam. '*Sell the property and sue their asses! Kaching!*' he thought as he took her keys from her red bag at the nurses' station.

In the dimly lit underground parking, a Peugeot 206 flashed its lights as Andrew pressed upon the key's unlock button. It was parked behind a row of BMWs and Mercedes. 'Greek doctors and their luxury German cars,' he whispered as he dashed to the white vehicle.

In a matter of minutes, he was free, set on the open road.

By midnight, he had arrived home.

Susan was about to take the last step to the top floor and drag her tired, aching body to bed when she heard the car engine grunting outside. Andrew dashed up the steps to the front door while Susan hurried down, back in her waiting position. The heavy door opened slowly, and Andrew appeared behind it.

A long moment of silence followed as they both stood starring at each other. Relics of the healthy people that they once were. Andrew pushed the door closed as quiet as he could.

'Are the kids asleep?'

'The kids are fine. Been sleeping for hours. Where the hell have you been? Is that a hospital gown?'

That night, the last night for the Fotopoulos family at the house could have been different if Andrew had only answered 'heart attack.' Susan would not have revealed the dark secrets of the past. Yet, he pushed a flat smile and waved his hand.

'Nothing to worry about. I crashed on a tree. I was driving to the morgue. I was in a right state and lost control. They wanted to keep me in as a precaution, but my place is here.'

Susan exhaled loudly and covered her eyes. She shook her head. 'Morgue? Penelope is dead?'

'Apparently, she has been dead for a week.'

Susan felt the need to scream. More weird thoughts. More strange happenings. Her remaining normal side wanted to ask for details. It wanted to hug her husband and tell him off for leaving the hospital at this ungodly hour. Yet, his words fed her paranoia more. Made her inner voices sure of their choice. Her fingers began to twitch as she built up the courage.

Andrew watched as his wife remained at a distance, both in body and in spirit. 'Is something the matter?' he asked as he took a few steps forward. That was when he noticed the bruises on his wife's face and arms. He rushed toward her. 'What happened to you?' Susan placed both her palms on his chest. 'We need to talk. There is something I need to... admit.'

'Admit?'

'Please, step back. I... I can't think... process... with you so near.'

Andrew took a reluctant step back while Susan went up

a step. With her eyes lowered, she spoke softly. 'Remember when I was pregnant with Maya?'

Andrew nodded. 'Is this really the time to dig up events laid to rest?'

'Please, don't speak for the next five minutes. Just fucking listen for once in your life.'

Andrew raised his hands. 'Okay, Suz. Go on. The stage is yours.'

'*Sarcastic, smug prick.*'

'Sshh.' Susan wasn't sure if that was aimed at him or her inner voices.

'I had blood from the get-go. Sex was off the table. That is when you and that brunette with the beady eyes got close. What was the whore's name? Julie. Yeah, that's it. Julie from the office.'

'Susie, I came clean about the affair. I left nothing out. I ...'

'Shut up, Andrew. This isn't about you. Your affair pushed me so far down, the bottom of the barrel was my ceiling. I gave birth knowing you were fucking someone else. Depression doesn't cut it to explain how I felt. I began drinking. A lot. Every day. I hid it well from you and the kids. I was out of my face when we had the talk. How you were sorry, how you broke it off, and how it was just a meaningless fling. You think if I was sober, I would have ever forgiven you? Ever agreed to another kid just to save our family...'

Susan scratched the railing. The words gathered yet could not escape easily.

'Susan, my mother is dead, and I am in pain. You are a mess. Let's get some sleep, and we can go over...' His cold voice finally came out. His fingers formed loose fists. He was losing his patience.

She raised her voice. 'I was drunk the night he died.'

'What?'

'It was the night you and the kids stayed at my aunt's house in Nottingham. You drove up there for a business meeting, remember? I... I downed two bottles of chardonnay as a starter. Eugene was sleeping peacefully, and I was all alone. I called my aunt, and she said the kids were all sleeping and that you had gone out to the pub with my cousin, Peter. I... pictured you meeting someone, flirting, dancing. I continued drinking. Bottle after bottle to get you out of my head.'

Andrew shook his head. 'Irrational little Susan. Playing stupid images inside her head...'

'Eugene started crying. I went to him. Comforted him. My head was heavy, drowsy. I gave him milk in case he was hungry. Can't remember if I heated it or gave it to him cold. I have no memory of him drinking it. I tried to change him. Slapped on a sloppy diaper. He just wouldn't stop crying. By that point, he was screaming. Then, it hit me. He was cold. I turned up the heater. I must have turned it up too much. And I just kept on covering him up. I thought I was doing the right thing. Blanket after blanket, I stacked them on his little body. He began to quiet down. I tucked them in tightly and put a few pillows around him...'

Andrew was now standing right opposite her. 'What are you saying?'

'I showered and when I came out, it was so quiet. My head was lighter. I went to check on him and the pillows were on his head...'

'Go on!'

'He wasn't breathing. I called for an ambulance and removed all the pillows and blankets. The paramedics... the paramedics told me... he... he was dead. I killed him. I killed Eugene.'

Andrew had never punched anyone or anything as hard as he punched Susan that night. Susan took the blow and fell back. Andrew knelt above her and wrapped his hands around her neck.

'Squeeze harder,' she begged. 'I deserve to be punished. I thought I was going to be arrested that night, but the doctors told us he had a weak heart and mild breathing problems and...'

Another punch. Andrew's hands returned to her throat. She did not struggle.

'The itchy bitchy spider...'

'Eugene? Eugene?' She gasped for air.

'It's okay, Mummy. In a minute, you will be here with me, forever.'

'What do you mean, baby?'

'Die in the house, stay forever in the house. Soon, we will be together. Don't struggle, Mummy. Let him choke you. He doesn't love you. He never did. He cheated on you. We don't need him. We don't want him.'

'But, what about your sisters? Your brother? I want them. I want them with us.'

Silence.

'No mummy. They have all their lives to live...'

'Die in the house, stay in the house.'

Andrew let go of her. 'What the fuck are you mumbling?'

'Die in the house, stay in the house,' she said and kicked him off her. Andrew fell back and felt his heart beginning to thumb against his chest. He couldn't stand up. From the corner of his eye, he watched as Susan walked into the kitchen and came back out with a crazy shine in her eyes and a sharp butcher's knife in her right hand.

As the pain spread, he struggled to speak. Susan walked straight past him and headed upstairs. 'Where... are ... you... going?'

'Die in the house, stay in the house.'

Olivia sat motionless and wearing well that feline not-caring look on the top step during their entire fight. Her devilish eyes opened wide as she saw Susan reappear with the knife in her hand. She sprinted for Sophia's bedroom, and with accuracy, she leaped onto the bedside table, stepping on the white iPod that was connected to the cylinder speaker. Some of Sophia's most prized possessions. Loud pop music boomed around the room awakening both girls in shock. With another tap from her front paw, peace returned to the bedroom. Enough peace for Sophia to hear her father's cries.

'Susaaaaan, leave the kids alone!'

Sophia ran to her door and peeked into the hallway. A crazy figure limping toward her frightened her. She immediately closed the door and locked it. Susan rattled the door handle.

'What's going on?'

'Nothing, Maya. Quick. Get up. Let's go scare Christopher. A prank. Yeah, a prank. Come on, get up.'

Sophia took the little girl by the hand and climbed out of the window. A narrow balcony connected their room with Christopher's. His window was closed, but he was awake. Susan's banging on the girl's door was enough to pull him out of his adventures in ancient Greece. He led his forces into the battle of Marathon, securing a Greek victory and pushing the Persians back into the sea. A recurring dream for the young boy.

'She has a knife,' Sophia said as she passed Maya to her brother and rushed inside his dark, warm bedroom.

'We have to make a run for it. You will carry Maya and go ahead. I'll follow with my baseball bat. We run for the door and keep running. We are faster than her.'

The two siblings exchanged a look. Funny how both felt ready for this. How they felt that they knew that this day was approaching. As if they were just killing time until the day their mother's sanity finally passed the limit line and fell off the cliff.

Sophia picked up Maya and lay her head on her shoulder. 'Close your eyes.'

Christopher opened his door slowly. 'One, two, go,' he whispered. The two girls went ahead, and Christopher tiptoed behind them. They had made it to the stairs when the banging on the girl's door stopped.

'My babies, where are you going? Come to Mummy. Come. I have great news. Eugene is waiting for us. He is here. Don't you just miss him? Miss him terribly?'

Christopher looked back and saw his mother approaching slowly with her right hand behind her back. 'Sophia, run!'

Down the spiral, the three went with speed and without looking back.

'Kids, help me.' Their father lay on the ground with his hand upon his heart.

'Get Maya out of here. I'll be right behind you.' Christopher tried to pick up his father, but his old man was too heavy for his young arms.

'Chris, we have to go.'

A loud scream came out of a wild Susan as she jumped down the last stairs and stabbed Andrew in the center of his chest. Both children choked in shock, unable to process what they were witnessing. Sophia squeezed Maya against her, hoping her little sister did not see. Both walked backward toward the door.

Susan pulled out the knife and let loose a sinister laugh. It sounded disembodied as it echoed around the dark room. 'Where are you going, little ones? Your father always locks the doors behind him,' she said and rattled the front door keys that Andrew held in his palm.

With their backs against the door, they watched as their mother walked toward them. Drops of their father's blood fell off the blade's end.

Christopher took one look to his left. 'The basement door has keys on it. Go!' He pushed his shocked sister and raised his bat. Sophia ran to the basement door, taking its keys into her hand. 'Christopher, come on.'

Christopher swayed the bat before his mother. 'Stay back, you lunatic. We are your kids.'

'But that is why I want you with me. I love you...'

She said no more. Christopher hit her with all the force his small body could master, dropped the bat and ran to his sisters. They closed the door behind them and locked it.

Susan took a step back from the blow. She licked her bleeding lips and turned her attention to Andrew. He was coughing up blood. 'Oh, no mister. You're not dying in here,' she said and unlocked the front door. She carried her husband out and kicked his dying body down the porch's steps. She returned to the house and called out to her children. She begged them to open the door. Her patience lasted three minutes. She picked up Christopher's bat and began banging against the door.

'The old handle isn't going to hold long,' Sophia said.

They headed down the stairs, and to their surprise, the

statues were missing and where they once stood, a hatch door was opened.

'A secret passage!' Christopher said with excitement.

'To where?'

Bang. Bang. Bang.

'Do you care?'

Sophia shook her head, placed Maya on the ground, and climbed down the wooden steps. One by one, the kids ventured into the black hole and down they went. A well-lit tunnel awaited them. It seemed familiar.

'It is just like the walls of the Necromanteio.'

Bang. They heard the door give way. Sophia picked up her sister and ran. Christopher looked up and smiled at the closed hatchet door. He had locked it behind them. He crossed his fingers and ran after his sisters.

Their mother's cries and howling faded into background noise and diminished as they hurried down the tunnel. A cold wind roamed toward them, pushing off their sweat and cooling their red, panicked faces.

A gate ahead swung open, whining on its hinges.

'Wait. We saw this gate. It was closed when Persephone brought us here.' Christopher stopped and placed his hand on the rusty metal. He looked around at the other two open gates. 'It's the third gate. The one that leads to Hades. The underworld. Sophia, it leads to our house.'

Sophia stroked Maya's hair and smiled at her sister. 'Christopher, just get us out of here. You know *who* could be behind us.'

'This way!'

Soon, the Necromanteio's entrance was before them.

'Let's get out of here.'

As the three children stepped outside to the chilly

summer breeze of the hill, strong lights fell upon them, freezing them on the spot.

'Who's there?' a familiar voice called out to them.

'It's us. The Fotopoulos kids. I'm Christopher...'

The car lights were switched off. In the car park, under the moonlight, Harry, the taxi driver, stood in front of his car. Persephone was behind him, fixing her skirt and blouse. She quickly pushed back her hair and ran toward them.

'What are you three doing out here at such an hour? Did you use the passage way?' None answered her. Besides trying to catch their breath, they were trying to catch their scattered thoughts and shake away their fear. 'Harry, we have to take them home...'

'No!' they shouted back in unison.

'Our mother has gone crazy. She killed our dad and came after us with a knife,' Sophia managed to say.

A single cloud passed above blocking the moonlight, and an owl hooted as its eyes shone in the dark. Persephone opened her arms and took the two girls into her warm embrace. 'It's okay, my dear. You are safe now.'

'I will drive you to the police station. They will keep you safe. Get you back to England. You have relatives to pick you up, take care of you, right?'

Christopher nodded. 'Aunt June.'

Persephone sat in the back seats with the girls, never letting go of them while Christopher sat in front with a worried Harry. They drove in silence until they reached the outskirts of the sleeping village. 'Erm, kids? Err, I will park down the road from the station and you will walk from there.'

Christopher looked back at his sister.

'You see, Persephone and I are friends. Close friends.

But... err... her husband doesn't see it that way, and we would prefer to keep our night meetings a secret, you see?'

Persephone smiled brightly at them. 'Just say you walked here from the Necromanteio. Don't mention us, okay, my dears?'

Both kids nodded in agreement.

Harry switched off his lights and turned down a quiet, deserted road. He parked behind an old building that transformed into a grocery store during the day. The police station was next door.

'Thank you,' Christopher said and got out of the vehicle. Persephone stepped out with the girls. 'Now, my pretties. Be brave. Go in and tell the officer everything that happened at your house. You're safe now. And remember...'

'Don't mention you or Harry.'

'No, my dear. Well, that too. But remember, to live your lives to the fullest. It is tragically short, and you never know what the Gods have in plan for you. Now, go. My brave little girls.' She kissed them softly on their cold cheeks. Her lips were warm. Her aroma was mesmerizing. 'And, you, my brave knight.' Another kiss. On his forehead.

And off the three little ones went.

Chapter Thirty-Four

Police cadet Christos Nicolaou was busy on his phone. It never left his right hand -or so it seemed to his girlfriend. He was checking the basketball results. As always, he had placed a bet. And lost. He sat alone in the renovated 19th Century building, enjoying the cooling air from the newly-bought revolving fan. With his feet up, he picked up his frappe and brought the straw to his lips. The sound of the front door opening startled him. Sixty-two night shifts he had served up to that point, and zero was the number of people that had walked through the door. He lowered his phone and coffee, sat up straight, and looked over the wooden counter.

His eyes widened as he saw the three ashen children walk in, dressed in the pajamas. His eyes fell to their muddy slippers. He had never seen these kids before, and he was born and raised in the village.

He sat them down on the sofa reserved for cops only behind him, listened to their story while covering his absolute shock, and called to wake up his superiors.

He made them three hot chocolates and turned on the television for them. '*Thank God, for twenty-four-hour cartoon channels.*'

Across town, office Daniel Maniatis crawled out of bed and began to dress at speed. Officer Nicolaou's words rang in his head. 'Their mother killed their father. Stabbed him in front of them. She went after them...'

Daniel crept down his house's steps, picked up his keys, made sure his hand gun was secure on his belt, and dashed outside to his car.

Eight minutes later, his vehicle arrived at the Fotopoulos mansion. He switched off his engine, and with his firearm in his right hand, he stepped outside. The countryside was quiet. Too quiet. The house stood before him in complete silence. He switched on his flashlight, and that was when he saw the body of Andrew Fotopoulos, still on the ground. He walked steadily toward him, his eyes wary, scanning the perimeter. He knelt and placed two fingers on Andrew's neck. Dead. His eyes freakishly opened forever.

Daniel took slow steps and approached the front door. He pushed it open with his right leg.

'Hello? Mesopotamos Police! Hello?' He proceeded inside. 'Hello? Is anyone here?'

A noise came from his left. 'Show yourself,' Daniel commanded and turned his flashlight toward the direction of the rattle. A black cat with bloody lips sat upon a side table and was looking up at the light switch. Daniel turned on the lights. He gasped at the sight. 'Oh my God...' The three words travelled upon his choked breath.

Susan's body hung from the top floor railing. Her body swung gently by the spiral staircase.

A bizarre smile imprinted on her face forever.

Epilogue

2019

I wish to believe that I did my best to distance myself from the story. A true story is always had to tell, never mind being wrapped up in the center of it. What to leave in, and what to take out? Whose side to present? All? None? Was the supernatural element there or was it just a ten-year-old's vivid imagination? A boy's desperate reach into a pool of reasoning to come to terms with a deranged, grieving mother, a violent, distant, money-loving father, a senile grandmother, and the days of horror he and his sisters experienced that summer in Greece?

I searched for answers for years.

I was twelve when I first wrote down my memories of those days.

As a teen, I would beg Sophia to re-tell everything she remembered. But Sophia just wanted to leave the past behind. Buried. Deep under the vast lands in Mesopotamos.

I needed to unearth it though. Sometimes she would find the courage and mention details that she brought to the surface. Other times, she would curse and stop talking to me for weeks. I guess some things were too painful for her. I could see she was holding back. Especially about our life before Greece. 'Dad was a violent cheater, and mum was a drunk!' she once yelled at me and stormed off. Another time, it slipped out. Dad hit her too. I decided not to ask about that further.

Sophia never bought into the supernatural side of things. She believed me a fool for believing the mutterings of a mad-woman or all the nonsense she had written down on her phone's notes. As if our mother found bloody letters and talked with Eugene! Just the thought made her laugh. Sophia blamed the alcohol for it all.

Maya, on the other hand, believed that every single thing we experienced in the mansion was because of the Looker. She became obsessed with the idea. The idea of a demon-ghost figure haunting the house. Her bizarre eyes stared straight at me when she told me at the age of six that the Looker loved to play dress up. 'He was dad's builder, mum's lover, Sophia's cat, your gardener, and my friend.' I wish Maya was older at the time. I feel like she understood the house better than any of us, yet she was barely a child back then -now an unstable teen into the occult. Sometimes, she would remember details from those days, yet I did not recall most of her memories. Did she really say, 'She was not our grandmother, and anyway, he will be back in another form soon,' or was that line made up by a high teenager to further feed her beliefs? I chose to omit that piece of *evidence*.

I was always somewhere in the middle. Stuck between

the paranormal and the real. My books and the real world. My family's tragedy, and my desire for our pain to have a Greek mythological spin on it. Was my Persephone the queen of the underworld? My inner Greek geek surely hopes so, though my sanity fears such notions.

I finished school last summer and when all my friends were presented with the dilemma of starting university immediately in September or taking a year off to travel the world, I had already settled on my plans. I booked my tickets to Greece the following day. Alone, I repeated the journey we took back in 2010.

My fluency in Greek helped me with the local police. Unfortunately, Officer Daniel Maniatis died from cancer during a cold winter in 2016. His wife left for Athens. Locals said they heard that she remarried a rich widow down there in the big city. However, I was allowed access to the case file and to local newspaper articles that were not available online. Most details were known to me. Some assisted memories in floating to the surface. The general census, also known as gossip here in the meadows of Greece, was that my father was responsible for his mother's death. Everyone loves a good story, and a good adventure is only as powerful as its heroes and its villain. Their words painted Penelope as the kind-hearted Greek yiayia (*grand-mother) and Andrew as the foreign son who came for her riches. Police officer Maniatis even stated in his report that he believed that it was my father who was messing with my mother's head to get rid of her without having to give up half of his inheritance. A lady from the nursing home seconded his thoughts, even going so far as to call my father unstable. I never had such bad memories of my father. It was a hard pill to swallow. The thoughts kept me up on that hot July night.

The following morning -a bright summer day similar to the one that welcomed us to the country all those years ago- I splashed water upon my face and gazed upon my reflection. I felt like that young boy again. Before he lost his childhood, his innocence, and his parents. A boy ready to return to places he never thought he would. I sat in my Ford rental for a good twenty minutes before turning the ignition key. In a matter of minutes, the hill housing the Necromanteio entrance rose from the horizon and dominated my view. Vivid colors painted everything in my periphery, yet the hill seemed dark, distant and unwelcoming. I parked in the visitors parking, flashbacks from that last night playing in the back of my mind. I could see those three helpless, scared children coming out of the darkness again and again. The site had not yet opened for the public. Too early, you see. Yet not too early for the tour guide to be in. A lone car at the end of the parking area revealed so much.

'Persephone? Persephone?' I called out as I stood behind the closed gate. A figure appeared in the dimly lit entrance. She was coming out. My heartbeat accelerated. I wondered if she had maintained her beauty. I wondered if she would remember me. I wondered if she could help shed some light as she did down those narrow corridors. The woman came out into the light and strolled toward me.

'We are closed, sir. Opening in ten minutes if you don't mind waiting,' the elderly woman said. The short, rather plump, silver-haired lady was in her late sixties, maybe even early seventies. She was also definitely not my Persephone. 'Sir? Sir?'

Disappointment.

'Err, I was looking for Persephone? She used to work here as a guide?'

'There is no Persephone working here. When was this?'

'2010?'

The lady tilted her head. 'Oh, I have only been here the last few years. Wanted something to boost my income. Pensions are awful nowadays. Crisis and all.'

'Do you know anyone that could tell me where to find her? Are you from Mesopotamos? Persephone would be in her...'

'My boy, I was born and raised here. Never had a Persephone in our village.'

She read the disappointment on my face. 'Who are you? Your Greek is excellent, yet you look too white to be from around here, if you don't mind me saying so. My grandkids are always telling me that I am, how do they put it, politically incorrect.'

'Christopher. Christopher Fotopoulos.'

She took a step back.

'And you were here in 2010, you say?'

I nodded.

'You're one of the Fotopoulos kids, right? Andrew and Susan's son.'

I sighed. 'I guess our murderous story was quite the news in this small place, huh?'

She licked her lips and nodded in agreement. 'Have you been to the mansion?'

'I was planning on going there after here.'

'Be careful. The place is cursed. Ever since Iphigenia built it with stolen church money. Tsk, tsk, tsk. Talk about inviting the demons in.'

'Who?'

She focused on my youthful eyes. 'Wait here. I've a book for you to read. I have no idea how it ended up here. It is Father Gregory's diary. Written before his suicide. It is kept here in our museum artifacts. I will lend it to you.'

I scratched my forehead, my nails scraping along my sweaty skin. 'Is that allowed?'

She waved her hand. 'Oh, no one is here. You deserve to learn your house's history. You know, my heart shattered when I read your story. Losing both parents in such a way. No, no. You deserve to know.'

Soon, I returned to my car with the old diary in my hands. I switched on the engine. I needed the cold A/C. I read the entire diary in half an hour.

I now knew what had to be done.

History could not be allowed to repeat itself.

With the old book on my lap, I drove to the mansion. I stopped the car at the exact spot that Harry parked back then.

I took my laptop and exited the vehicle. I shivered at the sight of the house. I looked away. I walked down a path well known to me.

Every word came from the weight on my chest.

Every word I typed made the pain feel lighter.

I sit here on my bench writing my tale, searching for my catharsis.

The mansion watches from a distance as I write about it.

I've been here for days. I haven't dared to step a single foot inside its walls. I sleep in my rental, until every word is put down.

I must go now. The book is finished. I must walk up to the house.

I must enter inside and empty my gasoline tanks.

Writing the story is not enough. The mansion cannot continue to exist. The curse ends here...

I need release from it.

- Christopher A. Fotopoulos

Also by Luke Christodoulou

vinci-books.com/TheOlympusKiller

In the Greek islands, the gods aren't the only ones demanding sacrifice.

A sadistic killer stalks the Greek islands, murdering victims and posing them as "Olympian Gods." Captain Papacosta and Lieutenant Cara race to stop him before myth-fueled revenge claims more lives—and the Olympus Killer becomes unstoppable.

Turn the page for a free preview…

The Olympus Killer: Chapter One

The bright Greek sun had just sunk into the ocean.

It had been a beautiful sunset. The way the light jumped upon the waves, en-flaming the waters of Vathy Bay, was spectacular.

'Eye candy,' Stacy thought as she ambled past the colorful, little fishing boats, all lined up, waiting for their masters to arrive, before setting off for the night's late catch.

Stacy realized that this was the first time she had truly been alone since her divorce was finalized last week, back home in L.A. Her socialite friends had persuaded her to get away from it all and the very next day, they were on their way to the Greek island of Rhodes.

It was so quiet and peaceful by the rock where she had sat and stared at the full moon. She gazed upon the shadowy still ships sleeping on the dark horizon, before taking off her red Manolo Blahnik heels and carefully climbing down to lie on the golden sandy beach, isolated by the rocks from the rest of the world. All the aloneness felt a tad weird after being surrounded by crowds of every age and color imaginable, just a few days ago at Faliraki, Rhodes main club scene. After Rhodes, the gang headed to the island of Ko, where they continued to party hard. She smiled as she remembered them all lined up on the bar counter at Jackson's Beach Bar dancing the night away. Now, she was enjoying the serenity offered by the island of Samos. Jennifer, Ginger and the rest of the girls had done a terrific job taking her around the Greek islands – island-hopping as Ginger liked to call it - to help her forget him. Him. She wondered what 'The God' was up to at the moment. That's what everyone called him at the company.

'Hmm... to everyone but me,' she thought out loud. Deep down, certain feelings lingered in her, but she could no longer bear the pain of staying with him.

'Cheating bastard,' she said and closed her eyes.

'Beautiful night.' A voice from behind her interrupted her reverie.

Startled, she let out a brief scream as she leaped to her feet and turned towards the direction of the voice.

'I'm so sorry. I didn't mean to scare you,' the handsome, black-haired man rushed to say, the moonlight revealing his sparkling green eyes as it danced across his face.

'I don't scare that easily,' she replied, trying to catch her breath. 'You surprised me, that's all. How long have you been there?'

'Oh, I'm not a stalker,' he joked, mocking her with his smooth, relaxing voice. 'I come here to write.' His whole face lit up as he produced a silver Parker pen and a thin red notebook out of his backpack as evidence.

'So, you live here?'

'No, only been here a couple weeks. I'm on holiday too. Alone,' he pointed out. 'Tom Smith,' he said, stretching out his right hand.

'Stacy Anderson,' she replied. Her hand fitted perfectly into his. It felt strange using her maiden name again. Even stranger was the fact that she felt comfortable with this man she had just met. Ginger would have been so proud to see them sitting side by side in the sand, making small talk as the warm Aegean Sea caressed their feet.

'So, what are you writing about?' Stacy inquired.

'It's a *thriller!*' he announced, deepening his voice and taking on a scary tone. They both laughed. It had been a while since she had laughed and meant it.

'I love thrillers,' she said with flirtatious excitement.

It was the last thing Stacy Anderson ever said. As the knife hit her chest and penetrated her heart, Stacy tried to catch a breath and scream out, but Tom's left hand quickly covered her mouth. His right hand lifted the knife again and the blade flashed silver in the moonlight. Blood was dripping from its sharp end as he stabbed her again with more passion this time and with obvious exhilaration in his devilish green eyes. All seven hits were to her heart. Tom leaned in close and slowly unbuttoned her bloody shirt, taking his time before turning his attention to the button of her jeans.

He gazed upon her beautiful, naked body and gently touched her fake breasts. They were perfect; probably the best money could buy.

Then, with savage fury, he plunged the knife between Stacy's legs, burying it deep inside her, before slicing viciously upward. Tom stopped, pleased that the pomegranate in his bag would fit. He stood up, admiring his work. He then walked into the water and with a smile of satisfaction upon his face, Tom swam away.

The Olympus Killer: Chapter Two

8:47 and as always, here in Greece, I was early. I laughed at the thought that New York made me quick. Apparently, the years of being a homicide detective in the Big Apple had left their marks on me. Athens was a jungle too, but a smaller jungle than my previous one. Just an hour ago, I had received a phone call from one of the many charming secretaries down at Headquarters.

'Captain Costa Papacosta?'

'Yes?'

'Good morning,' she said with a dull tone and proceeded to inform me that the chief had requested to see me. My office down Athinon Avenue, where the crime investigations department was housed, would not be seeing me today. I had to be at Headquarters at nine o'clock sharp.

'What is this about?' I said as I managed to interrupt her fast flow of words. *We Greeks talk fast, but boy, this girl took the cake.*

'Be there at nine. Have a nice day, Captain,' she said, and the phone went silent.

Captain. I still haven't gotten used to being called Captain. Since I quit the NYPD two years ago, came back to my homeland and joined the force here, I had been Police Lieutenant Costa Papacosta.

It was still a step back from being a N.Y. detective and the money, believe it or not, was even lousier, but I did not care. I wanted to get away. Besides, life here is cheaper than back in the States and you actually get to see the sun every day.

9:12, the clock said, and I was still sitting in the badly-lit hallway on the top floor of the huge, grey building with the hundred little windows that was the headquarters of the Hellenic Police.

A few minutes later, a tall girl with huge brown eyes hidden behind strict, black, reading glasses, wearing a tight 'woman's suit' and a fake smile, informed me that the chief was ready to see me now.

'Was he preparing himself all this time?' I said and earned myself a semi-confused, semi-angry look as she did not register my attempt at a joke. Maybe the tight suit squeezed all the humour out of her body, leaving nothing behind but the perfect police secretary.

'Enter,' she said coldly and showed me the slightly opened door with her right palm.

The office was huge compared to my own and just a little smaller than my filthy, rented apartment down at Ampelokipous. It was fitted with outdated, worn-out, Persian designed carpets. On the surrounding walls were portraits of past presidents, prime-ministers, retired chiefs, maps of Greece and various police symbols. The desk was made out of thick, dark Acacia wood and everything upon it was tidied in military fashion. The only thing that looked remotely homey in the whole place was a colorful, hand-made frame with a photo of the chief at a younger age playing with his two boys.

'Sit down, Costa. We need to talk.'

I sensed a level of anxiety in his voice that I had never heard before. This was, after all, a man capable of scaring away Charo, the ferryman of the underworld himself! Well, at least that was what police officers joked about during very long coffee breaks.

'Good morning. What's this about, chief?' I asked as I slowly placed myself in the maroon armchair opposite his desk.

'Do you watch the news, Costa?'

'Most times... yes,' I replied, slightly puzzled while picturing myself in my boxers sitting on my black leather couch with a kebab in one hand and a cold Mythos beer in the other, killing lonely nights in front of the TV.

'What do you know about the murder in Chania five days ago?' he asked.

'American tourist. In his late forties. Multimillionaire CEO of a major pharmaceutical company in Chicago. On holiday in Crete with a young, hotter-than-the-weather twenty-year-old. Also American. He was found dead a few kilometers away from his hotel in the outskirts of Chania. He was completely naked, tied to a tree, stabbed...'

'Stabbed? Now there's an understatement! His whole stomach and head were cut open with his guts hanging out all over the place,' the chief interrupted. He then asked in a slightly calmer tone, 'and what do you know about the murder in Samos three days ago?'

'Again, an American tourist. Early thirties. Rich, and if I may add, beautiful blonde woman. Police found her, naked on the beach, also stabbed.' As I answered, I realized the similarities, so the chief's next words did not shock me.

'It was the same killer, Costa.'

'And what facts do we have to base this on?' I asked.

'Always the Yankee detective,' the chief said, smiling at me. 'The two were married until a week ago. A young lieutenant down in Crete made the connection. You see, the woman was using her maiden name. Got the lab results too, this morning and it confirmed that the two were struck by the same blade. The lieutenant's name is Ioli Cara; she will be waiting for you in Crete tomorrow.'

Now his words shocked me.

'What? What do I have to do with all this?'

The chief looked straight at me and spoke with the tone of a father explaining to his son that some things in life we have to do whether we like them or not.

'You were a homicide detective in New York. You have seen freaky shit before.'

'Freaky shit? Sir, I don't...'

'We kept the gruesome details out of the media,' he admitted and took a deep breath that ended with a long sigh.

'The man's head was cut wide open and his brains were carved in half.'

He gazed at me to check that he had my full attention and added, 'the sick bastard even tore open the woman's vagina and placed a pomegranate inside her.'

'A what?'

'You heard me, Papacosta! It's July. There are more tourists on the islands than locals. The victims were American, and any potential witnesses will most likely be tourists. I want you on this. End of discussion. Get your flight details from Helen outside and keep me informed.'

Before I could say anything more, I was in my car, plane ticket and case files on the back seat of my second-hand, black Audi A3, on my way home to pack.

The Olympus Killer: Chapter Three

Olympic Airlines flight 308 landed at nine in the morning at the small airport of Crete's second largest town, Chania. I dislike flying as I am quite a tall guy at 6'foot or 1.84 meters as we would say here in Greece and I have broad shoulders, so the tiny space these airplanes call seats are a nightmare to me. Thankfully, this was no transatlantic flight, but a fifty-five minute 'up-have a drink-here are some stale nuts-down' kind of flight.

I picked up my black Samsonite bag and rolling it behind me, I exited the building.

Ioli Cara was not what I was expecting. Don't get me wrong, Greece has some of the most beautiful women I have ever seen in my life, it's just that you don't find many of them working homicide cases.

She was tall, nearly as tall as I was and that perfect kind of slim. It was not the 'too-slim' that turned me off (not judging, just a personal preference), but that healthy, athletic slim.

Her name definitely did her justice.

252

Ioli was a mythological princess and Cara meant black in Turkish. She had long, shampoo advert, shiny, black hair, dark, seductive eyes and sun-kissed skin.

I sound so Greek, explaining meanings of words. Greece is definitely winning my American side.

Ioli must have been at least fifteen years younger than me, in her early thirties. As she walked over confidently in her tight blue jeans, I could see the men —and most women— around us, turn and steal a quick look.

'Captain Papacosta?'

I nodded with a smile.

'Ioli Cara. I've been waiting for you. My car is over there,' she said and turned towards her car.

'*No handshake?*' I thought as I whispered a 'nice to meet you too' and followed her, trying not to stare at her figure and come off like some dirty old man. Having tucked my luggage in the back, I sat in the passenger seat of her navy-blue Opel Corsa. Ioli placed her hands firmly on the wheel and asked, 'do you want to go straight to the police department or do you first want to pass by the B&B we have booked for you to... freshen up?' as she looked at my unshaven face, my messed up hair, my deprived of sleep eyes and my scruffy looking grey suit.

'Take me to where the body was found.'

'Straight to business. My kind of guy,' she said, smiling and put on her black shades from Madonna's D&G collection. Mindless details but I have an obsession of knowing the makes of things.

Chania was a fifteen-minute drive away. We drove through town and headed towards the beach and the luxurious, five-star hotel of Antlantica Kalliston Resort and Spa.

'This is where Eric Blair stayed. The body was found five minutes away, over those hills.'

'Let's go to our crime scene then.'

Just a few moments later, we were in front of an enormous, thick-trunk oak tree. There were no buildings in sight. A hardly used dirt road led to the spot and as the murder occurred at night, the killer must have had Eric to himself.

I ducked under the police tape, took a few short steps forward and stopped to process the scene. My eyes started to scan the area. Stains of blood were scattered all over the ground and spatter from the blow to the head had painted part of the oak dark red. Besides the blood, there was nothing really else to imply that some wrongdoing took place here. Ioli stood patiently, a few steps to my side, examining my method or so I hoped. I closed my eyes, rebuilding the area in my head as I tried to picture the killer's movements. He must have been quite strong to have lifted Blair's body and then carried it up to the oak tree. Did he give a sedative to the victim or did he make him walk up to the tree and then tied him up?

I turned towards Ioli. 'So, Lieutenant Cara, you were the first officer to arrive at the scene, walk me through everything that you saw. Leave no details behind. There are no insignificant details when it comes to murder.' I did not intend on sounding so uptight.

'The body was found early Thursday morning by an elderly couple passing by on the way to their farm. The poor old woman broke down in shock and had to be hospitalized for the day. Thankfully, the old man had a cell phone and found the courage to call it in. I arrived ten minutes later. It was like nothing I had ever seen before...' She paused as to gather herself emotionally and then started to describe what she had seen. I just stood there, taking everything in and scribbling down the main facts in my small black notepad. I did not want to interrupt her at the moment with questions. I needed her to be my eyes to something that I did not witness.

'... the man was completely naked and tied to the oak by two pieces of thick rope. One piece was around his legs at knee height and the other piece was around his chest.'

She stepped up close to me and placed her index finger on my stomach. 'He was cut wide open from here to here,' she said as she ran her finger all the way across my beer belly. 'It was revolting. His guts were hanging out. Pieces from his insides had fallen to the dirt and were already filled with flies and a few worms. But the worst was the head. It looked like it had taken a blow from an axe. It was cut right open and you could clearly see that the brain had been carved in half. This is one sick fuck of a killer if you ask me.'

She stopped and looked at me to catch a reaction and as I did not move a facial muscle, she took in a small, soundless breath and continued.

'We found nothing else. And I mean nothing. It was so fucking frustrating. Not a single hair, not a single fingerprint, not even a goddamned footprint in the dirt.'

I looked down and noticed many footprints around the scene. Ioli quickly remarked that when she arrived, the whole area from the road to the tree had been raked to perfection. The footsteps belonged to fellow officers and the paramedics that took away the body.

'I obviously took pictures of everything and checked the grounds for evidence before allowing them near,' she continued and went on to state that she had a fellow officer working on a list with tourist rental cars, but so far nothing suspicious had come up.

'Good job, Cara. Did you personally speak to the girl-friend?' I asked.

'Yeah, I questioned the *girlfriend*,' she said.

'Girlfriend?' I repeated, imitating her tone and rolling of the eyes.

'Well, I wouldn't call her that, to be honest!'

'And what would you call her then?'

'She was a slutty, young, would-have-been-a-prostitute if not so gorgeous, woman. Clearly with him for his money. I mean, the guy wasn't that great looking, he was married until last week and was old enough to be her father.'

This girl sure did have a tongue on her. I realized that even though I had just met her, I liked this girl's attitude. We Greeks do swear a lot, but I was never good at the *sport*. Mama's training had worked well. Whenever a 'gamoto' used to slip from my adolescent mouth, a firm strike from mama's right hand would find me on the back of my head, followed by the line 'no need for language, young man.' I remember sitting on the stairwell of our apartment block in Astoria, New York, telling my mate Jimmy about mama's views on swearing. Jimmy looked at me like I was from another planet. 'Fuck. It's just a fucking word. It's even in the fucking dictionary, if you don't fucking like it, then fuck off,' he said and we both burst out laughing. Quite the char-acter that Jimmy. He was also, like most kids in our neigh-borhood, the proud offspring of Greek immigrants. We grew up together and both of us joined law enforcement. Jimmy was now an FBI agent; 'just like in the movies,' as his mother Toula proudly announced to everyone she met.

'His escort, one Lizzie McAdam, aged 21, reported that Eric had gotten out of bed after intercourse, had a shower, got dressed and said that he was going for a walk down at the beach to smoke a cigar. That was the last time she saw him. She woke up the next morning and realized that he had never returned.'

I flicked through the crime scene photographs that Ioli had given me as we exited her car. I looked at the close up of Eric's hand and noticed the faint yellow color on his fingers and nails. Clearly a daily smoker. 'Is she still here?' I asked.

'No, we let her go after questioning. The security cameras from the hotel showed them both entering their room and only Eric was recorded leaving a couple of hours later. The suite was on the top floor, so she could not have left the room from the balcony. Anyway, she hardly knew the guy, was too petite to have carried him and to be honest, we all found her irritatingly dumb. She could not have planned this. As nothing, though, is unlikely in this world, we kept all her contact details and checked that she arrived in New York after leaving Greece. Eric's sister is coming today to escort the body back to the states tomorrow. Hopefully, she will be more helpful with background details.'

'Let's get going to the body then, before questioning the sister.'

The Olympus Killer: Chapter Four

Alicia Robinson could not believe her luck. Winning Miss England two years ago was still her greatest success, but this came as a close second. She was in Cyprus soaking up the hot, sizzling Mediterranean sun, browning up her pale white skin with the rest of the youthful and glamorous models by the pool of the prestigious Columbia Beach Resort in the small, coastal village of Pissouri. They deserved a good bake in the sun after a morning-long swimwear photo shoot down at the beach of Pissouri Bay.

Columbia Resort was located upon the slope of a verdant hill that headed down to perfectly clear waters. Tall palm trees and green gardens surrounded it and the view offered was breathtaking. The resort offered every luxury imaginable and the girls, all young and most never having left their home country before, were enjoying the feeling of royalty. At night, all the girls came down together after spending a considerable amount of time on make-up applying, combing their hair and picking out dresses. They gathered around the pool area and were faced with a mile-long buffet dinner. All tables were set neatly with expensive porcelain plates and exquisite silverware. The tables were spread out under the night sky; a sky filled with countless stars that seemed to shine so much brighter in Cyprus. The buffet had everything your heart -or stomach- could desire.

Alicia mostly wanted to try the Greek-Cypriot cuisine she had heard so much about. Delicious, steamy kleftiko, wine-marinated pieces of pork called afelia, mousakka, golden oven-cooked potatoes and the freshest salad she had ever seen, soon filled her plate. Even Londis grocery store back in her home town of Canterbury did not have tomatoes this red. As she walked over to their assigned table, her plate drew a few gazes from the rest of the models who had mostly placed a few olive oil marinated croutons and some weirdly-named salad on their plates. She could sense the envy building up.

'What? I have a good metabolism. Anyway, I'm not going to keep it all in!' she joked, in an attempt to break the tension. Most girls smiled and the drop-dead-gorgeous, crazy Italian girl laughed out loud as they all sat down to enjoy their saladicious feast.

Pissouri was a quiet village and it literally stood up to its name. Pissouri in Greek meant pitch black and after ten o'clock, it was exactly that. Visitors soon realized that the tranquil village had no sign whatsoever of a nightlife. Most models did not care as they needed their so-called beauty sleep. After many air-kisses and wishes for sweet dreams, they scattered to their rooms.

'Living clichés,' Alicia thought. She did not feel like sleeping.

'I am young, on top of the world, with so much energy

from my youth or is it perhaps from the kleftiko?' she joked to herself.

She decided to take a walk down to the beach but thought to buy a triple-chocolate Galaxy ice-cream before heading down to the bay for a moonlit stroll in the sand.

Just a few minutes later, she was walking into the corner shop, Magnum ice-cream in hand. No one was to be seen behind the scratched wooden counter. She waited a full minute before hearing a screeching noise coming from the rear end of the shop. The owner was busy with his night duties. It was minutes after closing hour.

'Excuse me?' she called out discreetly.

'Well, hello there,' the owner said and quickly walked towards the counter, dusting off his hands upon his blue shirt. He offered Alicia a generous smile that lifted his heavy moustache.

'Just this, please,' Alicia said and placed her ice-cream on the counter.

'That will be 1.95, thank you,' he said, with his thick Cypriot accent.

'*Oh, what an idiot I am,*' she automatically thought to herself as she realized she had left the hotel without any money.

'I'm so sorry. I seem to have forgotten my money at the hotel. I'll be right back,' she apologized.

'It's ok. I'll pay. These too,' said the gentleman behind her as he placed his bottle of Evian water and a Mars ice-cream on the counter.

'No, no. No need for that. I'll just pop back to the...' Alicia rushed to say.

'I insist! Come on... Can't a guy buy a girl an ice-cream anymore?' he interrupted as his right hand pushed through his shiny black hair and awkwardly scratched the back of his neck. He had amazing green eyes and that voice, '*oh that voice, so smooth yet so masculine,*' Alicia thought.

'Thank you,' she whispered gently as they exited the shop together and stood on the bricked road that led down to the beach.

'Sam Newton,' the stranger introduced himself, and offered his hand.

'Alicia Robinson.' Her hand entered his.

'Care for a walk, Alicia? Before these melt?' he asked, ice-creams in hand.

Alicia nodded and smiled in reply. They walked downhill along the path, side by side, with the silver moon serving as their only light. Soon, they had reached the narrow stairs that led down to the sandy beach.

'Ladies first,' Sam said. He stepped aside and with his hand stretched out he showed her the way. Alicia smiled and thought, '*does chivalry still exist or does he just want to check out my derriere?*'

They slowly strolled further down and having finished their delectable and refreshing ice-creams, they sat down on a wooden bench and gazed at the sea. The waves were the only sound breaking through the silence and the darkness.

'Are you here on holiday with family, friends? Boyfriend?' he asked with a cheeky smile and a double raise of his eyebrows.

'Co-workers. I work for a London-based modelling agency,' she replied, trying not to sound pompous.

'That's fantastic! I should have guessed,' he said, and his eyes scrolled down her face and started to scan the rest of her body.

'You?' she quickly asked as to retrieve his eyes back to eye level.

'Oh, I'm a writer. I'm writing my next book at the

moment,' he stated and pulled out of his backpack a red notebook with a silver pen clipped to it.

'It's a thriller,' he proudly announced, with a mischievous grin. 'Here, let me read you a passage.'

Grab your copy…
vinci-books.com/TheOlympusKiller

About the Author

Luke Christodoulou is an Amazon bestselling author, a poet and an English teacher (MA Applied Linguistics - University of Birmingham). He is also a coffee-movie-book-Nutella lover.

His first book, *The Olympus Killer* (#1 Bestseller - Thrillers), was released in April, 2014. The book was voted Book of the Month for May on Goodreads (Psychological Thrillers). The book continued to be a fan favorite on Goodreads and was voted BOTM for June in the group Nothing Better Than Reading. In October, it was BOTM in the group Ebook Miner, proving it was one of the most talked-about thrillers of 2014.

The second stand-alone thriller from the series, *The Church Murders*, was released April, 2015 to widespread critical and fan acclaim. *The Church Murders* became a bestseller in its categories throughout the summer and was nominated as Book of the Month in three different Goodreads groups.

Death of a Bride was the third Greek Island Mystery to be released. Released in April, 2016 it followed in the footsteps of its successful predecessors. From its first week in release it hit the number one spot for books set in Greece.

Murder On Display came out in 2017 and enriched the series.

Hotel Murder, the fifth and 'final' book in the series, followed in early 2018.

In 2018, his box set of mysteries became an international bestseller.

Luke Christodoulou has also ventured into 'children's book land' and released *24 Modernized Aesop Fables*, retelling old stories with new elements and settings. The book, also, features sections for parents, which include discussions, questions, games and activities.

In 2019, *Twelve Months of Murder* came out, his first collection of shorts.

His first novel outside of the Greek Island Mysteries collection came in 2020, maintaining his love for a Greek theme. A supernatural thrill ride with the name of *Beware of Greeks Bearing Gifts*.

Pandora's Box followed in 2021. A mind-twisting whodunit set in his favorite Greek town, the seaside resort of Parga. The following year saw the release of the highly anticipated *Achilles' Heel*.

His first YA murder mystery, *Senior Year Murders* was released in 2024, hitting the charts for young adult thrillers.

He is currently working on various projects (which he is secretive about).

He resides in Limassol, Cyprus with his loving wife, his chatty daughter and his super-energetic son.

Hobbies include travelling the Greek Islands discovering new food and possible murder sites for his stories. He also enjoys telling people that he 'kills people for a living'.